POWERS REVEALED

the threat of angeals

BOOK 2

C. T. FITZGERALD

The Adventure Begins

IN

Crucibles of Power

Start Your Journey

The Threat of Angeals

BOOK 1:

Crucibles of Power

C. T. Fitzgerald

This is a work of fiction. Any similarity between any person is just coincidental. This book is the sole copyright of the author and can't be reproduced in any form without the sole permission of the author. To contact the author for these permissions or other engagements email the publisher:

editors@emerald-design.co

BISAC Categories:
FIC009020   FICTION / Fantasy / Epic
FIC009000   FICTION / Fantasy / General

Copyright © 2021 C.T. Fitzgerald
All rights reserved.
ISBN: 978-1-954779-10-5
Cover Art by Jimmie Carroll

Dedication

For Lachlyn, Shea, and Emilia:

Beautiful Little Women

Table of Contents

Dedication	V
Main Players	XI
Preface	XVI
Surprise Landing	1
Found	12
Toll Bridge	25
Maps and Plans	32
Misdirection	42
Powers Collide	51
Standoff	63
Dominance	75
Gorm Reborn	82
The Ancient Promise	91

Mik and Nik	97
Vespex Kee	104
Friends and Brothers	110
Overmatched	120
Questions	137
Retreat	144
Ambushed	152
A New Life	159
New Threat	168
Just Liam	178
Walking Away	182
Hope and Faith	188
Sailing Away	195
Slaughter	202
Taken	211
A Dangerous Gift	217
Command	224
Axtol the Great	230
Awakening	238

Catching a Ride	**245**
Forced to Fight	**252**
Lost and Found	**260**
I Am a Cow	**267**
A King Comes Forth	**283**
Ship and Crew	**295**
Treasure	**303**
Dancing Fools	**315**
Fire and Water	**321**
Cost of Doubt	**334**
On the Board	**351**
Who will live…	**360**
Darkness Falls	**368**
The Servant	**375**
Dark Fire	**386**
Heated Thoughts	**390**
Epilogue	**393**
About the Author	**395**

Main Players

Travelers: Seemingly all-powerful beings that wage an unending contest for control of planets and the life of those planets across the universe. Only two Travelers are known to exist, but there may be more. What they call themselves is unknown.

Mother: Every planet has a caretaker, an entity that is the planet, but is also self-aware as an active force. Her mortal enemies are the Travelers, who want to control and change her planet.

Celine: Celine was a woman who killed her husband in self-defense and gave her children to her sister. Then she was converted by Mother into Mother's "daughter", at which point she lost her humanity, and became Mother's Paladin to actively resist the efforts of the Traveler's and their surrogates.

Little Mothers: Celine selects four former "Sisters" to join her as surrogates in the coming war for control of Athlan. Their role in the coming battle is unclear, but they wield a terrible power that is meant to control and kill their targets.

Sisters: An ancient, informal group of women, mostly with families, who propagate all that is good within family life and, therefore, Athlan society. They have no special powers, other than the ability to shape the minds and hearts of their children, thereby influencing everything on the Sacred Island.

The Cath Angeal: A being of indeterminate sex, capable of being males or female, who is the ethereal general of the Traveler known on earth as the Traveler of Light. The Cath Angeal is associated with "goodness" in human terms, but on a universal scale, who knows?

The Dorchada Angeal: The opposite of the Cath Angeal. He, always a he, represents the other known Traveler, and is associated with the powers of Darkness, or evil. Again, how they see themselves and how they are seen across the universe is unknown.

The Warrior: For centuries uncounted, the Island Nation of Athlan was ruled and ruled well by "The Council", which was composed of four members and only four since its inception: The Priest, The Scientor, The Poet and The Warrior. Each member was tested by their own

"Angeal" before they took office. Each member wears the marks of their office on their arms or hands. These sacred signs are indelibly etched into their bodies and are the true sign of a Council member. The Warrior is the member who is responsible for the defense of Athlan, either on the Island itself, or anywhere in the world where forces are gathering that threaten the peace of Athlan. Traditionally, the Warrior is tested by and is loyal to The Cath Angeal.

Warriors of the Past: When a Warrior of the Council dies, a statue of that Warrior is erected in the Hall of Heroes. The Cath Angeal recognizes that the present-day Warriors-Kon-r Sighur and Cean Mak-Scaire, will need help in the coming battle. So, she recalls twelve of the Warriors of the past, Warriors who have already died, to help with the coming battle.

The Bas Croi: He is the creature of the Angeal Dorchada, and as such, leads the forces of darkness on earth. Croi is the latest in a long line of Dorchada's evil puppets, just like the Warriors have been the tools of the Cath Angeal. Croi's primary goal in the coming conflagration is to kill the Warrior and wipe out the Gardai.

The Twelve: Since time immemorial, Dorchada's champion, Bas Croi's spiritual ancestors, has had the use of 12 evil spirits that always use the same names, when one is destroyed, while they assume different bodies. In the coming battle, they are called Croi's Captains, and they lead his armies.

The Marfach Gardai: The Gardai is the military arm of the Council and is led by the Warrior of the time. Gardai officers and troops are the finest soldiers on earth and are seen as the guardians of everything that is good in Athlan society. The final defense of Athlan will fall on Gardai shoulders.

Torvyn Lok: Lok is a former Gardai Marine Officer and a friend to Kon-r Sighur. Lok, after resigning from the Gardai, is now the captain of a magnificent, innovative, ocean-going vessel, the Ban Colm. Lok is a successful trader who can't completely pull himself away from the Gardai, where is heart truly lies. The unbreakable connection to Sighur and the Gardai drives him to put himself and his crew in mortal danger.

Liam Mak Kross: As Athlan crumbles, slaves escape their bondage. Liam becomes the leader of a large group that call themselves the Outcasts. Mak Kross is marked by a green leaf tattoo on his chest and a plain white stone that hangs from a piece of worn leather around his neck. He has no idea what either means. He is more than he seems, but must discover that for himself, as the Outcasts die around him.

Vardar: Lizard-like King of the M'elan'i, also a wielder of a white Star Stone. Vardar is a throw-back to an ancient civilization, the last of his kind. His existence hints at life beyond earth. Vardar and Liam test each other in a battle for control and survival.

Wasir Obenga Owanga: Former farmer in Afrik who is subverted by The Angeal Dorchada and becomes the Captain of the Black Ships, tasked with rescuing The Bas Croi and his followers once the Warrior and Gardai are destroyed and Athlan self-destructs.

preface

"Who chases power, pursues death."
—Ro Fannin, First Warrior

Naked Power craves, then creates, bloodshed."
—Gardai War Manual

The Island nation of Athlan, once ruled by the legendary Council of Four, the Priest, the Warrior, the Poet and the Scientor, each marked with symbols etched into their skin by forces unknown, continues to self-destruct on a physical plane, as well as a moral one. Of the Four, only the Warrior, Kon-r Sighur, has survived and Athlanean society is tearing itself apart, as certain death stalks all of them.

The stellar Angeals, Cath and Dorchada, power brokers of the competing Celestial Travelers, have unleashed their players, willing and unwilling, on the dangerous gameboard called Athlan, under the blood-red skies of the tortured planet. The fight for control of the earth is heating up. Implacable foes advance across the burning face of the doomed

Island, and all converge, by design or by chance, on the last bastion of hope-The Ban Castlean—The White Castle of the Gardai.

A second Warrior, an impossibility according to Athlanean belief, has accepted his role in the coming war. Cean Mak-Scaire—a fisherman's son—has appeared unlooked for, bearing the sacred and indelible marks of the Warrior. His appearance has signaled a new epic in the Earth's embattled history: he has refused to offer blind obedience to the celestial forces fighting for control of the earth and humanity. In the end, even though he will fight, he fights for himself and his people-not for the Cath Angeal and the unimaginable force and unknowable reality she represents.

As Athlan continues to self-destruct, new, unlooked-for powers take the field and the once well-defined war between the dark and light now includes powerful combatants that are bewildering shades of indeterminate grey. The mayhem expands, and more and more ignorant Athlaneans are lead to the slaughter.

For the final confrontation, the Cath Angeal, the Angeal of Light, summons twelve of the long dead Warriors of Athlan, once Council members marked by the Palm and Fist, who shed their blood and lost their lives fighting to defend the Island Nation in the past, while The Bas Croi, infused with new power by the Angeal Dorchada, Angeal of the

Dark, summons his twelve Raver Captains, who have existed on earth as the tools of evil from the earliest of times, living in many bodies over time, to lead the voracious, mindless armies of the night.

And while the Angeals push their pieces across the board, Mother Earth and her newly created daughter, Celine, have spawned a small cadre of volunteer killers, The Little Mothers, who are dedicated to the preservation of the earth as it is, not as the Travelers and Angeals would have it.

The results of the inevitable conflict are unknowable. War is chaos. The good die as easily as the evil and the best plans go amiss. The deadly game plays on, as it has for millennia across the universe.

Chapter 1:

Surprise Landing

The vanishing sun sank behind the Westron mountains, and the *Ban Colm* sailed in a light breeze just over the horizon. Rigging creaked and white water surged along the ship's sides, as bare feet slapped on white deck planking worn smooth. The crew was excited. When night fell, the *Ban Colm* would turn inshore and sail toward the port city of Cala. Captain Torvyn Lok, leaning on the starboard rail, watched the sun go down and figured he could get within a mile of the port without being seen. He would raise sail soon and take the *Ban Colm* toward the harbor under its unique propulsion system. Instead of sneaking into the harbor itself, there was a small fishing village just south of the Luath River called Bailiag. The port of Cala surrounded the mouth of the river, but the village was less than a mile south of that. He would lower a boat from the *Ban Colm*, take Rok Tan and six men, then make land just north of Bailiag. He'd leave two men with the boat, then walk across the Cala-Bailiag Bridge into Cala, and begin searching for Vespex Kee. The former Gardai, famous seller of information, lived on the northern side of the river, where he had his supply business. Once across the bridge, things could become dicey. Lok would take one man and find Kee's business or house, while Tan would take the rest and search the taverns along the waterfront for news of the one-armed trader. They would meet at the north end of the bridge in three hours with or without Vespex.

Lok couldn't think of a better plan. Much would be left to chance once they crossed the bridge. If they didn't find Kee, Lok would learn what he could about Athlan and then decide. He wanted to empty his holds of goods and refit the ship, but if it was too dangerous, what then? The sun was almost gone, and he wasn't sure. *What a mess.* He had told KT, his adopted daughter, to go to Arcasaid, the seaport that supplied the Ban Castlean, home of the Gardai, if he didn't get out of Cala. She must find Kon-r Sighur, the Warrior of Athlan. Maybe that's what he should do, too. If things were bad, he'd probably lose his cargo, and maybe his ship, but it was either that or turn away from Athlan and find a new home elsewhere. Through trade and war, he had learned of plenty of acceptable destinations with good weather and better people.

Lok knew he wasn't thinking straight. He should just turn the *Ban Colm* and sail away, period. Something held him back. He had to know what was happening to his country. He promised himself that the people on the *Ban Colm* would make it; he wouldn't endanger them, but, if that was the case, why was he even thinking about Cala, and Arcasaid, the Ban Castlean, and the men who manned the walls? He felt a deep sadness. After all these years, after all he had seen and done, he was still one of them, still Gardai in his heart. Even so, he needed to do what was right for his crew, which meant he had to do everything he could to off-load his cargo, re-fit the ship, pay his people, and take them to safety.

Out of the corner of his eye, he saw Rok Tan, battle master, walk toward him along the rail. He was an amazing young man, and Lok had always hoped Rok Tan and KT would have a life together. Tan bounced up the stairs quickly and began talking. "The men are ready, sir, and the boat is loaded. Just give the word."

Lok asked, "What about Lanterns?"

"White in the fore, green at mid-ships, red aft," answered Rok Tan. The lights would allow them to find Seoult and KT before dawn.

"The men?"

"Steady and smart, Tor. Tough enough if we have to fight."

"Let's hope we don't, Tan. This isn't an invasion. If we must fight, something has gone very wrong. However, make sure every man is armed,"

"Yes, sir."

Lok asked, "Have you ever been to Cala, Tan?"

"Yes, sir, once. We marched from the Castlean to Cala on a training exercise when I was new to the Gardai. We were given a night's leave. I can't say I remember much of the layout, sir, although I do seem to remember there were a number of drinking establishments along the waterfront."

Rok Tan was no angel, but neither was Lok. "I seem to remember the same thing. But this trip will be different. Cala may be dangerous if things have continued to deteriorate on Athlan. We have a ship and food, and we'll be outsiders. Watch your back. Speak as little as possible, and in the name of all the gods large and small, *don't* let the men drink."

Tan said, "I'll do my best, sir."

Lok knew he would. "Alright, Tan, we'll continue for another hour or so, then lower the boat. Make sure the men eat something. We may have an exciting night ahead."

Lok turned toward the wheel. Seoult stood with massive hands on the spokes, head tilted up, studying the sky. Just behind him to the right was KT. It was clear she had been watching Lok and Tan speak. It was also clear she was not happy about being excluded from the conversation. Lok walked across the softly rolling deck and stood behind KT's left shoulder, so both she and Seoult could hear him. "We'll be leaving the ship in an hour or so. Mr. Seoult, start making your way toward the beach north of Bailiag. Keep her about a mile offshore. Look for us near dawn off the same beach. If we aren't there, sail over the horizon and come in again the next night. If we aren't there, then you know what to do. Both of you: understood?"

Seoult's "Aye" was the only answer Lok heard. KT didn't say a word; she just glared at him.

He had to say something. "KT, I know you want to come, and I know you would handle yourself as well as anyone in the boat, but I need you here. If I don't return, this ship is yours. The papers are in my cabin, in my sea chest. You two will make a good team, and the men will follow you." KT remained silent. "We've talked about this before and agreed it's the best way. I don't want to leave..." He stopped as KT walked away from him. Lok watched as she ran up the rat lines and into the darkness atop the mainmast, where she sat with her back against the masthead, looking out over the empty sea. Lok stood in shock, his mouth open.

Seoult, the wise, said, "Better close your mouth, lad, before some nasty creature flies in to make a nest. Ah, don't worry. She ran because she didn't want to cry in front of everyone, not because of you, sir. You know that; besides, you'll see her in a few hours, and when you do, she'll treat you like a small child, give you a terrible tongue-lashin', and the matter will be forgotten in a few days. Go do your job, Captain, and we'll do ours."

Lok went down to his cabin. He made sure the ship's papers were in his trunk, and then thought about the coming mission ashore. He changed into a dull black outfit. What should he take? They had to get in and out quickly. *Dagger, killing sword, and....* He reached into his sea chest and pulled out a lightweight, leather harness that he wore over his shoulders. The harness had four small sheaths on the front. He reached in again and took out an oiled rag. He opened the cloth to four six-inch throwing knives. The knives had two razor cutting edges and each came to an extremely fine point. They had been made for him by the head armorer in the Castlean when he had been a young Gardai officer. They had saved his life more than once. Their real value became clear when someone had to be killed quietly. He put each knife into its sheath and hoped he didn't have to use them. He thought about putting on his fine chainmail vest, which would turn the sharpest knife or spear point, but nighttime, small-boat operations were not the best time to weigh oneself down with armor. He put on pair of soft, lambskin gloves, dyed black and cut away to clear his fingers. Lok also put an all-purpose dagger in his boot, because you never knew. He grabbed a black cloth and wrapped it around his head, tying a knot in the back. Lok remembered doing this the first time many years ago; he was young and excited and a little scared. A lifetime later, he was just scared.

Lok took a deep breath and went topside. Seoult was still at the wheel, two seamen standing behind him, waiting to take their turn. *They'd have a long wait,"* he thought. Seoult wouldn't consider handing control of the ship to someone else at this crucial moment, and Lok was glad he wouldn't. He saw Tan and his men gathered around their boat. He knew what they were feeling, what they were doing. He went down onto the main deck and joined them.

"Sir, the boat is loaded and the men are ready to go," said Tan. As he said this, Tan gave a small jar to Lok, along with a smaller smile. Tan and his men had blackened their faces, and Lok's stood out like a big, bright moon. Tor dipped his fingers and smeared lamp black over his face.

He gave the jar back to Tan, smiled, and addressed to the crew. "Thank you for volunteering, men. Our mission tonight is simple. Find a man named Vespex Kee. We'll land on the beach south of Cala, walk north over a bridge into the city. We'll split up. Tan will take three of you and I'll take one. Two will wait with the boat. Tan, who will go with you?" Three men raised their hands. "Okay. Who waits with the boat?" Two men raised their hands. Tan had done a good job. One man was left. His name was Sandine. "Sandy, you're with me. We'll go to his home and, if he's not there, we'll search his business and warehouses. Tan, comb the waterfront inns and alehouses for him, or word of him. We'll meet back at the northern end of the bridge over the Ruath. If you find him, bring him with you, whatever it takes. We'll do the same. We aren't here to fight. We want to get in, get what we need, and get out. After we meet at the bridge, we'll return to the boat. Any questions?" There were none, and the men, civilian sailors, still snapped to attention.

 Tor got the same feelings he always did when good men stepped up to do dangerous work: pride and humility. "Right," he said. "Tan, lower the boat, and let's get moving." He turned aft and shouted, "Shut down the drive, Seoult." Seoult echoed the command and the crew acted. The *Ban Colm* slowed and began to wallow in the soft sea. Lok, Tan, and the rest climbed in, while other crew members got ready to lower the boat. Lok shouted "Away!" and the boat went down into the sea. Six men put oars into the water and began to row toward shore. Lok sat in the bow, while Tan sat aft with his hand on a small tiller. No one spoke, but everyone turned back and watched as the *Colm* slipped into darkness. The men had the same thought. *We'll see you soon,* Colm, *if we're lucky.* The surf was light as they approached the beach. They were making good time; the men put their backs into it. Lok watched the sea because none of them really knew this stretch of coastline well. Water could shoal quickly. Lok saw a sparse twinkling of lights to the south. *That would be Bailiag,* he thought. To his right, he saw a dim red glow in the sky, and that was Cala. *Why red?* Fire was the only answer that came to mind and that wasn't good. He could hear waves breaking on the shore, which meant they were getting closer. This was the tricky part: pulling through the surf in the dark. *One mistake, one missed stroke, one rogue wave, or...* There was a loud crack, and Lok pitched over the bow into the sea. His last thought before hitting the water was *Rock*, and that rock had ripped the bow out of the boat.

Lok was a strong swimmer and clawed his way to the surface. The moon was hidden, and he couldn't see anyone around. He got his bearings and swam toward the shore, wondering where the rest were. The noise got louder and he soon found himself battling through the surf, trying to keep his head above water, trying to breathe as he stroked madly toward the beach. Lok lowered his feet and touched bottom, although the force of the waves wouldn't allow him to walk in. He found himself on his hands and knees crawling out of the surf and onto the sand like a giant crab. He was exhausted and flopped onto his back. Breath came in great, ragged gasps. After a few minutes, he propped himself up on his elbows and looked up and down the beach. He saw one man standing a hundred or so yards toward Cala, but that was all. Lok checked his knives- chest and boot- and realized his boot knife missing, as was his sword. He still had his throwing knives. Not happy, he stood and began walking toward the figure on the beach. After a few steps, he recognized Tan, and when the moon came out, he saw six men and the shattered remains of their boat lying on the sand.

Both Tan and Lok began checking their men. After a few moments, four of the remaining six were on their feet, a little worse for wear and thankful to be alive. Two men didn't move. The surf had brought dead men up onto the beach. The Colmers gathered around to say goodbye to their shipmates. A quiet prayer was said quickly for Lans and Targ, and the men got busy again. No one reached the beach with the weapons they left the ship with, although everyone was armed in some fashion. Tan had his long sword and nothing else. *It could be worse,* Lok thought. They could pick up weapons in the city. Getting a boat to return to the ship, however, could be difficult.

"Alright, let's go. Tan, put two men out front. We'll find the road that runs along the beach to Cala and follow it to the bridge. If anyone comes along, get off the road and let them pass. Understand?" Everyone nodded. Tan picked two men and sent them towards the road. Lok and Tan waited a few minutes for the scouts to get ahead and then lead the others off the beach along the same track. They had lost considerable time already, so both scouts and Lok's group double-timed as quietly as they could. Luck was on their side. No one came from Cala or Bailiag and the moon hid behind clouds again. Silently, they ran- shadows more than men. A night bird whistled and the small troop dropped to the ground. After a few moments the bird whistled again, and Tan stood tall, as if waiting for something in the dark. In a few seconds, one of the scouts materialized before him and whispered something.

    Tan pointed back up the track, and the scout ran back the way he'd come. Tan said to Lok, "The bridge is just ahead around this bend. There is a two-man guard at this end and the area is well lit with lanterns. The guards don't seem to be expecting trouble, but they aren't sleeping and they can see anything coming towards them. Not good, sir."

Chapter 2:

FOUND

Thousands of years of law and social custom crumbled, destroyed by the basic animal need to survive. The Marfach Gardai, the deadly guard that had kept Athlan safe for centuries, had no experience with civil insurrection or riots. The Gardai had always stayed out of civil affairs, and wisely so. Early on, as the island began to die, the Gardai had tried to create some measure of social stability, but the result was a long-running battle between them and the distraught citizens they were sworn to protect. Brother fought brother and father fought son in the streets of Cathair. In the end, the Gardai had been recalled to Ban Castlean by Kon-r Sighur, after having, however reluctantly, killed their share of citizens. Instead, the Gardai spent time preparing the fortress for whatever might come. The withdrawal of the Gardai had dire consequences. A power vacuum had been created by their absence. Like all vacuums, this one needed to be filled and, unfortunately, was being filled in a terrible way.

Citizens banded together in small, ravenous groups, constantly searching for food and weapons, which were essential if they were to slaughter the people who had food. If they were to defend their booty from other, like-minded bands, they needed weapons. Human packs roamed the burning plains, searching the remains of gutted farms and estates; they scoured the city and combed the waterfront, hungry for anything of value. There were no older pack members. They were incapable of keeping up or defending themselves. Consequently, these packs were comprised of the youth of Athlan. They were young, tough, and feral.

There was a force at work among these groups, something sinister. Each group was slowly but surely working its way toward the Ban Castlean, although none of them were organized. No one knew how or when, but each group of Ravers—for that's what they called themselves—had been joined by men who were distinct from the gang members. These men were neither old nor young, and each had a hard, military appearance. They were giants in their own way, and they carried weapons and demonstrated their expertise often. These strangers dominated their groups, eliminating anyone who disagreed with their leadership. They taught their young charges how to fight and kill. They taught them how to torture, how to make the pain last until their victims could no longer scream. These men carried strange names: Ture-el, the giant, and Neqael, the snake, and Akabek, the slayer, who was the most bloodthirsty. His murderous cadre didn't just kill, they tortured and stole minds and souls. Akabek, The Slayer, left a trail of beheaded corpses held upright by spear shafts that impaled the dead bodies, keeping them upright and ghastly.

There were twelve of these man-monsters marching through Athlan, gathering young men, training them to kill, all inexorably moving towards the Ban Castlean, exhorting them to destroy the past, destroy what the Council had built. After all, who was responsible for their troubles? Who should have protected them? Who should have found answers that would have saved them, their families, and their country?

Who of the Council remained? Kon-r Sighur, the Warrior, who was safe and well fed within the ivory walls of the Ban Castlean. He needed to die! He must be dragged from the fortress and made to pay for the failures of the Council. He must pay for the deaths of loved ones; he must pay and pay and pay! Revenge! Revenge became their battle cry. Death became the Ravers' god; they killed every person or animal that got in their way. Like slow-moving waves of white-hot magma, the mobs closed in on the Ban Castlean, the Marfach Gardai, and Kon-r Sighur.

Weaving through these death squads, sliding along their flanks, hidden, watching, was another group of Athlanean youths, a group quite different from those who they shadowed. These young men were all slaves who had been brought to Athlan as young children, taken from their homes as hostages, as treasure, as currency to be sold for leather, wool, or straight profit. Many had no idea where they had come from, or who their families had been, or what their real names were. They numbered well over two hundred and were led by a young slave like themselves. His name was Liam, usually called Li, and he had taken the surname of Kross. Taken from a far northern isle as a young boy, Liam had worked in chains for the last eighteen years. His wrists and ankles were covered in scar tissue, like the others in his band. They wore their scars as a reminder of a life they would neither forget nor return to. Liam alone wore another mark, a shape that was burned into his skin, over his heart as a child, before he was stolen: it was the shape of a three-leafed plant with a thin stem. The leaves and stem had been stained bright green and had faded with time. Liam had no idea what the brand meant, but it had always felt right in some way, and for that reason alone, he felt proud to wear it.

His unique brand was one of the few things that set him apart from his slave brothers. Liam was smaller than average. Like the others, he'd become hardened and tough. He had been trained as a blacksmith and his iron grip attested to his profession. Although he preferred not to, Liam could fight when necessary, and only fools challenged him. Sadly, the world was populated with fools, and Liam reluctantly exercised and sharpened his fighting skills. There was no quit in Liam Kross. If you started the fight, he would finish it. However, he wasn't violent by nature. Those who knew him loved him. He always had a good word, would stop what he was doing to help anyone in need; he laughed and smiled and befriended old and young alike. His light-brown hair framed brilliant blue eye—eyes that drew people in- freedmen and slave alike- eyes that said, *Here I am, alive, bright, and warm, let's have some fun.*

Liam was no savant, although he instinctively knew that people could sense his concern for them. He was a positive influence, a bright light in the brutal, dark world of slavery. Never the smartest, never the best athlete, still, they liked him. More than that, he was trusted. The other slaves trusted his blacksmith strength and honesty.

The slaves called themselves Outcasts for obvious reasons. Unlike the rampaging gangs who were burning their way to a specific end, the Outcasts moved through the husk of Athlan with older men, women, and children—all former slaves. They would not leave their people behind. They had suffered together: they would die together. Now, though, for the first time in their lives, freedom was a possibility. They would not give up without a fight. The prospect of imminent death didn't worry them. They considered themselves to be on borrowed time. Each day free from chains was a bonus.

The group of dependents—older men, women, and children—moved slower than the main group of Outcasts. Liam had asked for volunteers to stay with and protect this group. Aside from protection, they needed to be fed on the run, and they were incapable of foraging through Athlan's ruins. Some of Liam's strongest men volunteered to stay back. They were led by one of Liam's best friends: Ka-an Tal, a black man, who was unique in Athlan, even among the slave community. Liam had selected Ka-an because of his steady nature and quick intelligence. Trained as a stone mason, Ka-an stayed cool under pressure. He had borne the brunt of Athlan cruelty for most of his life and never responded rashly. It was this ability to stay calm, disciplined, and unbowed in the face of pain that drove his Athlanean slave masters wild. Compliant because he had to be, Ka-an never broke, and the Athlanean slavers hated him all the more. He was a thinker who would never abandon his charges, and Liam depended upon his natural valor. Ka-an kept his group as close to the main body as he could, but even on a good day, a considerable distance separated Liam from his friend. Ka-an sent messengers to Liam on an hourly basis, as did Liam to Ka-an. In this way, they stayed close, and confusion was kept to a minimum as they worked their way through a tortured, forlorn and deadly landscape.

A third group of Outcasts had formed of necessity—the Scouts who ranged forward looking for information and enemies and guarded the Outcast flanks. Responsible for the safety of the group, they were led by a slight man lovingly called Rat. Rat had been a slave since he was a baby. With olive skin, dark eyes, and raven black hair, Rat had been trained as a miner because of his small but strong physique. Rat could fit into holes no one else could enter. More importantly, he had the nerve to go into holes that scared everyone else. He also had another life when not in the mines: he was a master thief. He was legendary within the slave community. The poorest would ask him for things they needed to survive, and Rat would often deliver. He could climb any surface, and he moved silently and confidently through the dark.

Over the last few months, Rat had learned through trial and error to move through the blasted fields and cities of the island nation. He and those like him had learned the importance of dark clothes and sharp knives, about silence and speed, about life and death. They had learned to remain still for hours as sweat dripped into their eyes and bugs crawled over their skin. They would hide in the rubble, an enemy sometimes only feet away: no movement or breath, only patience and fear. The Rat and his men were a special group of soldiers, young men who took pride in their abilities and responsibilities to the group. They were soon called

Shadowmen by the rest of the Outcasts. The Shadowmen had kept Liam's people safe, avoiding traps and pitched battles by taking the risks. They were the best, and each ex-slave was willing to die to prove their loyalty to each other and the group.

Evening approached, and Liam sat before a low fire hidden from view by the crumbled corners of a burned-out house. The Rat and Ka-an were with him. Liam was troubled. Something was happening on the island beyond the eruptions and death. He sensed it, but was unsure how to articulate his feelings. He called this meeting to pick the brains of his lieutenants. He needed to know where to take his people. *My people,* he thought. *When did that happen?* Once just three young men scrambling along a coast road to nowhere had turned into his people—almost three hundred strong and growing. Everywhere they went, survivors crept from under a collapsed wall or pile of rubble. Only a few were men of fighting age, most of whom had been sent back to Ka-an to protect the growing number of defenseless refugees. Liam stared into the flames. *Where to go?* he thought. *We must get off this island, but how? And who leads these small armies that constantly cross our path?* These armies—crazed young men, but well-armed, and trained—posed a threat because they killed what they caught. They weren't as skilled as the Rat and his men, but they didn't have to be. Their numbers were far greater, and life was not precious to them.

He looked across the flames at the Rat, who sat on the ground, his back resting against a large masonry block. He looked tired, but Liam knew he would never admit it. Rat was tough, and taking on more than the rest was a matter of pride. "Rat, how are your men getting on?" Liam knew the question would get him the truth about the Shadowmen.

"They are well, Liam. Tired, maybe a little bruised here and there, hungry as usual, but there can't be any fat Shadows, can there?" Everyone smiled at his joke. Just like the Rat. He would die with a maddening grin on his face. Nonetheless, if the Rat revealed those weaknesses, Liam knew that the situation was worse. "We could use a few nights' rest and some good food, but we can continue as needed, Liam. Don't worry about us."

Liam slowly nodded. "And you, Ka-an? How are your charges?"

Ka-an chuckled softly. "We are ready for the spring solstice races, Li—fresh as daisies." That would be all the mason would reveal. Really, what was there to say? Everyone was tired and hungry. Everyone's nerves were on edge.

"Rat, where are your pickets tonight?"

"I have a dozen men in a rough circle around us, about two hundred yards out, then a staggered inner circle of the same number half that distance away. Young Tomas is on point with the marauders we slipped behind yesterday."

Tomas was a boy, about thirteen or fourteen, who had followed the Shadowmen night and day for almost a week before Rat decided to catch him. When he did, Tomas fought like a young tiger, but quickly tired; he'd been starved for a long time. The Rat took a liking to the boy and began his training as a Shadowman. Tomas was born for the work. Small and wiry like the Rat, Tomas knew no fear, which was good, but also not so good. He tended to lack the one thing Shadowmen had to command: patience. The Rat hoped it would come with age and experience. As point man, Tomas would creep up to the enemy's position every night to get a fix on them, then slip back and report to Rat or one of his men. Rat's instructions were clear: do not get close; do not get captured. No heroics. Get in and get out. Tomas was proud of the work he did, and the other Shadowmen considered him their lucky mascot. "Isn't he a bit young for that job, Rat?" asked Liam.

Rat didn't hesitate. "He's young, but he's good. If I didn't think he could do it, Li, I wouldn't put him out there. Together, yesterday, we waited under a pile of burnt rubble and watched a group of Ravers pass us, no more than thirty feet away. He didn't move a muscle, and it was damned hot under that garbage. Not many men can say they've done that or even could do that."

Liam had asked the question, not because he was worried about Tomas, he trusted Rat to know his business. He had asked the question to stall for time.

Ka-an Tal solved his problem. "Li, just tell us what's bothering you. What's on your mind?" Ka-an was always one step ahead.

"Alright, Ka, you know me too well. Something is wrong with all of this—not the destruction of Athlan, I could care less if this island sunk to the bottom of the sea, and I know you two agree with me. No, there's a strange undercurrent dragging everyone, us and them, toward something, somewhere, and I can't get a handle on it. We are being pulled, maybe herded, toward something for some reason that I cannot comprehend." Liam saw that they didn't understand him. "Rat, you lead us every day, so I ask you, where are we going?"

Rat's jaw dropped. "I thought..., I mean, you tell us, but...." His thought petered out.

"Ka-an, what about you? What do you think is happening?"

Ka-an, sitting on rough wooden box, lazily poked the fire with the tip of his blade. The former stonemason was careful not to damage the true temper of the weapon. He considered the question. "That we are here at all is amazing. We should be dead like the thousands of other slaves who died in chains. But we did not. Instead, we gathered people of all ages—survivors. Your questions are good ones: why do we live, and where are we going? The second question is easier to answer: we move steadily toward the sun. We run from certain death or captivity. We run toward the high ground along the western ocean. The first question, why do we live to do so? I have no answer, Li, because I have no religion, no belief in anything not of this earth. We were slaves, now we are free. These are the only things I know."

    Wood smoke. It was a good smell. There was something about campfires that made Liam feel calm, almost content. He looked toward the night sky and saw stars dimly through the smokey haze that covered most of the island. Liam's men surrounded them, politely staying by their own fires, talking in low voices, an occasional laugh escaping into the night air. Liam knew they trusted him to make the right decisions. That made it worse. What would he do if he were alone? He'd go to the western seaport of Arcasaid, just south of the Ban Castlean, and he'd try to get on a ship to anywhere. He began to rub the green tattoo on his chest. He'd caught himself doing that more often lately. He did it without thinking. He would find his hand on the mysterious marking, sometimes rubbing so hard that skin would rub away and fine beads of blood would outline the three-leafed talisman. *That is what we'll do, then*, he thought. *We'll make our way across the plain, fight if we must, scrounge for food for the three hundred or more hungry mouths, pick a pass through the mountains, march down to the coast, and what? Simple, we'll find a ship for three or four or five hundred, take it and sail somewhere, even though none of us know a boat from a brick. Brilliant, Liam, just brilliant.* The funny thing was, there were no alternatives, and the really funny thing was, when he told the others, they would just agree and get on with it, as if he was asking them to walk down to the stream for water.

"Here is what we'll—" There was a disturbance at the edge of camp. Liam, Rat, and Ka-an jumped up, hands on weapons, ready. Rat recognized three of his men who'd been on guard duty. They carried something wrapped in a cloth. Liam felt his stomach drop.

Rat met his men. They whispered. One of them handed the cloth to Rat and put his hand on Rat's shoulder. Rat slowly turned away and walked to Liam, who saw tears on Rat's deeply etched face. Rat held out the wrapped shape, and Liam took it from his hands, knelt before the fire, and opened the cloth. Ka-an leaned over to get a better look. As the last rag was removed, both Liam and Ka-and cried out in horror. The wild eyes on the severed head of Tomas glittered in the firelight.

Chapter 3:

Toll Bridge

Lok and Tan got their men in order. Tor explained their course and two groups set out along the road to the Cala Bridge, Lok with two men on the seaside of the road and Rok with the other two on the land side. They moved quietly and kept to the shadows as much as possible. Lok still didn't have any idea what he'd do when they got to the bridge and guards. *Whose guards? Would the city still post guards on a far bridge when Cala was burning to the ground? And what kind of guard would stay there? For what? What were they guarding?* Lok tried to count the possibilities, but the only real option was that these guards were simply brigands trying to steal whatever they could.

Lok heard laughing ahead and waved Tan over to him. "Can you hear them, Tan?"

"Who couldn't? If I'm not mistaken, I think they're a little worse for drink, too." Both smiled in the dark. They were the smiles of predators with dinner in sight. They began a slow crawl to the bend in the road and watched the guards cavort on the bridge. Tor noticed how the shadows fell around the bridgehead, how far the lantern light extended beyond the last plank.

"Alright, here is what we'll do. Give Tan and I a three hundred count to get within throwing distance of the guards. Rona, Bondon: you are now drunken sailors. Give us your weapons. Once we're in place, start singing for all you're worth and walk to the bridge. Stumble, mumble, laugh, stagger, but don't stop when they tell you to. Keep going. Get as close as you can, then collapse and laugh like the demented drunks you are. Telk, you and Sandine get as close to the bridge as possible, but do not let them see you. If anything goes wrong, I want you to cover our retreat back down this road. I'm not sure if the guards are the only armed men in the area. Rona, when you fall, we'll take out the guards while their attention is on you. Make it good."

Lok looked at Tan and said, "How do you want to do this?"

Tan didn't hesitate. "I'll take the left side, you take the right. When Rona goes down, I'll be in position to throw my knives at the guard on my side of the bridge, then I'll charge."

Lok nodded. "Alright, I'll carry our two spears and take out the right guard, then do the same. Rona, keep an eye on those two. If we don't finish them quickly, they will try to kill both of you before they die. Any questions? No? Good. Remember, give us a good three hundred count before you move off."

The former Gardai began stalking their quarry. Tan would have to get much closer to throw his knives. Lok could throw a spear accurately for thirty yards or so. The roadway approaching the western edge of the Cala Bridge sloped toward the river on each side. The bridge end rested on natural rock. The road had been constructed to match the level of the bridge. The slope was severe enough to create deep shadows on both sides. However, the road was funneled to the bridge by a row of hills on the land side, then flattened out for fifteen yards or so before the edges sloped away to the river. This created a serious problem for Tan, because he had to cross that open area before he was in range of his knives. On the other side, once Tor passed the last bushes, he had a shorter crawl through flat, empty ground because he could launch his spears from further away. Discovery would spell disaster for both men.

Tor and Rok moved slowly, chests flat on the earth. They kept eye contact the entire way. They got to the level ground at the same time and paused to check on the positions of the guards, who were sitting with their backs to the bridge stanchions, facing the road. As many soldiers have learned, alcohol is a terrible thing, and with any luck, these two would learn the lesson again. Loud, horrible singing was heard coming up the road. Rok and Tor froze, trying to become one with the earth. *Blast them,* Tor thought, *the clowns are early.* And they were, and, if Tor didn't know better, he would have thought they were stupidly, undeniably drunk, all sheets to the wind.

Rona and Bondon continued their inebriated stroll toward the guards, who struggled to their feet, not quite believing what they saw. Tan made a gesture with his hands as if to say, *What now?* Lok knew there wasn't much choice: he and Tan had to crawl across the flat and get as close as they could, hoping the guards concentrated their diminished mental capacities on the drunken sailors. He looked over to Tan and wiggled his fingers, as if he was moving across the ground like a snake. Tan understood, and they both began to low crawl, faces in the dirt.

The guards shouted the command to halt, but Lok's men never stopped, as ordered. They slowed, walked in a few drunken circles, but continued toward the bridge, arms draped over one another. A short distance behind, Lok and Tan crawled closer to their quarry. The guards shouted again, and the foremost brigand launched a short throwing spear, which sunk into the ground inches from Rona's foot. Lok thought, *Alright, this is it; they can't go any further. Fall down you fools! Fall!* But he kept his mouth shut, and Bondon, laughing like a loon, picked the spear from the ground and started to dance with it, always inching toward the bridgehead, always with Rona staggering behind at arm's length. Both men were laughing, shouting obscenities at each other as they continued their diversion.

Lok and Tan also continued to close in and were a few yards away from getting within range, when the other guard, the one closer to Tan, reached behind a bridge stanchion, pulled out a war bow and steel-tipped battle arrow, and with considerable skill, sent the deadly shaft into Bondon's chest. Bondon dropped the spear, grabbed the shaft with both hands, but didn't have the strength to pull it out. Blood gushed from his mouth, and he pitched over, face in the dirt, dead before he hit the ground. Silence was followed by laughter. The guards were having fun. Lok and Tan jumped up, took two steps to gain momentum, and launched their weapons. At the same time, Rona grabbed the spear and charged the bridge. The lead guard died with one spear through the throat. The archer took a knife in the thigh, but he knocked another arrow and would have shot Tan, but at the last second smoothly readjusted his aim and put an arrow into and through Rona, who was much closer to him. It happened so fast, neither Lok nor Tan knew Rona was dead on his feet. Both Gardai thought the archer had missed. The arrow had been nothing but a flicker of light. Tor launched his second spear and was as good as his word. The archer caught the spear in the stomach and was driven over the rail into the river below. Just as the guard went over the rail, Rona silently collapsed. The bridge was cleared.

Tan bent over Bondon, and Lok gently rolled Rona onto his back. They didn't even hear the pounding footsteps of Telk and Sandine running to their friends. Neither Tan nor Lok shed tears. They'd seen too many good men die in combat. Telk and Sandine imitated their officers, and stood, heads bowed, quiet, useless. "We can't let them lie here in the open, Tor."

Aye, he thought, *more dead. My plan…again.*

"Let's move them down the slope to the riverbank."

All four men moved off with their dead mates, and gently laid them on the bank. Lok folded their arms over their bloody chests, closed their eyes, and said a few quiet words. The other men prayed as they would. They took a last look at their shipmates and began scrambling up the bank to the bridge, Tan in the lead, Lok the last to leave.

They re-armed as they could. Tan took the dead archer's war bow and a few shafts lying on the bridge, along with one of his throwing knives. The other was stuck in the archer's thigh, there to rust on the river bottom. Once armed, they moved across the Cala Bridge and came to an intersection of main thoroughfares. Vespex could be anywhere. Lok called for a halt.

He recognized the roads. "We'll split up. Tan, you and Telk go down to the waterfront and ask around for Kee. I don't have to tell you to be careful. Sandine and I will go up the hill to his house. If either of us finds him, we bring him here. If we can't move him, find out what he knows about the Gardai, Athlan, and whatever else you can get out of him. Maybe he knows somebody who will buy our cargo. Either way, meet back here in three hours. I want us gone before the sun rises. Remember, we still have to steal a boat to get back." Lok and Tan nodded to one another and went their separate ways. Simple.

Chapter 4:
Maps and Plans

Liam began to wrap the young boy's head when he noticed a shape carved into Tomas's forehead. It was crudely done, and he couldn't clearly make out what it was, but it didn't matter. The message was clear, and it had been efficiently delivered. Whoever was running the Raver unit they had slipped behind yesterday hadn't been as stupid as they had thought. They must have set a trap for Tomas, or whoever might show.

Liam asked Rat's man, "Where did you find the body?"

The scout, Bentai—a short, squat, muscular man with almond eyes—answered. "There was no body, Liam, only the head. It was stuck on a metal pole jammed into a rubble pile."

Liam thought, *No body*. Gods only knew what they had done with the boy's body. Thinking about it wasn't going to help anybody. "Bentai, Rat, bury his remains, will you? Rat, when you're finished, come back to me. We have decisions to make." Rat met his gaze over the flames, and

Liam could see the anger in his eyes, flickering in the firelight. Rat wanted revenge and would go for it tonight, if Liam let him. Liam couldn't let that happen. Maybe later, but now Liam had to keep Rat focused on something else while he decided their future course. For all he knew, the Ravers could be mounting an attack right now on Ka-an's group.

"Give me some time, Li. I'll come back," Rat answered.

Rat, Bentai, and half-a-dozen men left the light, carrying what was left of Tomas into the night. Tomas had been a good kid. They would do what was necessary. As brutally tested as these people were, Tomas's murder shocked them. A killing like this was personal. They were all survivors, sensitive to everything around them. Their danger was palpable. Tomas's death was a challenge, a threat laid down by savage killers. Liam furtively looked around the camp. He could see men checking their weapons and packs. Where a sense of calm had prevailed before, there was now a sense of urgency. Voices were quieter, and laughter was a thing of the past.

Liam said to Ka-an, "The map you found, An, do you have it with you?"

"No, Li, it's in my pack, but I can get it and be back by the time Rat is finished. I'll also check on my people to make sure they're alright." He vanished into the night.

Liam put more scraps of wood and debris on the fire. They would need better light. He sat down on the rubble and began to think. He stared into the flames, poking around the edges of the fire with his long walking staff. He had found it in a burnt-out shrine to one of the many gods of Athlan. The wood was black and highly polished. A circular knob had been worked at one end and a metal tip protected the lower end. After many nights around campfires, Liam had found he couldn't burn the staff. He wasn't sure if it was a good thing to carry. There was something wrong with wood that wouldn't burn, and sometimes it felt greasy in his hands.

Smoke swirled around him in the light night breeze, forming a fragrant curtain of solitude. No one approached. He needed to be alone, and his people knew it. They would leave at first light, cross the mountains and make it to Arcasaid. But he needed the map; he needed to see the passes. He needed so many things, including luck. He was drawn deeper and deeper into the fire. He could feel the heat on his face. He leaned forward toward the flame. He was alone, but he was standing on a mountain; it was night, it was cold, and a steady rain blew into his face. Lightning shattered the darkness, and thunder rolled over the sea. He saw a ship cutting through the storm and a light, maybe a lantern, in the rigging, and he knew the ship was coming for him.

He sent his thought out over the water. *Who comes for me?* No answer. He turned his back on the light and walked into the dark, into the heat that now singed his eyebrows. Liam jerked his head back. He sat bemused, shaking his head and rubbing his eyes. Nothing like this had ever happened to him. Liam's feet were always firmly planted on the ground. He had experienced neither visions nor vivid dreams. His mind held no illusions. His right-hand fingers began to trace the green mystery on his chest. *What does any of this mean?* No answer came; no answer ever came.

Liam snapped out of his reverie and noticed Rat and his men coming back. At the same time, Liam saw Ka-an slipping through the darkness. The Outcasts were eager to avenge Tomas, and they expected quick action. Liam planted the staff into the ground and waved Rat and Ka-an to the fire. "I need your patience and brains tonight, Rat. The welfare of the group means more than vengeance upon Tomas's killers. Do you agree?" The issue wasn't so clear for Rat, but he knew his duty and nodded in agreement. "Ka-an, take out the map and both of you come over by me." Ka-an opened his pack and took out a square piece of cloth that was folded many times. The three friends sat close before the fire and opened the map onto their laps. It was unbelievably light, a thing of beauty and great age. Ka-an had found it while searching an abandoned home for food. And even if none of them were experts in the arts, they all recognized the artistry of this map. Athlan had been stitched into thick, silken cloth with fine threads of gold and silver; reds and greens and rich blues made the mountains, plains, and rivers burst to life. Cities were in place and roads major and minor. The detail was exquisite, and they wondered who the owner had been, how long the artist had worked on it. For a moment, they studied it in silence, respecting the beauty.

Neither Rat nor Ka-an could read. They were never taught. Liam, however, had been taught to read by his master's youngest daughter. Since none of them had ever been away from Cathair, reading a map was something of an adventure. Rat asked first, "Where are we on this thing, Li?" Ka-an remained silent but attentive. Liam put his finger above a small river where it emptied into the sea on the southeastern corner of Athlan. He didn't let his dirty skin touch the wonderful, white silk surface.

"This is where our village was, Rat, right down here at the mouth of this river. We know it as the Bogha, but this map calls it the Tana: same river, different times. This map is at least a hundred years old, I'd guess. We lived on the north bank, here," and he pointed again.

"Where do you think we are now, though, Li?" asked Ka-an. The fire's imperfect light and the folds in the silk made it difficult to see clearly. Squinting closer to the map, while tilting it toward the fire, Liam studied the landscape and tried to remember their movements over previous few weeks. They had trekked sporadically in search of food and to avoid the larger armed parties that seemed to be everywhere. They had been essentially wandering in a zigzag pattern with no clear destination.

"I'm not sure, An. We moved south across the river first, walked along the coast for a few days, then we cut inland across abandoned fields, and through burned out villages. We walked, stopped, searched for everything we could, sometimes we waited for Ravers to clear out. My best guess is that we aren't all that far from the coast, maybe twenty miles or so, right about here." He moved his finger over the map toward the center plains. Rat and Ka-an could see they were almost in the middle of nowhere, somewhere on the great plains of south-central Athlan. Food was going to be a problem. The women would keep up because they were the tough ones.

Ka-an asked the obvious question. "Where are we going, Li? And once we get there, what do you think we should do with all these people?" Rat sat back, waiting for Liam's answer.

Liam continued to study the map but choices were limited. "This is what we'll do." He ran his finger along the river they knew as the Bogha from the sea until it disappeared into the foothills of the Westron range. "Water will be our main concern all the way. We must stay near a ready supply for the children and older people. We might be able to get fish out of the river, too. We can follow the Bogha as far as these foothills. I'm not sure how far that is, so I'm not sure how long it'll take us to get there. Everyone we meet seems to be moving northwest, in the general direction of the Ban Castlean. We can avoid them by going straight west along the river. When we get to the end of the Bogha, we'll have to turn north, follow the Westron hills on our left, and find"—his eyes searched as his finger moved— "this pass, the first one, Whistling Gap. It may be high; no, it *will* be high, dry, and cold. The climb won't be easy, and if the pass is held against us, we'll have trouble getting through. Once we come out of the mountains, we'll turn north again and march along the coast." He checked the map but found few villages of any size along the west coast. That didn't mean there weren't any. "We need to make it to the port of Arcasaid, the seaport for the Ban Castlean. It looks like a few miles separate the harbor from the Castlean, but who knows? The Castlean will be the last place on this cursed island to go down. The Gardai call the Castlean home. If there are ships to use, they'll be here. The Gardai won't simply lie down and die."

Ka-an and Rat continued to look at the map, but neither was really seeing it. The fine details and wonderful colors meant nothing to them. Instead, they were imagining what their duties would be, how they would use their men, how they would find food and travel across the landscape.

They worried about weapons, skins to carry water, medicines, and clothes. Where were they going to get clothes to cross the pass without freezing to death?

Rat stood up and began to pace before the fire. He was the first to break the silence: "Li. Do you have any idea what you are asking us to do?" He bent down, studied the map, and pointed. "Listen. Why don't we get back to the river, follow it to the coast, and run up to this town, here, and take our chances? We'd be there in half the time it looks like, and we wouldn't freeze, that's for sure. And if everyone is going that way,"—he pointed at the Castlean—"we'd be going the other way. This must be better for us than trying to cross those mountains. We don't know anything about Arcasaid, no more than we do about any other place."

Liam said nothing as he continued to study the map. Ka-an answered for him. "Rat, we can't go back. Nothing is there. We know this. If this city was any kind of great place, people would be heading toward it, but they aren't. I don't like Li's idea any more than you do. I'll lose more people than you. The elders won't make it. Liam knows this. But our journey is about the future, not the past. Li is right. If there is any place of hope, it will be near the Castlean and the Gardai. And hope is all we have."

Liam began to fold the map. "An, can I keep this with me for a while?"

"Sure, Li."

Liam stood, dropped the folded treasure on the log, put his hand on Rat's shoulder, and looked into his eyes. He could see pain and doubt through the reflected flames. "Rat, I'm not happy about this either. I don't have all the answers, and I can't bring Tomas back. I need you and An to help me get as many to Arcasaid as we can. That means we walk away from Tomas's murderers and don't look back. We go at first light. We can't fight a straight-up battle, and those Ravers won't be satisfied with just Tomas's head." Liam watched Rat blink away the tears, but neither of them looked away. Liam could see Rat struggle with the idea of running, and for a moment, he wasn't sure which way Rat would go.

Finally, Rat said in a low but steady voice, "I'm good, Li. Tell me what you want me to do." Liam knew the price that answer cost the Rat. So did Ka-an. The three young men, slaves no more, moved closer together and grasped each other's arms in friendship and support. They were brothers.

They looked out over the fire into the quiet camp and realized all eyes were on them. No one was sleeping. The Outcasts waited for their orders. "Let's sit down again and go over what we'll do in the morning and what we have to do tonight," Liam said. Before he could sit and open the map, someone began to scream for the Rat.

Powers Revealed

A young man, one of the Shadowmen, ran through the camp toward the fire. He was out of breath, but managed to gasp, "They're coming! They're coming now, the ones who killed..." No more words came forth, as a long, red arrow pierced his body and stopped inches from Rat's own heart. Shafts whistled through the darkness from all directions. Ravers. The Outcasts had run out of time.

Chapter 5:

Misdirection

People were shouting. Death was in the air. Invisible shafts screamed in from the night sky. It wouldn't be long before Ravers charged the camp. Liam scattered the fire with his feet and he, Rat, and Ka-an moved quickly through the deadly rain, shouting to each other as they ran.

"Ka, get to your people and get them moving toward the river. Rat, gather your scouts and guide Ka to Arcasaid. Here's the map." Li threw the map to the running mason who caught it and once more vanished into the dark, followed by a hail of red shafts.

Rat and Liam knelt in the shadow of a tumbled roof. "What will you do, Li?"

"I'll stay here and try to get us organized for what comes next. Get out of here. We'll try to find you along the river. Don't leave Ka-an and his people. Guide them west as fast as you can. Follow the river. They'll need you if they're going to have any chance of making it. Don't come back for me, Rat. Do you understand?" The Rat gave Liam a long look and left in silence. Liam marveled as he disappeared into the shadows, and if anything was certain on this night, he knew the Rat would gather his people and find Ka. Liam hoped the main attack was here on his people and that there wouldn't be a second one on Ka-an's group at the same time. That would be a disaster, but there was nothing he could do about it.

When they bedded down for the night, there were close to a hundred men with Liam, but they weren't the best fighters. Rat and Ka-an had the best. Liam's group had learned through trial and error to construct a defensive perimeter every night when they stopped. Some positions were better than others. This night, they had settled between two tumbled down homes with about fifty feet between them. Liam, Rat, and Ka had been sitting around a fire that split the distance. Liam saw his people still milling about, illuminated by their fires. "Put out the fires! Put out the fires!" he cried. "Put them out and lie down." Hearing his voice, they rallied. The fires sizzled out, and they got down on the ground. Liam tried to get them in a line which would be anchored at each end by a wrecked house. "Archers, to me. Archers, to me." A few bowmen came to his voice, and he divided them. He wasn't sure how many went where, between the two homes. Arrows continued to fall, but fewer cries were heard. They weren't easy targets anymore. He moved up and down the line in a low crouch and made every other man face away. "Stand when I say stand. Stand when I say stand." Liam knew the enemy would come from both directions at once. They were surrounded.

But by whom? Sure, it was the group of Ravers they thought they had evaded yesterday, the same group that had delivered the message with Tomas's severed head. But why would they double back to attack Liam's harmless travelers? Why send a message at all? And who had trained these men? They had gotten past Rat's Shadowmen to launch this attack. How did they do that? Were Rat's men dead? They must have had many trained archers because the marksmanship in the dark and the number of arrows shot were impressive. How many did they have out there? How many would make the charge and what weapons did they have? These thoughts swirled in Liam's brain and he had no answers. None. Was this what they called combat? He felt helpless. Should they just wait for the attack? Should he attack, or should he run? Where would he run to? Where were they gathered? He might run right into them and be slaughtered out of hand. Maybe he could lead his troops to break through somewhere and keep on running. Which way, though? He knew the general direction to the river was south and west, and that's where Rat and Ka-an would eventually hook up, but was that where he wanted to lead his attackers? No, he couldn't do that. The best he could do was to charge in the opposite direction, which meant he would try to break out to the north and east, back towards were they had originally come from. His only hope would be to break free, then loop back around to the south by making a large circle to the east. He shook his head. All this was guesswork. He didn't know anything. But he did know that no one was coming to help him and the more he thought about it, the surer he became that sitting still meant certain death.

We go, he thought. *How? We crawl in the dark as far as we can to the northeast but send a small group as a decoy to the northwest. They will make a noisy charge while we run like hell as silently as we can, and hope for the best.* Liam knew many would die, and everyone in the decoy group would surely die, but that was their job. It would have to be volunteers. He couldn't pick men to go to their deaths without hope. He felt ill, guilty, knowing he couldn't go with them. Liam crawled along the line calling for twenty volunteers. "I need twenty men; twenty men on me." Men along the line began to crawl toward him. In fact, as far as he could tell, everyone volunteered.

Tears burned his eyes. Liam began to tap people on the shoulder, saying "Over there," as he pointed to a shadowed area. The chosen moved off. Liam joined them in the dark. "Listen. This is not easy, but I won't lie to you. We need you to launch an attack in that direction." He pointed to the northwest. "And I hope you make it through their line, but your main job is to draw attention to yourselves. Fight whoever you come up against for as long as you can. If no one's there, come back to us until you find someone to fight. Make it loud. Scream as you go. While you attack, I'll lead the rest out to the northeast. I don't know what we will find, but we can't stay here. I'm sorry. I don't know what else to do."

Liam could sense their eyes on him. The arrows had stopped. There wasn't much time left. A voice came out of the darkness close to Liam. "No one likes it, Li, but we understand. Go ahead; get the others ready. We'll do our part. How will you tell us when to go?"

Liam had difficulty getting the words out. These people deserved better. "We'll begin to crawl towards them as soon as I can get the word up and down the line. Can you count?"

The voice answered, "Yes."

"When the last of us disappear into the dark, count to one hundred and go. Make as much noise as you can and get in amongst them. After you go, we'll wait a bit, then make our break. If any of you make it through…." And he thought, *Can I tell them where we are going? If they get captured, will they talk? Of course they will, but to lie to them…?* This was getting worse and worse. "We'll be moving north across the plane. Try to find our trail and meet up with us." *God help me*, he thought.

There was silence for a short while, then a chorus of "Good luck, Li. We'll meet again; get them out, we'll be alright." Liam couldn't help himself; he moved into the small group and began to touch the people there, grasping their hands, taking hugs, feeling their arms wrap around his shoulders. They had gone through a lot together, and he realized that each was fully aware of his fate, yet no one regretted volunteering, and no one held their coming deaths against him. They would die free, and if that was their end, that would be a good end. He had to go. A final "Thank you" and he was gone, feeling guilty as hell.

Liam ran in a low crouch to the western end of the line and began to touch each man and issue the same command. "Come with me, stay low. Come with me, stay low." He collected the remaining men who could still move, which left more than a few dead or wounded on the line. He realized he couldn't leave the wounded. They would have to carry them. Liam took a quick count. He had about seventy good men left, and figured he had to carry about five or so injured. Not good. He grabbed men, and they went back down the line checking the wounded, grabbing them roughly, and carrying them out.

"Listen to me. We're going to crawl that way," he instructed and he pointed to the northeast. "Stay flat to the ground until I start running. Those who are hurt, don't to cry out. Keep your eyes on me. We'll try to get as close to them as we can, but I don't know where they are or how many they are. Don't stop to fight if you can help it; just keep running. Try to get through their line. Once you do, keep going and loop back toward the river. We'll gather there." There was a low murmur of assent, and the Outcasts drew closer together. Liam figured he would be one of the first to die, along with most, if not all the wounded. Why bother to discuss the obvious? They needed hope; they needed to believe they could escape; they needed a leader to get them to safety. He would try.

Li put his hand around the white stone at his neck. It felt warm. What did it mean, if anything? He'd worn it since he was a baby. He covered his tattoo with his right hand and felt it pulse on his chest. He drew energy from the odd mark. For the thousandth time he wondered what the mark meant. Why did he always feel different from others? No time for doubt now. He dropped to his stomach and spoke to those behind him, "Wait!" Liam waited for the others to attack. What a waste. Soon, though, he was thinking to himself, *Come on, come on, go, go*. He was committed and needed to get on with it. Seconds seemed like hours as they waited. He found himself breathing heavier. And then he heard the screaming, saw shadows moving out standing tall and brandishing whatever weapons they had. His men ran willingly to their deaths so he may live; he was consumed by guilt. But he felt terribly alive; there was a job to do, and he'd do it. Waiting a few counts longer, he said in a hoarse whisper, "Now!" and he began to belly-crawl across the darkened earth. Shadow shapes flowed across the land with Liam on point. He moved forward, stopped to listen, moved forward, and stopped to listen. He could hear the fight his men were putting up, but he couldn't think about that now. Move. Listen. He was surprised they'd gotten so far without contact. Were they just lucky? Was no one in front of them? He continued forward. They had covered fifty or sixty yards across flat ground, and he had to decide. Continue to go low and slow, or should he make a break for it? The twenty wouldn't last much longer, and once they were dead, the enemy would begin searching for the rest of the Outcasts. He worried about his wounded. They must be in bad shape. How far could they run? How far could they be carried? Not far. Not fast. He could only go as fast as the slowest man. No one would be left behind.

Liam raised his head and tried to penetrate the night. He could see no cuts through the landscape where they could sneak unseen. They would have to go up and over the ridge before them and that meant they needed to stay flat to the ground, otherwise they'd be outlined against the night sky. They were so close. He couldn't believe their luck. "Stay low, straight ahead." He began to crawl and he could hear the others behind him. In his mind, they sounded like a noisy herd of cattle, but he hoped that was just his nerves. He could hear their breathing and the sound of cloth sliding across the earth, but there were no cries of pain, no jangling metal, no talking. He was so proud of them. He stopped, listened, and looked at the low rise. Nothing. Once over the swale, they would make a break for it. They would make it.

As he began to crawl forward again, a picket line of spears thudded into the earth before his eyes. Liam didn't know what to do. The spears burst into flames and lit up the night, exposing the Outcasts. As if by magic, the ridgeline sprouted armed men in such numbers that Liam lost all hope. More spears fell and ringed the group in a circle of fire, trapping and utterly exposing Liam and his people. Sinister laughter filled the air. More spears fell and ignited. The tiny ring was lit as if the sun had risen. The Outcasts stood in their new prison, waiting for the onslaught. They couldn't see into the darkness beyond the ring of flame. Blind to the night and helpless, they were surrounded, penned like animals awaiting slaughter. The dream of freedom was over.

Chapter 6:

Powers Collide

Liam could hear their enemy coming down the slope. Shading his eyes, he caught glimpses of the men surrounding them, but he couldn't make out clear details, nor could he count how many there were. A voice echoed through the night: "Lay down your weapons or die." No Outcast dropped their weapon. They all looked to Liam and waited. What should he do? What could he do? If they fought, they died. If they surrendered, they died or became slaves again. Whatever he decided, he would be wrong, but he chose life, because with life, there was hope. He dropped his sword and stuck his long knife into the earth. He realized he had lost the staff during the escape. The rest followed his lead, and weapons clanked and thudded on the ground. Sections of spears disappeared, and armed men rushed in to shackle the Outcasts. Once secured, they were thrown to the ground. Liam struggled with his captives, determined to resist, when the same voice bellowed, "Leave him alone." Liam's guards backed away. He sensed a large group approaching on the other side of the fire. A half dozen armed men entered the circle, but Liam hardly noticed them. His attention was trained on the huge warrior in their center. This was their commander. There could be no doubt, and the giant laughed as he approached.

He stood within a few feet of Liam, hands on hips, a smile on his rugged face. His eyes were black and empty. Firelight flickered in them, and Liam had the strangest thought that they weren't eyes at all. No, they were eyes, but something *else* was looking at Liam through them. Something that hated him. Liam knew why these Ravers had come back to kill his people. They weren't after them—they were after *him*. He could see it in this man's empty orbs; he could feel the malice, but why? He was nobody, nothing. The giant spoke, "My name is Akabek. I have served the Black Death for thousands of years, small man. You thought yourself clever, but your plans were revealed from the start. We slaughtered the pitiful force you used as a decoy, but some of them still live. Yes, some live, and they will regret that bad bit of fortune, Liam. Oh, yes, they will scream and scream until they have no voice, and still they will not die. And *you*…well, we just had to wait for you and your scum to crawl to us. We laughed, as you crawled, worm."

And the men around Akabek roared with demented glee; they beat their spears into the earth and began to chant: "Akabek, Akabek, Akabek...!"

The giant held out his hands for silence. "You have come to the end of your journey." He paused and tilted his head as if listening to someone, but no one spoke. Then he continued, "Liam, you will die and so will your useless army. Did you think that you could sneak around us whenever you wished? You are an ignorant thrall, Liam. You play a game you do not understand, and now you will pay the price, as Tomas did—so young and so stupid. Did his death distress you, slave king? Did you cry for the boy? He suffered, you know. He called your name, oh yes. He cried and called your name. But you didn't come for him, did you? You didn't help him, a boy who shouldn't have been playing with men. He was so disappointed, Liam. As he died, I think I heard him whisper your name. Did you wonder why his body was never found? Why we only returned the head?" More laughter came from his guard.

Liam was shaking with rage. He ground his teeth. He wanted to fly at this pig. He no longer cared if he lived or died, but he was determined to kill the giant bastard. "Ah, the anger, little slave. Yes, you wish to kill me and rightly so, because I came to kill you. You want to fight me and so we shall, but it won't be that easy, Liam. Oh, and as for Tomas, we tossed his body into a pit of human waste. I thought that was an appropriate ending for a headless piece of garbage."

Then Akabek shouted to his men, "Line them up!" And the Ravers lifted the shackled Outcasts from the ground and marched them before Akabek. The Outcasts were made to stand in a line that ringed the inside of the circle, their backs to the flaming spears. Akabek shouted, "Hold him!" And the six guards rushed Liam, grabbed his arms, and put spear points to his throat. Liam couldn't move. Akabek began walking around the ring, stopping before certain Outcasts, shaking his head, looking back at Liam, and smiling.

Liam felt sick. *What was he...* Akabek drew his curved sword and made a swift cut. Liam watched in horror as the head of a man named Jjon toppled from his shoulders and bounced on the ground. Jjon's body crumpled, blood spurting from the severed neck. Akabek's guards went crazy, pounding their spear butts onto the ground, chanting his name. "Akabek, Akabek...." Akabek looked directly into Liam's eyes and smiled. With a flick of his powerful wrist, he sent Jjon's blood flying from his blade, and with a dismissive kick, he sent Jjon's head rolling to Liam's feet. Enraged, Liam achieved nothing by his struggle to reach Akabek, other than to drive spear points into his neck, causing his blood to run down the sharp-edged blades. The guards withdrew their weapons and laughed again. The wounds were shallow and their prisoner would live to meet his fate.

Akabek continued to walk around the ring, deciding on his next victim. No one noticed the two figures that had appeared on the low ridge line. They were utterly still and seemed to be wrapped in shadow. They watched and listened to the disgusting spectacle. After the giant had beheaded a second victim, the smaller of the pair asked, "Who are these people, Mother, and what is happening here?"

Mother answered, "What do you sense, child, not see, but *feel*?" Celine turned back to the ring of fire and closed her eyes. Her senses travelled through the earth and invaded the ring. She felt the horror of death and the life force of many humans, she.... *Ahhh, what is that, what... and another one, but different, much different.*

She withdrew from the circle. "Other than the dying humans, two powers exist, one of which I've never met before. One comes across as the power of fire and death and is quite dangerous. I met this power at a stream crossing. The other is different. It seems less threatening, but it's still dangerous. The giant is red and black, while the slave is white and green. Their power is deadly—quite real."

Mother nodded. "Perceptive, daughter—what you were feeling are the representatives of those that battle for our planet. I believe they are both minions of the Travelers, but I am not sure. My sense in this matter is somewhat confused. There is something strange in that circle. Look closer. Do you see the giant warrior who stalks the ring selecting victims?"

"Yes, Mother."

"He clearly represents the power of the Bas Croi and his master. The other threat is less clear, dear. I can't quite identify it. The young man with the spear points pressed into his neck—he is the one radiating the other strength you felt, and he is strong, but why does he submit to those animals? He could easily reduce them to cinders." She extended her senses into the circle, concentrating on the captive. She rushed through the earth and entered his body through his feet. Liam screamed at the invasion. He felt as if he was losing his mind, like he was dying. Total fear gripped him, causing his will to explode through his frame and crash into Mother's spirit, stopping her cold. Liam didn't know what he was doing but was determined to fight. He concentrated. Sweat dripped down his face. His body trembled with effort. The guards backed away from him, ignorant and frightened. Liam, hands clenched and body rigid, howled like a tortured animal, and even Akabek paid attention, forgetting his bloody inspection.

The Great Mother continued to force herself into Liam's body and mind. She couldn't believe his ability to resist. Who was this boy, and what was the power that thwarted her? She strained, yet made no progress. This was ludicrous. And she found herself being ejected from his mind. She felt the power, and she knew fear because this was something new, something she couldn't overcome. Liam. That was his name, and he was a new player in the game but who did he play for? There were only so many choices, at least there used to be. Mother found herself back on the swale with Celine. Gaiea, unshakable power of the earth, stood in shock, defeated. By what? That was the question. She said to Celine, "I brought you here to test your powers against those of the Travelers, or rather, of their minions. I knew there would be a confrontation between them. However, we've found something quite different, and I don't know what to do. I have been defeated by the boy held captive. He is not controlled by the Travelers. Why does he submit when he wields such power?"

Celine considered her words and asked, "Is he good or evil, Mother?"

"For us, there is no distinction, Celine, but this one is not part of the game. He fights for himself. Remember what I taught you. No matter which side wins, we lose. Our goal is to keep things the way they are, and this means that we need to defeat both sides—all sides. But this boy, his is something new; he belongs to neither side. What does he want?"

This was all very strange to Celine. Mother had become her entire world. That she had been defeated was inconceivable. What did this mean for her? If Mother could be beaten, *she* could be beaten. But Celine had been chosen for a reason—she had the will to fight. "Mother, what is my power? You never told me what I was supposed to do here. Are mind tricks my only weapons?"

She was right, thought Mother. *I wonder if it will be enough now.* "Our great power, Celine, is to preserve things as they are, as they should be. From me, you have the strength to hold things in place. Your human ability was to fight back and kill. Combined, I believe you can negate the challenge of the Travelers—more precisely, the actions of their minions on earth."

"What about that boy down there? What will happen with him?"

"I honestly don't know, girl. Think again: what sense did you have of him?"

Celine considered the question. What did she feel? "His was a cool force, not aggressive, but powerful anyway. His was the strength and danger of a dark forest, while the giant's was the power of fire. And I wasn't threatened by the boy."

You should be, girl, thought Mother. They stood in silence and watched the scene below. Akabek killed another Outcast, this time by cleaving the man's body from skull to belt with one murderous stroke.

"Mother, I've had enough. Maybe you can stand here and watch while those people are slaughtered, but I can't."

"What will you do, girl?" But Celine was already running down the hill in body and spirit. No one noticed as she slipped behind the last row of soldiers, and no one noticed when each of the men slowly sank to the ground, suddenly too exhausted to stand. She stood before the burning spears and watched.

Akabek grew tired of his game. He turned toward Liam and shouted to his men, "Let him go and give him a sword!" Liam couldn't believe it. He would have his chance. One of the guards offered him a sword, but Liam ignored him, searched the ground, and found his own. It felt good in his hand. He bent down and picked up his long knife. One of the guards tried to stop him, but Liam's knife flashed, and the howling man's arm hit the ground. Akabek smiled as he began to stalk Liam. They circled each other, sizing each other up, looking for openings. Liam surged forward, but Akabek not only moved as fast as Li, he moved with skill.

The strokes of both were deadly, and they would have killed each other, but a powerful voice boomed one word: "Stop!" And Celine walked into the light.

Neither Akabek nor Liam understood what had happened. Both realized they should be dead. Each had seen the other's blade coming for him, and in a split second of recognition, each was resigned to death. Akabek felt no remorse because he was following his master's will. Liam, with nothing to live for, took comfort in the justice of Akabek's death. Neither was able to finish his stroke. They were within arm's reach of each other, struggling mightily; Celine walked between them. No one else moved. Even the spear flames froze in place.

Liam thought, *This is not possible. Is she a witch, a sorceress?* She stood on her toes, looked into Akabek's eyes and placed her hand on his chest. He tried to scream but no sound came from his open mouth. He struggled against his bonds. Celine turned to Liam, looked into his eyes, and put her hand on his chest, on his brand. Liam recognized the same power that tried to dominate him before. He concentrated his will and pushed against her pressure. His brand burned in his chest, and Celine screamed in pain. She jerked her hand away and looked down at her palm. The three-leafed brand marked her palm. Celine's eyes widened, not in fear but in wonder. Liam broke the spell. Sword held high over his right shoulder, body coiled, ready to cut her in half, he...hesitated and took one step back. He lowered the sword and studied her face. She was beautiful- summer and spring combined, warm winds and blue sky, soft rain and the wonderful scent of fall.

It was a very strange tableau. Akabek stood still, an impotent giant bent on murder. Not even a foot away stood Celine, her right hand singed, and two steps in front of her stood Liam, still as stone. He didn't know what to do or say. "What are you?" she asked.

Liam, struggling to answer, replied, "I'm a person. My name is Liam. I was a slave, as were all my people, but now we are free."

Celine shook her head. "No, *what* are you, what power do you serve?"

Liam was seriously confused. His anger began to mount. "I should be asking you that question. Who or what are *you*, and what power do you serve, and what gives you the right to enter my body and mind like you tried to do?"

Celine was taken aback by his anger. She found herself studying his face and eyes; they were blue like the sky with gold sparkling around the edges. She took a step closer to him; she couldn't help herself. "My name is Celine. I serve the earth, boy, and I'm no threat to you if you are no threat to me." Liam found it hard to concentrate. They looked deep into each other's eyes, then embraced. Their kiss lasted long. Deep knowledge passed through that kiss.

Liam pulled back, although he still held her loosely. "Celine, you aren't human, or, uh, you're more than human, or less than human." Celine had a fleeting memory of her husband and family, now long gone.

"I could say the same of you, slave boy." *But you aren't aware of your power, are you?* she thought. *You're just a sweet boy shouldering responsibility that shouldn't be yours.*

As she reveled in the warmth of their embrace, she felt the strain of sustaining her strength. Akabek and his men still struggled to be free, and she exerted her will to keep them in stasis. Another thing she had just learned: her power had limits. What was she to do?

"Liam, I must go. When I release your people, take them, and go where you will. Akabek and his underlings will remain in place." He didn't know what to say. Who was Akabek? Who was she? What was she?

So much to know, but instead of asking questions that might help the Outcasts, he asked, "Will I ever see you again?" and she smiled.

Chapter 7:

Standoff

Liam stepped back from Celine and realized he wasn't breathing. He was stunned by her kiss. She seemed to melt into him, become one with him, and he had let it happen. He couldn't move and didn't want to. But what was he to do? What about his people? "I can see it in your eyes. You want to run, but you want to stay. You must go, Liam. Take your people and go now: right now. This filth will not move as long as I can hold them. I will not stop you."

Liam snapped out of his warm trance and looked at his troops. "Suki, Jenar, get everyone moving. Grab all the weapons you can carry. Take water, food, cloaks—anything we can use." Liam wondered for the hundredth time who she was. And how did she do what she did? He didn't know whether he could trust her, but she'd saved them and she was letting them go.

"Which way do we go, Li?"

That was Jenar, he thought, *a good man*. "We go southwest. Stay together, put scouts ahead, and look for sign of Rat and Ka-an. Stay quiet. We don't know who else is out there, or where." Liam never took his eyes off Celine, as he listened to his people gather what they could. What would he do with his dead? He reluctantly broke eye contact with her and walked to the Outcast bodies: such a waste. He had to bury them; he couldn't leave them in pieces.

He found Celine by his side. "I'll take care of them, Liam." She opened the earth with a wave of her hand, and three graves appeared in the bloody soil. Liam's people looked on in stunned silence. Was she a god or a demon? She was beautiful but dangerous.

"Put the bodies into the earth," Liam said in a soft but powerful voice. Hands lifted the slain Outcasts and gently lowered them into their graves. The Outcasts sobbed, stunned by what had happened—what was still happening.

"Get your people back, Liam!"

Liam nodded and gestured for everyone to move away from the graves. As they did, Celine drew her right hand across the burial ground. This time, the graves filled in and the bodies disappeared. Green vines and white flowers sprouted from the ground and the mounded graves were covered in seconds. "Do you wish to pray for them, Liam of the Outcasts?"

Li thought for a moment, and honestly didn't know what to say. He had no prayers of his own. He couldn't ever remember a slave having their prayers answered, even those that begged for a quick death. "If anyone who knew them wants to say a prayer, go ahead, but make it fast." No one stepped forward, which bothered him for some reason.

While the Outcasts continued to arm and provision themselves, Liam turned to Celine again. "Thank you. They followed me, and I couldn't protect them. Would you tell me who you are? Will we meet again?"

She smiled. "As to whether we will meet again, Outcast, I have no idea. I am not a god. Who am I? That's still a mystery to me, too. Once I was just like you and your people, a slave of sorts, and maybe I still am, but I have been changed by the strength and will of the earth, and I'm here to test my power, against all of them," she pointed to the Ravers held in stasis. She shifted her gaze to the massive warrior who clearly led the band of killers. "I have come to test myself against him. You, you were an accident, Liam, but I did try your will, and you resisted me. You resisted my mistress, too, and she is far more powerful than me. Perhaps we should be more concerned with you than him."

They stared at each other, and neither realized they were getting closer and closer. Liam broke the silence. "You will never have anything to fear from me, Celine. I owe you my life, as do these poor people." Inches separated them. Each felt the other's sweet breath on their face, yet they did not touch.

Something kept them apart, as if they both knew there was a barrier that should not be broken. "I don't know what is to come, Li, but I cannot make the same promise to you. In this I am not my own master. I protect the earth because no one else does. Things may be different if we meet again." She hesitated, then said, "Go."

Liam nodded. He called the others and gathered them for their escape, checking everyone and taking a quick inventory of weapons and food. He had become a commander and didn't even recognize that he was doing what every warrior does before and after a battle. He had learned the hard way, and certain actions had become habitual. He circled the Outcasts, herding them together, saying a word of encouragement here, making a small joke there. He thought of Rat and Ka-an. Did they make it to the river? Had they found one another? Would they find a safe place and wait for him? He chuckled. Why were there always so many questions? He looked at the others and realized he considered them to be "his people." No, they were thinking too, thinking about what just happened, where they were going, what they would eat. He understood they were thinking and questioning as hard as he was—they were just thinking about themselves. He realized the major difference between those who led and those who followed: leaders thought of their people first, while followers thought of themselves first. He couldn't blame them, but that central fact was what separated him from them, and always would. He smiled again. *Stop thinking, mighty slave*, he mockingly thought to himself, *time to go.*

"Jenar, Suki: southwest to the river, get going!" Liam turned to the others, as his point men moved out. He yearned to say something to Celine, but the earth began to shake and a tremendous roar filled his ears. Everyone was knocked to the ground. The Ravers fell where they stood. He turned to Celine. Had she betrayed them? Was she playing with them? She stood calmly, unaffected by the quake. Liam looked back toward his people and couldn't believe what he saw. A giant wall of earth was encircling both groups, Ravers and Outcasts alike. He watched the wall as it formed a complete circle, a writhing prison of dirt and rock. He was stunned. Could she do this? And even as he thought she could, another being materialized from the earth itself. She—yes, it was a she—stood at Celine's shoulder, more severe, taller, dressed in green. Her eyes burned with a dark green fire as she took in both groups of humans. Liam had a sense she wasn't happy. The quaking stopped, dust settled to the tortured ground, and the men dusted off and stood. Instinctively, they backed away from the two creatures standing in the center of the newly created arena. Liam was on edge as he observed that the Ravers were also moving and there were far more of them than there were Outcasts.

The two groups faced off. Only the fact that Liam's Outcasts were now better armed kept the Ravers from attacking immediately. Even this fact didn't deter Akabek. Grabbing a broken spear shaft from the ground, he rushed toward Liam, chanting in a guttural language. His eyes glowed with an evil red light, and Liam took a step back. Nonetheless, he gathered himself. He drew a sword in his right hand and a long knife in his left, bent his knees, stood on the balls of his feet, and readied himself for the onslaught.

Akabek began screaming in a different voice as he closed in. He raised the shaft above his head to drive it through Liam, but a huge voice echoed across the bowl: "Enough!" Akabek froze again; the scream of death strangled in his throat. Eyes bulging, he was helpless. Liam held those maddened eyes, and he saw things he would never forget: endless evil and all-consuming hatred. But there was another being within Akabek's eyes, and that being wanted to destroy and kill everything and everyone.

Liam was surprised to see that he could still move. He relaxed his stance but kept his weapons ready. He turned to Celine and the other being walking toward him. They stopped a few feet away in silence; he was sure they were talking to each other without words, and, of course, they were. Liam began to think of the larger woman as Mother and knew for some reason that he had it right. He watched her as she walked over and stood directly in front of Akabek. She raised her arm and spread her right hand over the Raver's face. He seemed to go mad at the contact. His eyes rolled back and he gasped. His body began to quiver so much as if to shake itself apart. He struggled mightily to break the spell that held him in thrall. Mother tightened her grip on his contorted face and Akabek howled in frustration and pain. Liam shuttered at the sight. He couldn't imagine the battle that was taking place within the Raver's body. He wasn't even sure who was fighting—Akabek or the creature within him. What did it matter? Mother was merciless in her interrogation—if that was what she was doing—and then it was over. She dropped her hand and returned to Celine's side. The Raver captain seemed to lose consciousness, but he couldn't fall to the ground. Mother's power held him upright, as if she wasn't finished with him.

She looked into Celine's eyes once more, and without audible speech, said, *Have you tested yourself against these two, child?*

Yes, Mother, I have.

And what did you find?

Celine hadn't really considered the matter. What did she find? That was a very good question. She thought back to Liam and her attempt to gain control over his will. He had fought her to a standstill, but she never felt threatened by him, and she didn't really understand where his power came from. She was certain that he was just a man, a young man at that, but his will was like supple steel. He felt cool to the touch and could not be broken. More importantly, he did not try to invade her mind. He did not seek control. This played heavily in his favor. On the other hand, the Raver, who called himself Akabek, had felt hot and diseased. She felt darkness when she had penetrated his mind and there was something else there, another power she couldn't name. Danger radiated from the core of his being, and it tried mightily to break her will, to control her spirit. Mother waited patiently for her answer.

The boy has incredible power but is far less dangerous than the other. This one, who calls himself Akabek, wields the power of others, power that is deadly to all beings, including us. I can sense it in his body; he is simply an extension of that greater power, like I am of you.

Mother considered her words. *Do you remember when I told you that both sides in this conflict were equally bad for us in the end?*

Celine nodded. *Yes, I remember.*

Why do you hesitate, then? We came here to test your power against both sides. Do you not know what that means? We didn't come here so you could practice freezing people in place, although that can be a useful ability. We came here to learn the limits of your power. And what is the ultimate limit of your power, Celine? Celine knew the answer. Mother wanted her to kill both men. How would she do it? She considered her ability to hold people in place. If she could stop them in their tracks, perhaps she could stop...their hearts from beating? Oh no. She saw Mother nodding. *Yes, Celine, that is why you are here. Kill them. It must be done. Sooner is better than later, girl.*

Celine approached Liam. She could not deny the Mother. Liam's death was not what she wanted, nor did she think it was necessary. The boy was strong in an obstinate way, but he wasn't a threat to Mother. His was an isolated strength. But Celine had no choice. She concentrated her mind on his body and, specifically, his pounding heart, which she could feel, so close, so close... beating, beating, blood coursing, life flowing, warmth... She began to squeeze, and squeeze... Liam gasped as he felt the first pain. His chest felt as if someone had hit him with a heavy hammer to the heart. He staggered. Both hands covered his heart reflexively. Another blow seemed to crush his chest; Liam felt as if a giant hand had reached into his body and grabbed his heart. He fell to his knees and cried out. Then he got mad.

"Celine, no!" he shouted. She was doing this. She was killing him. His anger raged as he fought the pain. Breath ragged, he clenched his fists and exerted his will. Celine's eyes widened in surprise; she saw a flame burst forth on his chest. It was a green flame and it burned hot, as if his skin fueled the fire. She recognized the form of a three-leafed plant that grew in the far north of the world. Why did it burn on this boy's chest? She didn't have time to think. Liam snarled like a wounded wolf and forced himself upright. She felt herself being expelled from his body, and she saw him stagger toward her, long knife and sword out, ready to end her life. She uttered a cry, and it was her turn to stagger backwards, repulsed by his power.

Mother had seen enough. Through Celine, she felt Liam's might. She had seen the fire raging in his chest. For the first time in a very long time, Mother had experienced something new, something she did not fully understand. This boy's ability was staggering. A new force walked the earth, but the type of force was unknown. Who he served was also a mystery. Why she hadn't come across his ilk before confused her, too. Was she already losing control of her earth to an enemy she wasn't even aware of? Mother knew Liam represented neither the dark nor the light, as she knew them. He "felt" completely different. His strength didn't come across as aggressive in any way. She also had the feeling he would have no idea what she was talking about if she questioned him on the celestial war being waged on Athlan. She joined her power to Celine's and created a wall of energy between Liam and themselves. Liam could see the shimmering curtain. He stepped up to the translucent wall and slashed it with his sword. He cried in pain as the blade rang on the ephemeral light and dropped from his hand. He stood in amazement, glaring at the two earth creatures. He retrieved his weapon and tried to relax, breathing deeply. Stalemate.

Celine waited for Mother to finish her thoughts. She had learned she could be beaten. Her power was not all-encompassing. In the end, she felt Liam could have killed her with his weapons and determination. She had turned on him, broken her word, and he had reacted. The green fire amazed her half-human sensibilities. What was this boy?

Good question, Mother chimed in. *But whatever he is, he is beyond us for now. We will let him go and think about his power.*

Is he good or evil, Mother? Does he side with the light or the dark?

That, too, is a good question, girl. I'm not sure. Right now, I'd say he has the capacity to be both, but he is no threat to us. He fights his own battles and follows not the ancient agenda of power. Maybe the green leaf burning on his skin bodes well for us. Tell him to gather his people and go.

What about the others? asked Celine.

We still have work to do there, Celine. Get that boy out of here.

Celine approached the wall of power and stood directly before Liam. "I will not apologize for my actions. I had no choice, and I will have none in the future. I told you this. If you harm the earth, we will try to kill you again. If you do not, you will have no contact with us. Take your people, Liam, and leave this place of horror."

Celine felt deep pangs of sadness as she spoke. She recognized her emotions for what they were: she loved Liam. It had happened even as she tried to crush the life from him. She had become one with Liam the Outcast. Softly, she whispered, "Please go, Liam. Please."

Liam took one long last look, sheathed his weapons, and watched in awe as the earth wall opened to the southwest. "Jenar, Suki; off you go. Tamar, Garron, bring up the rear of the column. Watch for stragglers and guard our back. Follow me." Liam walked out of the bowl and never looked back. His heart ached for the woman who had almost taken his life. In a way, perhaps she had.

Chapter 8:

Dominance

Mother and Celine watched Liam and his people leave the enclosure. A few threw wary glances back at their inhuman saviors, fearful of their abilities, while others kept their attention on the Ravers that still strained against their bonds, knowing they would attack given the slightest opportunity. The last of the Outcasts had left the circle. Celine had hoped that Liam would give her one last glance, but he had not. *Just as well*, she thought heavily, *nothing could ever come of my feelings for him except heartache, or worse.*

Mother cut into her thoughts again, a habit that was fast becoming annoying. *You're right about that, child. You have no future with humankind, although I don't know if that boy fits the name. I hope not. Be that as it may, we have other work to do this night. We have met our match once, now we—you—must test yourself against that.*

She pointed to the giant warrior in stasis a short distance away. Celine cringed at the thought of entering that body, as she had Liam's. She now understood the dangers of possession and how she would absorb the feelings and thoughts of those she entered. She had no desire to taste the evil madness she had seen in Akabek's eyes. But she had no choice. She must know if there were others who could resist her, or worse, kill her. She knew she was also possessed by Mother and her will was no longer her own. So be it.

They both stood before the Raver. *Celine, be careful with this one. Can you feel the evil? Can you sense the Other within? This is the darkness, Celine. This one must die. He will fight: his will is not his own. Another, a greater threat, governs his body and mind.*

Celine considered Mother's words. *Will I be killing the Other, or the man in front of me, Mother?*

I don't believe you can kill this animal's master, girl. His name is Bas Croi, and he is evil's emissary on my earth. If you face him in the flesh, I believe you could die. I'm not sure what my fate would be, but we will stand together in this deed. Because he must work through this surrogate, his power is reduced accordingly. How much, I do not know. One word before you begin: do not stop for any reason once you start. No matter what thoughts enter your mind, no matter what you feel in your heart, do not stop, for if you do, open as you will be to their minds, they will turn their power on you faster than thought itself. Celine, there is real danger here for you and, perhaps, for me. I will shield your mind if you need help, if I can, but I make no promises. You are my warrior and you must test yourself in this battle.

Akabek quivered in an effort to free himself. Sweat ran down his face and dripped to the ground. His eyes burned with the madness of pure, red hatred. Celine shivered despite her resolve. Mother put her hand on her shoulder: *Steady, girl. This is what threatens our world. If it helps, get angry. He deserves no mercy and will show you none.* Celine steeled herself to the task and for the first time in a long while, she remembered her abandoned children, made the connection between her crazed husband and this piece of filth, and cold rage took over. She raised her arms and placed both hands on the monster's face, holding the sopping head as her fingers dug into his disgusting flesh. She began to concentrate, feeling the blood course under her fingers, feeling the lungs labor, the muscles straining to break free. She penetrated deeper and found the heart pounding with effort, strong and wild. She began to squeeze, her mind picturing her fist crushing the heart, crushing, crushing... And then she felt it: her power was rebounding on her. She sensed mad glee coming from Akabek's mind. She felt coldness penetrating her body; first her hands and then her arms went numb, as if death was slowly freezing her. She cried in pain and fear. "Mother!" But there was no answer; there was no help.

Unwanted images invaded her mind. Akabek was cracking her will and suddenly, there he was. Not the giant brute struggling against her grasp, but "him"—the master. Fire filled her head. She saw images of dead bodies and heard laughter in the back of her mind. The earth burned and was covered by a dark cloud. An unbearable pressure filled her skull and tried to beat her to the ground. She began to sink and felt her hands slipping from the Raver's face. She knew if she let go, she was dead, and she could feel Croi's dark joy as he exerted more pressure on her psyche. She was weak; she had killed her husband and abandoned her children; she deserved to die; she was useless. Celine moaned in despair. Was there nothing good in the world? And then, of all things, she remembered Liam, Liam the Good in her mind, and she felt better. Her strength began to return. She calmed herself and began to fight back, like Liam had fought back. Her anger returned. They would not win; they could not win. She pushed and pushed. Sweat gushed from her own face as she struggled with evil incarnate. She straightened and dug her fingers deep into his face. She found his heart again and exerted all her will, all of her force, all of her love for Liam, the man she tried to kill.

The Master slammed her mind with raging force once again, but she grabbed him, grabbed his mind and squeezed harder still. Her power grew as her anger and determination increased. Akabek screamed in pain and terror. He felt his heart constrict and his breathing become ragged. A thundering voice filled her head: "I see you, woman. You have changed. Your power has grown, but not enough, no, it will never be enough." Insane laughter filled her head, and he attacked her again, but she held fast. Love and hate gave her the strength she needed to complete her task. With one final effort, she exerted her full will, everything she had, and crushed the mighty heart in Akabek the Raver's heaving chest. She didn't stop there. Celine grabbed the massive body and lifted it over her head, held it, then slammed it onto the ground. A huge crack filled the earthen arena. She had broken his back as well as his heart. An eerie wail filled the earthen ring, and power sparked and crackled over the smoking body, which ignited into an intense flame. A wind came up from the south and blew the last sparks and smoke away. Celine looked down at the smoldering remains and then at her hands. For a second, she thought she could see his blood on them, blood up to her elbows, but that was illusion. And that was the last thing she saw before she hit the ground.

Mother knelt and lifted Celine's body. Actual tears dropped from the corners of her eyes and fell onto her daughter's strained face. Her warrior, her creation, had fought for her life, for their lives, and had given everything she had while she, the Mother, had stayed out of the fight, even when Celine had called her name. Mother, in the end a pitiless master, felt pride in Celine like she had never felt for any of her creations. But Celine wasn't perfect. Mother knew she had fallen in love with the boy called Liam, and Liam was a threat Mother had not been prepared for. So, she was still human, at least in this respect: she could feel love for another human, if, indeed, that was what he was. For Celine, love of anything other than the earth presented a serious weakness. What would she do if they met again? There were so many questions.

The world was changing and that, after all, was exactly what Gaiea was trying to stop. The Bas Croi's minions could be killed—at least one at a time. Mother had taken images from Akabek's mind in his struggle to overcome Celine, and those images were mixed with those of his master. A great battle was coming, but she knew that already. It was part of the ancient pattern. The images had centered on the great fortress of Athlan, the Ban Castlean, as Akabek and Croi had thought of it. Good. Maybe they would kill each other to the last man, and she and Celine could get on with tending to the earth. A nice thought, but Mother knew better. Her fate was in the balance and she would keep a close watch on the castle of man. And Celine, well, she, too, would stand sentinel after she had recruited her army of followers. Yes, Mother could see that now. Celine needed help, and she would teach her what she needed to know. More women would join earth's cause, and more men would die. With a wave of her hand, Gaiea Mother returned the earth to its former shape, burying, and thus killing, most of Akabek's depraved humans. Their deaths meant nothing to her.

Chapter 9:

Gorm Reborn

Deep in the northern ridge of mountains, a castle had secretly been carved within a solitary peak. The tower of this hidden fortress was, in fact, the mountain peak itself, and windows had been cunningly cut into every side, allowing someone standing in the tower to see in all directions. The castle was named the Krake Dolas, the rock of despair. No one left the Krake who wasn't a very changed person. A man walked alone in the tower, stopping occasionally to look west by southwest, where he saw the shining towers of the Ban Castlean. He muttered to himself as he circled the chamber. He could see the mighty fortress but the Gardai couldn't see him. Only a cruel, forbidding, mountain peak was visible to all who chose to look. Adventurous Athlaneans had tried to scale the peak, but the bodies of those brave souls were never found. Eventually, the people of Athlan lost interest in the "cursed" mountain.

Loss of interest in the Krake Dolas was fine with its present owner, the Bas Croi.

The Bas Croi had had a very bad night. His plans had been progressing excellently—the destruction of the Warrior, of the Ban Castlean, and final victory. His captains roamed Athlan, each one in command of an angry, violent pack of Ravers, all bent on carrying out his orders. The noose was tightening on schedule and Athlan tore itself to pieces, some of the destruction his doing, but most of it unfolding as nature willed it. And then, last night, that idiot Akabek had gotten himself killed. He would be replaced. What worried Croi, however, was the woman. Twice they had met, and she had become immeasurably stronger. In fact, when he tried to save Akabek, she had grabbed his mind for a shattering moment before he could get his defenses in place. No one other than the Bas Mor had ever taken possession of him. She had a capacity for violence, that one, and there was more. When she entered his mind, he had entered hers. She was a new force in the great struggle for control of the earth. Her power was strange to him, and none of the masters who now lived within his mind recognized its source. But any being that could override him and kill one of his minions, who had considerable strength themselves, was a formidable enemy.

There was also the boy. Croi continued to pace. He wasn't as sure about this one. Croi had drained Akabek's mind before he died and taken his memories, and the story of the Outcasts bothered him for two reasons. First, apparently the boy and girl, one called Liam by his people and the other named Celine, a name Croi had dredged from Akabek's blasted mind, seemed to have a relationship. The second reason was more disturbing. Watching the boy through the Ravers' eyes, he had seen the boy's chest blaze with green flame, as he and the girl apparently struggled with each other. Whose power did he wield? He withstood the girl, while the girl had killed Akabek and almost beaten down his own resistance. So, there were other players in the great game, more unknowns, and that was bothersome. The Bas Croi considered the new situation as he trod the ancient stone floor. He didn't need complications at this stage, and yet he couldn't fully assess the threat either of them presented. Neither strength, boy's nor girl's, felt like the power of the "light." That power left a bitter taste on the senses and burn marks on the brain; he knew this from the past experiences of the collective mind of the masters in his head. And another thing: the abilities used by these brats were completely different from each other. How strange: two threats, completely unknown to him and to each other, appeared from nowhere at a most critical time.

The Bas Croi didn't believe in circumstance. His collective memory screamed *danger*. Centuries of plans gone wrong raced through his mind. Instead of the traditional powers of the light and dark continuing their exclusive quest for mastery, there were now four challengers for domination, each contestant clearly capable of vanquishing the others. The added players vastly complicated the deadly, eternal game. Croi couldn't help himself. His mind raced with possibilities, most of them negative. He was sure that they both sought utter control. They had massive power, therefore, they would use it to conquer. Did they have armies hidden around Athlan like he did? Were they following their own agenda or were they being directed by others? So much uncertainty when he could not afford to be ignorant. He would have to watch closely. He would send a message to his captains, demanding information about both creatures. If they could be captured, good; but if not, death was just as good. That reminded him: his captains. He was one short, and there was an army out there without a commander. He knew they would fall apart, worthless scum, and disperse quickly, but he had to keep them together. They would all die, but no matter; they would serve their primary purpose, which was to draw attention at the appropriate moment.

The floor of the keep was black basalt. In the center, a smaller, blood-red circle had been etched into the hard stone. The sphere glittered with a light of its own, but instead of heat, a deep cold existed within the crimson space. The Bas Croi left the window and walked to the center of the circle. He raised his arms and uttered a guttural incantation, then sat down. The cold increased, but Croi didn't seem to notice. Arms folded across his stomach, he closed his eyes and cast his mind from the tower, looking for his leaderless army. Across the plain he traveled, moving south to the river Ruath. *Yes, yes, there, there is where Akabek died, killed by that young witch.* Croi saw the earthen arena. He saw the deep gouges in the ground. He studied the fresh earthen walls filled with boulders and old roots. He saw the gate-like opening to the southwest. What strength had created this thing that had trapped his captain? Had that troublesome girl done this? The creation of this arena had taken enormous force. He searched his memories for past contact but found none. This riddle would have to wait. He hovered over the area and came in close to study Akabek's body. There were deep depressions all around the edges of his face—fear and surprise emanated from his still unclouded eyes. The Bas Croi looked to the west, found nothing, then east. *There, there they are, the fools; Ravers, indeed.* They had travelled no more than a few miles from the spot where death had taken their captain; out on the open plain they camped, as if they didn't have a care in the world. He would change their attitude significantly.

The Bas Croi floated above the earthen wall and out over the plain. He couldn't materialize a physical body before them, but he could do the next best thing. Croi's spirit floated to the ground in the center of the Raver camp, and his image stood in the middle of a blazing fire. He appeared with a thunderclap and those around the fire were blown back. The Ravers, squinting through a terrible, reddish-white light, saw fire blazing within his body, and tongues of flame shot from his eyes and mouth. The frightened Ravers screamed, panicked, and began to run in all directions. Croi spread his arms and white lines of smoking fire ran from his fingers through each Raver. He turned every would-be warrior to face him. The Ravers existed in their own private hell of pain and fear. Croi had laid their minds bare, and he was reading each story in turn, looking for his next captain. He smiled for the first time since leaving his tower, and that smile was ghastly.

Looking down from the sky, the camp looked like a fiery spiderweb, and Croi was the deadly spider at the center. He continued to shred the minds of the unfortunate Ravers, until he found his man. Then Croi found a disgusting pervert of debauched appetites. He had done things before and since Athlan began its fall that were worthy of Croi's other captains. He was large, young, and very strong, but not exceptionally bright. His name was Gorm, and not only had he killed more than his share since becoming a Raver, but he had greatly enjoyed doing so. Croi read his memories, felt his passions, and learned that Gorm preferred to kill slowly, slashing his victims with a sickle blade that still hung from his belt. Then, before they bled out, while they were still conscious, he would slice open their chest cavities, ram his stiffened fingers into the opening, and rip out the beating heart. Gorm loved the rush of hot blood, the slimy feel of pulsing organ, and he lived for that sensation. Yes, Gorm would do.

Croi mentally reeled in the line of power that connected him to Gorm, and his new captain-elect seemed to float above the ground as he approached his new master. Gorm was drawn into the flames and held there. Croi could see him screaming within; Croi could feel the pain because he was in Gorm's head. As Gorm burned, Croi put one hand on Gorm's forehead and the other on his heart. Through his incorporeal limbs, Croi exerted his malignancy, and Gorm literally lost his mind. Croi replaced it with his own, and Gorm ceased to exist. He became the latest version of Akabek and continued to burn for the privilege. Croi spread his mind and the knowledge that Gorm/Akabek was their leader, and he reinforced the message with the burning pain their new captain suffered. All of the Ravers imagined they were standing in the fire with Gorm, and their brains were irrevocably damaged by the experience.

They were completely conditioned to obey Gorm's every word or suffer the consequence of fire. None had the strength to resist the Bas Croi. He found this thought ironic. He had no trouble managing thousands of killer sheep like these, but in one night he had been challenged by two children, both beyond his control.

There was one more thing to do. He would doubly reinforce the lesson. Croi made a mental suggestion to Gorm, then severed the lines of control. The Ravers collapsed as one, but Gorm's voice whip-cracked over their heads: "Stand, you useless bastards." They stood, as if pulled upright by invisible strings. Gorm pulled his wickedly curved blade, took two steps toward a strikingly beautiful woman, one of the few female Ravers who'd survived the last few months, and repeatedly slashed her breasts and face. Blood flew in great gouts as flesh was carved from her bones, but she did not fall, nor did she move. Sound did not escape her lips. When Gorm had had his fun, he shoved his hand inside her destroyed body and ripped out her beating heart. Holding it high before the group, blood dripping over his face, Gorm laughed loud and long. The lesson was complete.

Croi gave Gorm silent instructions and transported himself back to his keep. *It was an interesting and enjoyable evening*, he mused. Thoughts of, victory, and revenge percolated in his mind. The boy and girl were complications he could not afford to ignore. He wanted more information. He needed to direct his pieces across the board. There was much to do; time was running short.

Chapter 10:
The Ancient Promise

Arcasaid was the major harbor on the western coast of Athlan. The Blackwater River, which originated as a crystal-clear pool of icy mountain water within the walls of the Ban Castlean, ran under the walls of the castle and continued underground for close to a thousand yards before it surfaced and flowed in a gently curving line through the harbor business area and then down to the sea, another mile or so to the west. Ships of all shapes and sizes sailed in both directions on the deep and wide waterway. Large hulled cargo dromons navigated all the way to the massive stone docks at the head of the Blackwater and had done so for thousands of years. Ancient roads made of expertly cut and fit flagstones ran from the wharfs of Arcasaid up to the Ban Castlean. Every other watercourse on Athlan was lined with burnt-out hulks and the detritus of a dying nation—not so the banks of the Blackwater. Marfach Gardai lined the river on each side. Guard posts were manned at regular intervals, and heavily armed two-man Gardai teams walked the river's edge day and night, keeping civil order. The more important reason for their vigilance was obvious to Kon-r Sighur: the Blackwater was their only escape route to the sea, if flight became necessary. If the Gardai didn't keep it safe and clear, as well as Arcasaid itself, the Gardai and the people they protected would be trapped on a sinking island. And so, the Blackwater was protected and the people of Arcasaid and the Ban Castlean felt safe.

Not all was as it seemed, however. Athlan was an ancient land. Tunnels, sewers, and drains still existed underground, extending from the docks of upper Arcasaid into the Ban Castlean. If these old passages had ever been mapped, those aged scrolls were long gone, or buried in some dusty archive within the castle. Many knew the stories about these subterranean passages, but few knew the truth: one man on Athlan knew the tunnel system better than anyone else had ever known it and that man was the Bas Croi. Because his master had burned the details into his mind, he knew the only way into the castle would be the tunnels. The massive gate and the indomitable walls were impenetrable. No matter how many Ravers he could recruit and direct, the Gardai and Kon-r Sighur would safe behind their sacred walls. Croi considered this as he studied a map of the underground world he had drawn over the years based upon many trips through the forgotten passageways along the Blackwater. His lips drew back in a rictus of a smile. If only these sheep knew the slavering creatures of the deep like he did, things hungering in the dark… perhaps they would know soon.

Croi concentrated on the map. He began circling areas all over the island—twelve circles to be exact. These were the armies trained and led by his captains. Each army of Ravers was closing in on the Ban Castlean; the farthest unit was about five days away. Others were much closer, but they were under his orders to stay hidden in whatever ruins they could find until directed to do otherwise. The Gardai had not come out from behind their walls. The great and last real Warrior had retreated to the safety of his fortress, not wishing to become involved with the hordes of citizens destroying Athlan, as physical Athlan destroyed itself. He didn't have the stomach to slaughter his own. That was good. The Gardai could have caused Croi serious problems. Sighur had sent out scouting parties, who had easily been disposed of. Many of the bodies ended up in these tunnels, feeding the creatures that hunted in the dark for warm blood and sweet meat. None of his armies, even those led by the captains of his own mind, could have withstood a direct assault by a determined Gardai brigade. He chuckled. Even a company of dedicated Gardai would have caused serious problems for any of the Raver units, no matter how large and feral they were. Timing was everything now. The Bas Croi leaned back into a creaky chair, at one time a fine piece of the wood carver's art. He closed his eyes and consulted the dead masters who "lived" within his mind. Fine generals and beings of infinite subtlety offered their insights by reviewing for him what they had accomplished against the Light when they led the powers of the night. Knowledge, surprise, speed, a total lack of mercy—these were the keys to victory. The Warrior must die. And he would. Croi's plan was good. There would be tremendous bloodshed on both sides. That didn't matter.

What did matter were the ships he had gathered far to the east in the land of Afrik. Three large, fast battleships were, he hoped, even now sailing toward the west coast of Athlan. They were made from almost indestructible hardwoods and manned by fierce black warriors who worshipped him and those who had come before him as gods of the Night. These ships should have already sailed from their jungle river berths and would, at the appropriate time, cruise into Arcasaid harbor; they would take on the Bas Croi, his captains, and those soldiers who lived, and were worth saving. Croi didn't expect much resistance once in the harbor. Croi's minions would take care of the weak Gardai harbor guard by the time his small but powerful fleet made landfall, and by that time, the Marfach Gardai would be no more. Any resistance would consist of fleeing peasants and fat Arcasaid merchants trying to buy a ride to anywhere. They would die. Croi decided to make the journey from the gates of the Ban Castlean to the sea above ground, instead of beneath. He thought he would lose too many men in the tunnels, as amusing as that might be, and he needed followers where he was going. There would be fighting wherever they landed. Once dominant, he could recruit and train new followers. His power after the defeat of the Warrior and the final destruction of Athlan would be unchallenged across the earth. That was the promise made to him by his divine master; the ancient promise made to all of them. He felt emotion rising within as the old masters clamored for final victory—the vindication of all they had done, every life they had destroyed over the long, violent centuries.

Croi studied the map again. Only one path led into the Ban Castlean. The path had been dug out by his people and followed the original, tiled sewer line that ran from the center of the Castlean to the Blackwater. The sewer line had been filled in within the castle centuries ago and was long forgotten. In a few days, his men would be directly under the castle waiting his order to dig through the final layer of earth to the surface. When he gave the order, Croi expected to have more than a thousand fully armed Ravers in the tunnel. He almost had that now. They would be led by one of his captains. Rooms had been carved out of the rotting subterranean city and his army lived in the dark: human rats fighting the real rodents for their food. Croi took great satisfaction in the fact that the great Kon-r Sighur had no idea his destruction lay directly below his feet. The Gardai would get what they so richly deserved. Croi took a second map from a packet he kept close to his heart. He gently unfolded the seamed cloth and studied the faded lines. He took this map from an informant who had bargained hard with Croi, believing he could squeeze the great man for tremendous riches and, maybe, find a way off the dying island. After a suitable amount of haggling, Croi promised him what he wanted, but once the map was in his hands, the novice spy met a very bad end in the tunnels less than one hundred feet from where the Bas Croi now studied the layout of the Ban Castlean. Each area of the fortress was clearly marked—market, barracks, cistern, food warehouses, but most importantly, living quarters for the Gardai officers, including that of the Warrior himself, who took great pride in living as his officers lived. *So inspiring*, thought the Croi, *and so stupid*. He would die first, of course, and the rest would follow. Coming to the end of his campaign, it all seemed so simple, thought Croi, poring over the rest of his plan.

Chapter 11:

Mik and Nik

Tan and Telk began trotting down to the waterfront of Cala, once an important port city of Athlan. Both men had been there in better times, and they were shocked to see the utter devastation along the wharves and piers. Warehouses once filled with expensive goods transported to and from Cala were burning pyres, or grey piles of ash. Beautiful ships of all sizes were burned to the waterline, never having left their berths. Bloated bodies floated in the harbor, a rolling raft of rotting humanity. Tan grabbed Telk by the arm and stopped him. For the first time, Tan noticed small groups of men standing in shadow along the waterfront. Once aware, he saw them everywhere. Silent and still, they watched and waited. Tan knew he and Telk were in trouble. They had come too far too fast. They were surrounded.

Rok Tan looked for an escape. They could always run off a pier and dive into the ocean, but that seemed cowardly, and besides, those bloated bodies would soon attract sharks, and they had seen what sharks could do to a man. Neither sailor wanted to face that option. Further down the quay, Tan saw lights—what looked like a tavern. What kind of tavern could still be open in this place was anyone's guess, but it was better than being caught in the open. "Telk, don't run yet, but stay close. We're going to get to that tavern. If I say run, run like hell. Got it?" Telk nodded. They began to walk, as if on a brisk, evening stroll. Tan slipped his throwing knife into his hand, and Telk dropped his right hand onto his sword. Tan thought about unslinging the war bow, but that would be too obvious and might provoke those he wanted to evade. Nonetheless, shadows began to move to their left, in front of them and behind. The sea blocked any hope of escape to the right.

Just as Tan picked up the pace, a shout came from behind. "Stop!" He ignored the command and walked a little faster, Telk in tow.

Then, from their front, a voice commanded, "Go no further!" Which he also ignored, and they began to move faster. Tan could see men wrapped in black coming down from the warehouses, converging on them, trying to steer them away from the tavern ahead.

"Telk, run!" and they ran. Black figures emerged from the smoke and shadow, their hands clutching, trying to stop the sailors progress, for he was in the lead, fighting off their attackers with knife and sword, shoulder and fist. Telk now ran beside him, more hindrance than help. Telk continually got in the way of Tan's sword arm. But they managed to get through, and as they got closer to the tavern lights, the crowd flowed into shadow again, as if they had never existed.

How strange, thought Tan. *They used no weapons. They wanted to take us alive.* And that sent a shiver down his spine. Any real soldier would feel fear going into battle—what sane man wouldn't. No soldier, however, wanted to be captured, particularly when the enemy had no respect for life or the virtues of war, however dubious those may be. Most would rather die than suffer torture and humiliation. Tan was no different.

The Colmers finally stood before the tavern, the Hazard Inn, feeling relatively safe within the pool of light cast by the lone lamp above the door. It was once bright red, but had faded, and now was the color of brown, dried blood. Windows on both sides of the door had been painted black and were blocked by dark drapes within. No light escaped. The building itself was the last standing along the quay. The two looked at each other, shrugged, and moved to enter, Tan taking the lead. The door, extremely thick and heavy, opened easily enough and they entered. Without thinking, Tan said, "May the gods bless all here," which he had said a thousand times in taverns across the known world, and in all of those places of drink, large or small, someone would always answer with a variant of, "and you." It was how things were done; a sign of peace, the same as saying, "I want no trouble, I'm here to relax." But no sound came from the patrons of this place. In fact, no one even looked up from their cup.

Tan and Telk went to the bar, a wide wooden plank resting on a barrel at each end, which lined the left wall of the establishment. Rok took it all in within seconds: large fireplace on the right wall, no entrance on the back wall, a door at the end of the bar, probably leading to the kitchen, if there was one. There was a haphazard collection of tables and chairs scattered about the room, and about eight or nine shabbily dressed men of indeterminate age sat among them. Tan could hear his own footsteps. The room was eerily quiet. The barman, a nasty-looking brute who had seen his share of bloody brawls, easily a full head taller than Tan and almost twice as wide, made his way towards them and said, "Who are you two?"

Tan knew the type: sly but not smart, tough but not courageous—a bully, in fact. Not to be trusted. Yet, Tan knew he deserved an answer because it was his turf. "I'm Mik, and this here's Nik. We're shipmates. We travel together and were supposed to sign onto a ship, the *Ocean Star*, a few days ago. We could get outta here that way, see? But, there ain't no ship, and it doesn't look like one's a-comin' soon, so we came in here, hopin' someone could tell us somethin' about what's goin' on, or if there be another ship comin' in."

The barman stared hard at him. The stranger's story might be true. They had the look of seamen. But something wasn't right. What... and then he saw it: what sailor carried a war bow? Knives, pikes, pins, cutlasses—those were the weapons of a sailor. The barman, Kleg by name, nodded and asked, "What will it be mates?"

Tan answered, "Two ales, friend." And he put the only coin he found in his pocket on the bar—a gold florin stamped with the Council of Four likeness on one side and the Ban Castlean on the other. Kleg grabbed two battered pewter mugs and filled them from a cask beneath the bar. He placed them in front of the sailors, splashing foam carelessly.

The coin was worth far more than the drinks, and Kleg, who pictured that coin in his pocket, said, "I'll have to go in the back to get change for that."

He put his hand out to grab the coin, but Tan grabbed his wrist. "It's not that I don't trust you, me lad, but you know what change ya need to bring out. Leave the coin be, and when you've brought me my money, you can have yours. How's that now?"

Tan wanted to see Kleg's reaction to a little prodding. Kleg turned fire-red, and Tan knew that under normal circumstances Kleg would probably be over the bar and at his throat, but something wasn't normal, and Kleg restrained himself, growling, "I'll be right back, fine sir, don't you worry. Yes, I'll bring exactly what you deserve—yes sir."

Kleg went through the door at the end of the bar. Both men grabbed their mugs, drank deeply, and regretted their haste. Neither man had ever had such a foul brew. Both began to retch and cough and for the first time, and the denizens of the tavern laughed, breaking the silence. They had been waiting for the joke; now it had come. They laughed hard and long. Tan and Telk became suspicious because the joke wasn't that funny. Something wasn't right in this tavern, something Tan couldn't put his finger on, but his gut was rarely wrong about such things.

Telk elbowed him in the side. "They're up and moving," he whispered. Tan pretended to drop something to the floor, and as he bent to pick it up, he glanced around the room. Telk was right. Half of the patrons were moving between them and the front door of the inn. Not good. The others were spreading out in a rough circle behind them. No one had drawn a weapon, but Tan guessed that would happen soon. No sense in waiting. Surprise in situations like this was everything.

When he stood up, Tan leaned on the bar and said in a low voice, "We have to get out of here. If we try to go out the front, we'll be caught between those four and the others who will come in behind us. We'll take a chance. I'm going to say something about finding my change, and then I'll begin to walk towards the door at the end of the bar. Count three, then follow. We'll run through the door and hope we can get out the back. Don't stop running. If something happens to me, get to the bridge and tell Tor to get back to the ship. Will you do that?"

Telk didn't like the idea of leaving his shipmate, but he was a good man and would obey orders. "Okay, Tan. I'll find him." But neither man really believed he'd make it to freedom.

Chapter 12:
Vespex Kee

Tor and Sandine began walking uphill, towards the residential area above the docks. Cala's wealthiest had homes here, and those beautiful buildings were still there, although many had been gutted by fire. The main thoroughfares of Cala had been well lit by street lamps tended by night watchmen. This area, called Upper Ward Road, was always one of the safest neighborhoods in the city. While the homes were not enclosed with massive stone walls, each household normally had a security detail, and adventurers from the docks knew better than to seek excitement up the hill. Rough men who decided to ignore the word in town were often found lying on an abandoned wharf, their heads cracked, if not worse. Now, the street lamps were a thing of the past, their multi-colored globes shattered, and ruthless gangs roamed the darkened streets looking for easy prey. The dim light emitted from flames burning houses, or mounds of dying embers and the overall red glare cast by the burning city itself.

Tor flashed back to battlefields of his past, cities conquered and burned in the name of the Gardai and their merchant controllers. Sparks filled the air and waves of smoke came and went just as quickly. The wind swirled in off the water—a nightmarish scene from hell.

Lok and Sandine came across numerous bodies killed in various ways—some nailed to trees or hung from repurposed lampposts. They had been men, women, and children. Many lay in the street, naked or sprawled across lawns, as if they were dolls, broken and discarded. Was Athlan like this everywhere? The Colmers moved in a loose, back to back, two-man, fighting formation, and were constantly on guard for danger. They remained in shadow whenever possible. Each had a knife in one hand and a sword in the other. Lok knew, or thought he knew, where Kee's house was. "I think we have to go up this street for a short way, then cut north on a smaller lane. Kee's house should be at the end of the lane. Stay close. Yell if you see anything, Sandy."

"Right, Tor. Did you expect things to be this bad?"

Lok shook his head, although his partner couldn't see him. "No, not even in my nightmares could I have envisioned this. Our country seems to be falling apart quicker than I thought. Keep your eyes open. I don't want to fall apart with it. Let's go."

They continued to crab their way along the unlit street until Lok found the side street he was looking for. Once a neatly gardened corner, the entrance to Seashell Lane was a burned-out abattoir, filled with smashed furniture and mangled bodies. Lok stopped to search the dead, hoping he wouldn't find his former Gardai sergeant. After a while, he shook his head and said, "No, he isn't here. Come on." They continued up the lane, slowly, alert to danger. Lok's senses were wide open, and Sandine watched their backs. After a while, Lok grabbed Sandine and pulled him down. He pointed with his knife but said nothing. Sandine looked ahead through burned bushes and swirling smoke. He saw one man fighting against many, wielding a large broadsword, using only one arm as the other was missing from the shoulder. He was not doing well. Fighting in the red light generated by his burning house, Lok and Sandine could see blood running from numerous slashes and punctures on his body. He was exhausted and near the end of his endurance. Nevertheless, he fought on; his back was forced up against the remnants of a burning tree; his attackers darted in and out, avoiding the ever-slowing former Gardai, and they laughed at the swordsman's frustration and pain.

Lok's breath caught in his throat. It was Vespex and he was still a fighter, but Lok had to decide. Did he drag Sandine into a fight they may not—no, probably would not—win, or did they let Kee die alone, sacrificed to these animals in the name of caution? Vespex was Gardai. He was a friend. Lok grabbed Sandine by the shoulders and looked him in the eyes. Neither man said anything and each knew his odds of getting out of this one. Lok raised an eyebrow; Sandine nodded yes. Lok studied the area. The brigands had their backs to them. With luck, they could get close. "We go. No noise. You take as many as you can on the left, I'll take the right. Don't hesitate. This isn't about being fair. Kill as many as you can from behind, Sandy. There'll be no mercy for either one of us. Understand?" Sandine nodded. "Let's go."

Trying to balance speed and silence can be difficult. Lok wanted, needed, to get to Kee for information, but also because he was Gardai and Lok was Gardai, and as he ran, the feelings Lok had shut away for so many years came crashing back on him. Fear, exhilaration, anger—they all returned with a vengeance and he felt alive, really alive, for the first time in years. He drove his short knife into the back of the first man he came to. The world turned red. Lok left the knife in place and began slashing with his long sword. It wasn't much of a weapon, coming as it did from the ship's stores, but it had weight and length and the *Colm*'s armorer always kept a good points and edges on the ships weapons. Brigands began to fall like wheat to the scythe. Lok risked a quick look for

Sandine; he was in the center of a frantic knot of men, but that was all Lok could see. Lok continued to kill like the Gardai he was.

Lok could still see Vespex, his back pushed against the smoldering tree trunk, sword held defensively before him, but Kee's time was short. The rabid gang had finally taken full notice of Lok and Sandine. Some charged and died. Some began to edge away from the big man. Once that happened, it didn't take them long to break in full panic. They weren't soldiers; they were scum. They ran. Lok bellowed a war cry, separated another piece of garbage from his head and found himself standing before Vespex, who was now leaning on his sword bleeding, exhausted and dying. Tor grabbed his friend and lowered him to the ground, gently leaning him back against the tree. Sandine, breathing heavily, staggered to them. He, too, was bleeding from half a dozen wounds, but said, "Not to worry, Tor, they look worse than they are. Tend to your man, before he gets away from you."

Lok quickly assessed Sandine's injuries—an old battlefield habit—agreed with him, and turned to Vespex. "Ves, Ves, it's me Torvyn Lok; open your eyes, Ves, open your eyes."

Kee's eyes flickered open and slowly focused on Lok's face. Vespex smiled, "Torvyn Lok…I never thought to see you again…." The effort of speaking seemed to drain Kee. "Lok, take my sword; it's Gardai—the only thing I have left from those days. Take it, take it." Lok reached down and picked up the Gardai blade, much better than his own. "I've got it, Ves. It served you well." Kee smiled a small, small smile. His breathing became labored. His eyes snapped open, and his hand grabbed Lok's arm with desperate strength. "Lok, get to the Castle. Get to Kon-r." Vespex was breathing faster now.

"Why, Ves, why, what should I tell him?" Vespex forced out the words, "They're coming. They...they have a leader...they aren't what they seem...they come for Kon-r, they come to......" He never finished. An arrow whistled through the night. It pinned Kee to the tree. Lok dove away as a second arrow flashed through the space he left behind. Lok rolled behind the tree, just in time to see Sandine topple backwards, an arrow meant for Lok buried deep in his neck. Lok dragged Sandine behind the tree, but it was too late. Sandy died ugly, drowning on his own blood in panic. Lok folded Sandine's hands around his sword hilt and placed hands and weapon on Sandy's chest. It was all he could do for a friend. Lok knew he had to get away. Who was coming for Kon-r? Lok slid Vespex's sword into his own scabbard, lowered himself to the ground and began to slither through the grass, finding shadows and looking for a way out.

Chapter 13:
Friends and Brothers

Lok could count the number of times he'd fled a fight on one hand and still have five fingers left over. But today, he slithered, crawled, and flat out ran. Cala had gotten to him like no other place or battle. The best word he could come up with was *spooked*. He was spooked, which was different from being afraid. Fear was something he had dealt with. Fear never went away, at least not very far away. One learned to deal with it. When asked what courage really was, Lok knew, as did any experienced combat soldier: courage was doing your job even when you were scared to death. Courage wasn't about uniforms and medals and promotions. Lok was afraid, but that was normal. He was spooked, though, and that was new.

He felt things were happening around him beyond his control. He suspected someone or something was looking over his shoulder. He thought he was being driven, herded by an unknown shepherd. In short, he saw himself as a puppet, and he didn't know who was pulling the strings. He could feel the slime of evil surrounding him, rubbing against his body in the smoke, but he couldn't pinpoint the cause. The deaths, destruction—those things were horrible, but he'd seen worse. No, it was more than that; he suspected a purpose behind the evil. Maybe that was what Vespex had been trying to tell him.

"A leader," "not what they seem..." these were among Kee's final words. He was dying, but his grip was incredible and his eyes bright as he uttered his last warning. Tor knew he had to get back to the Cala-Bailiag Bridge. He had to find Tan and return to the *Ban Colm*. Charging across Kee's lawn with weapons in hand, he realized he belonged with the Gardai, with Kon-r. He couldn't run away. Once in, never out. The decision had been fast and final. Making it work with Seoult and KT was going to be a problem, but first, he had to get out of this damn city. He made his way down the hill, through the burning neighborhoods, staying in the shadows as much as possible. He avoided everyone he saw or heard. He felt like a hunted animal running away with its tail between its legs. At least he still could run.

And he did. He came to a point along the road where he could see down to the bridge. One dim lamp lit the eastern end, while the Cala River flowed beneath like a giant, glistening, black snake. The bridge was deserted, but Lok waited in the bushes, watching, trying to discern if there was a trap. He waited for a while and just as he was about to step into the light, a group of men emerged from the darkness and converged on the bridge. They were all wearing black robes with cowls over their heads. He saw no weapons, but he knew they could be hiding under the robes. One man stood at the end of the bridge facing the rest. Lok assumed he was the leader of forty or so men. The leader was talking, but Tor couldn't make out the words, couldn't see the face concealed in the darkness of the hood.

Lok wanted to hear what he was saying, so he crawled back into the greenery and slithered down to the men. His cover ran out five or six paces from the robed group, and he heard the words of the Master:

"All of our plans have been destroyed. We can't leave Cala as we wished. Our ship lies at the bottom of the harbor. Reaching Arcasaid and the Ban Castlean must follow a different path, one I can't foresee. The Great Danger still exists, and we must join this battle. If we cross the bridge, we will have to cross the plains of Athlan weaponless, which is our way, but also without food. You know what roams those plains. You know what will happen if we are caught. I have no choice. I will go alone if I must. We have been instructed by our god: The one, true god of all things. Search your hearts, brothers—who will come with me?"

Every man dropped to his knees in the dust of the roadway. One voice answered for all: "We are one; we will come. The final struggle draws near. Lead the way, Brother."

Lok had heard enough. These travelers were holy men, not scavenging brigands. They may be able to help each other. "Stop!" shouted Lok, as he walked down the road. The robed brothers formed a defensive line facing Lok with their leader at the center. He stood still with staff in hand.

"We seek no trouble, sir, but we can and will defend ourselves."

Lok had to make this quick. Tan may need him. "I bring no trouble. Who are you and where do you go?"

"I could ask you the same, friend, but you do not have the look of evil upon you. I am Brother Vivane, and these are the brothers of Our Sacred Lord, or, more correctly, all of the brothers still walking this ravaged earth. Many have been killed. We travel to the Ban Castlean."

Questions flooded Lok's mind, but he had no time. "My name is Torvyn Lok. I'm captain of the *Ban Colm* which, right now, is anchored just beyond the outer harbor. She waits for me and the rest of my men. Tell me, have you seen two men tonight along the waterfront?"

Brother Vivane turned to his people and a clipped, hurried conversation took place. "Yes, we have. Earlier this evening we were searching the quay for transportation when we saw two men approaching the Hazard Inn, an evil place if ever there was one. A few of us tried to stop them, but unarmed, we were no match for the taller one. Our good deed was paid for in blood. We decided to let them go. They entered the Inn. We watched for a time, but they never came out. We have our own problems, Captain, and we went our own way. Hence, you find us here."

Lok's mind raced. "I have a proposition for you. I need to find my men, and you need transportation to Arcasaid. I also need men to work my ship. Like you, I have lost many friends. Help me get those two men back, and I'll take you to Arcasaid, as long as your men work the ship for me."

There was a quiet murmuring in the group. At last Brother Vivane answered: "We are not sailors, Captain, but we will work for our passage, and we'll help you find your men. We believe you to be a gift from the Lord."

Lok grimaced. "I don't know about that, Brother, but let's get moving. Show me where this tavern is." The entire group began to run.

Lok ran next to the robed leader, who kept up a fast pace. Lok couldn't help himself. "Vivane, who are the Brothers of the Sacred Lord?"

After a few more strides, the holy man answered, "Call me V. That's what these men call me. We are a religious order. We believe in one God. We believe in an aggressive policy of goodness." He let that one hang in the air, knowing Lok would bite, which he did.

"What does that mean?"

"It means, Torvyn Lok, that evil must be aggressively fought wherever it is found. It means good men cannot stand aside and ignore what happens around them. Unlike some, we do not turn the other cheek. We fight when we must and we fight to win." Lok began breathing harder because V, in his zeal, had unconsciously picked up the pace while he spoke. Lok checked; V seemed unfazed, his breathing almost normal, and there was a small smile on his face.

They ran on. A million things passed through Tor's mind concerning the Brothers, Rok Tan, and Telk, the ship and the Gardai—always the Gardai. He could barely get the words out, but he managed. "Why do you have to get to Arcasaid?"

V responded quickly: "Evil goes to the Ban Castlean, and we will not miss the fight."

"How do you know that?" asked a winded Lok.

V turned and stared at Tor long and hard. "Perhaps I know some things about Athlan you do not. But, even if I don't, what does your heart tell you? You have been walking in the dark among the dead of Cala; what have you learned? What do you feel?" Lok knew exactly what V was talking about: the cold, clammy touch in the smoke, Vespex's last warning, his decisions all going bad. V was right: evil did walk the land, but Lok couldn't put a face to it.

Before he had time to answer, V brought them to a halt. They stood where Tan had been earlier, watching the light leak from the last building on the quay. There seemed to be a nimbus of color surrounding the forlorn structure, but that could have been the reflection of firelight in the smoke. "Your men went in there," V said, pointing to the building. "We waited, but they did not leave."

Lok was trying to formulate a plan. How many men could there be? How many might they have to fight? He was tired of making mistakes and watching men die for his lack of judgment. As if reading his thoughts, V said, "We do this of our own volition, Tor. Our lives are our own. Tell us what you would have us do, and we will do it."

Tor was starting to like Brother V, and just as he was about to explain his plan, a body came flying through the Hazard Inn's front window. Glass shattered across the quay. At that point Lok's only plan was "Run!"

As they did, Lok pointed to the rear of the Inn, and Brother V shouted, "Brother Boque, go to the rear and enter." Men sprinted for the back entrance of the Inn. By this time Lok and V were close to the front door.

Lokvyn said, "Through the door!" He was first and slammed into the thick wood. It didn't move, and he bounced back into the street only to see the Brothers of the Sacred Lord piling in through the smashed window. Instead of being first, he was last. He got up, went through the empty window, and found a melee in progress. The room was packed, all were armed in one way or another facing to the left, where Rok-Tan and Telk fought in the cramped quarters behind the bar. There were bodies everywhere. His men had done well so far.

With a shout, Brother V and his men charged the bar. Lok stood in wonder. The robed religious fought like holy demons, kicking and punching their way through the toughest scum of the Cala waterfront. The denizens of the Hazard Inn never knew what hit them. Before Lok could even pick an opponent, Boque's men burst through the back door and pummeled those that had tried to escape the whirlwind attack. The battle officially ended when Tan lopped the head off the last brigand standing. The Brothers stepped away from the bar and regrouped behind V, while Lok made his way to his winded men. Both had suffered cuts and bruises.

"Having fun, gentlemen?" asked the Captain.

Tan turned to Telk and answered, "Three things, Captain: first, it took you long enough; second, the situation was well under control, and third, who in the wide world of the Four are these maniacs?"

Brother V and his men began laughing. They laughed at Tan's description of them, they laughed as men fresh from battle do once they realize they're still alive. Lok realized he was remiss in his duty. "Rok-Tan, Battle Master of the *Ban Colm*, and Telk Freem, first mate, let me introduce Brother Vivane and the Brotherhood of the One, Sacred Lord."

Tan answered for himself and Telk, "Thank you for your help, Brother. You fight like Gardai masters. I would like to hear more of this "Lord" you serve. After watching you, I have an entirely new perspective on religion." They all laughed. Friendships were made. A good fight could do that.

Lok broke the good mood. "Gentlemen, this is heart-warming, but we have to get out of here. There may be more scum waiting in the dark. We must get back to the ship. Tan, Brother V and his men are coming with us. We'll go back to the Cala-Bailiag Bridge and try to make our way to the village. Maybe we can find fishing boats, or some craft that haven't been burned."

Rok was nodding in agreement, but asked, "Sandine?" Lok silently, slowly shook his head. "Kee?" Lok answered, "No." Tan shook himself and said, "Telk and I will lead. Try to keep up. Brother V, can you run in those skirts as well as you fight?" V smiled. "I'll be standing on the bridge when you get there, son. Ask me then." Telk and Rok-Tan laughed, vaulted over the bar, and made their way into the street. Lok, V, and the Brothers followed.

Chapter 14:
OVERMATCHED

The wind has picked up, was Lok's first thought as he hit the street behind Tan. The air was oppressive, hot and humid—like running through a warm fog. The smoke seemed denser, too, filled with the smell of burning homes and wasted lives. *It might rain soon*, he thought, trying to keep Tan in sight; the Battle Master sprinted along the docks, darkness closing behind him. Lok turned and found Brother V a pace off his left shoulder, his men running easily behind in pairs. The Brothers of the One Sacred Lord were a mystery. Lok was a well-traveled man. He didn't come from money, hadn't had anything given to him. He'd sailed to every major port in Athlan and marched across the rest of it; but he had never heard of the Brothers. *How could such a formidable band of men remain so active yet hidden?* he thought. When they were safe on the *Ban Colm*, he would have time to talk with V.

Leather sandals beat time on the ancient cobblestones. Lok's body automatically fell into the well-worn Gardai rhythm. The men ran in step, as if they had trained together for years. *This feels good.* They ran through the surreal night. The docks were empty. The people were gone, which was a relief. Lok was sure they'd be attacked when they left the Hazard Inn. He wasn't happy about the smoke. Rok-Tan and Telk were running somewhere up ahead, and Lok couldn't see them. "V, could you send two men to link up with Tan? Tell him to let us catch up."

V nodded and called out, "Billus, Tome! Go ahead, find Tan; tell him to wait for us." The two men were the youngest of the Brothers. They sped off into the smoky darkness, cubs finally allowed to play.

The tight group ran, reaching the corner that led uphill to the Ca-la-Bailiag Bridge. Just as they began to climb, Billus and Tome, with Tan and Telk on their heels, sprinted out of the smoke. Tor held up his hand and the group stopped. All four men were breathing hard. Tan walked the final few steps, hands on his hips, trying to catch his breath.

Lok asked, "Is there a problem, Battle-Master?"

Tan nodded a few times. "Yes, I think you could say that, if hundreds, if not thousands, of armed madmen trying to kill you could be considered a problem."

So, they were waiting, thought the Captain, *waiting where they knew we had to go; but so many?*

"That isn't all" Tan added, "They have a leader. I couldn't see him clearly through the haze, but he's a giant. Shield, sword, axe, helm—that's all I could see. One other thing: he was laughing."

Lok was dumbfounded: An army? Who were these people? "Tan, were they chasing you? How long do we have?"

Tan shrugged. "They weren't running like we were. When I looked back, the giant was walking after us, and his men remained behind him. He must think we have no place to go."

Lok needed to know if they were, indeed, surrounded. "Brother V—" He didn't finish his sentence. V and his men were in a heated, but muted conversation. Lok didn't interrupt, even though he wanted to. After a few moments, V turned to Lok "There is something you must know. I told you that evil goes to the Ban Castlean. I didn't tell you how. We know there are bands, small armies, led by extremely large men in full battle dress—giants, if you will. They kill for pleasure; destroy whatever they can. I—we—have fought them but we failed... every time. We can kill the rank and file; they are only people gone mad, but these giants, they're beyond us. Their power is not only in arms; they command, or *are* commanded, by a force beyond our strength."

Lok wasn't getting it. He didn't understand what V was talking about. "V. stop talking gibberish. I've seen your men fight. What are you talking about? What is so special about the giant? If he is a man, we can kill him."

V stood face to face with Lok. "He is not a man, Lok. We don't know what he is, but he isn't a man, not like any men we know. His eyes burn red, and he is fast—faster than anyone has a right to be. He blocks our blows and strikes with ease, as if he knows what we will do before we do it. And the blows we land, he shrugs off. His laughter is inhuman. He is evil incarnate. I don't know. Another thing: there are more than one of them. How many, I'm not sure, but they walk the earth in the same way: leading crazed, blood-thirsty mobs. They all move towards the Castlean."

Lok didn't know what to say. He'd been gone too long. This was beyond him: giants with strange powers? Maybe this was what Kee was trying to tell him? What had Athlan come to? Nonetheless, he was in command. He had to do something. "V, send runners. We need to find a way out of here."

V called names and men ran east into the night. He shouted, "Return soon. We may have to move." Lok knew V was right. They did have to move, but to where? They either had to escape or find a strong defensive position, which was another way of saying they would die, only more slowly. He looked down the quay. Nothing but debris from destroyed ships and cargo, and empty piers extending into the bay like skeletal fingers. The Hazard Inn? They could defend from inside, but in the end, the brigands could easily burn down the structure around them. Lok hated the feeling of being trapped. Maybe that's why he loved the sea. "V, let's run down the quay. We need some distance." They ran like men determined to survive, men still in control.

Lok knew the quay dead-ended into a wall of natural stone that formed the curved, northern arm of the bay. The wall was a ways off, but it did limit how far they could run. He didn't want to be pinned against it. Judging he was about halfway there, impossible to tell in the smoky dark, Lok called a halt at the head of a long pier called Grimpen Claw, because it reached out into the bay for more than five hundred paces, then curled in on itself, creating a wide, sweeping claw. Ships found it easy to dock at the pier, or along the claw itself. The wooden jetty disappeared into darkness; Tor couldn't see the Claw. There were no lights, only the sick, red glow from the burning city. Perhaps the jetty could be defended, if they could build a barricade across its width. Should he begin or wait for the runners to return? *Now, Captain Lok, make up your mind,* he thought.

But he was spared the decision because the runners returned, and their story was grim. They reported armed men coming from all directions. There was no escape. In an odd way, Lok was relieved. Now his choice was made. "Right, we need to build a wall across the pier. Fifteen paces back from the quay. Bring anything we can pile or lay across the stone. Tan, if you can make it back to the Inn, that bar would be a great start." Tan smiled, grabbed five Brothers, and ran toward the Inn. The rest scattered along the docks, searching for anything they could carry back. The men carried, pushed, and dragged a surprisingly large amount of rubble back to their position, and Tan and his men returned with the bar, running like death itself was on their heels. They began to build their haphazard barricade. Sailors and Brothers have two things in common: they can take care of themselves and are good with their hands. The wall, using the bar as the base, began to grow. Ship spars and rigging were intertwined with smashed furniture, carts, and crates until, in a very short time, a square wall—three paces wide by two paces high—completely blocked the pier. A step on the bay side had also been created for Tor's men, allowing them to attack over the wall.

Lok and Brother V stood back and examined their work. "It will hold for a while," said Lok.

V answered, "I hope they don't have archers." Archers could line the other piers and shoot across the water, making the wall useless.

Lok said, "I wonder if they have battering rams?"

V thought and answered, "Perhaps they'll create balls of fire."

Lok, nodding in agreement, answered, "That would be bad, but what if they had Elaphs from Afrik?" Both began laughing loud enough to make the men stop working and wonder if they had lost their minds. Rok-Tan and Telk, now inseparable, were sitting on the fighting step, watching their leaders doubled over with laughter.

Telk asked, "What do you think, Rok?"

Tan waited a few heartbeats, and then replied, "I hope everybody on this side of the wall knows how to swim, Telk, because those two lunatics have gone around the bend." Lok, V, Tan and Telk were laughing when the first arrow hit the wall.

Lok and Brother V shouted at the same time. "Archers!" They ducked behind the wall.

"Tan, take some wood off the top and build walls along each side of the pier, understand?" Tan did, because he realized what everyone sensed: if the archers got on the piers next to them, everyone would die in place behind the useless wall faced to their front. Men worked furiously as arrows sped into and skipped over the wall. No one was hit, mainly because it was dark. Eventually, two walls were constructed along the pier, roughly three paces long and chest height, but the main wall was also chest height now, and everyone had to crouch, which wasn't bad, but the forward wall could be scaled more easily. Lok risked a peek and saw the enemy moving down the pier under cover of the archer's barrage. They didn't have to hit anyone; they just had to keep firing. There was nothing Lok could do but wait.

Tor's mind worked furiously—a rat in a trap. To make things worse, Brother V's men wouldn't use weapons. How the hell were they to fight over the wall? The answer was simple: unless they changed their beliefs, they couldn't. V's men were only good at hand to hand, which meant the enemy had to get over the wall before the Brothers would engage. There wasn't much time. They'd be on them soon. And once again, Lok was shocked by V and his followers, who were on their knees receiving Brother V's blessing. When finished, each man grasped the hand of the one next to him, as if to say goodbye, but there were no tears, only smiles.

Tan, who had been watching the enemy advance, shouted, "They're here!" And before the crazed horde could slam into the makeshift wall, six Brothers leapt over the barrier and were fighting the crazed enemy before their feet hit the ground.

Lok screamed, "No!" He grabbed V and shouted, "Get them back. What are they doing?"

V shrugged away, "They are doing what they have been trained to do: they fight evil, which stands before us. Do you still not understand?"

Lok didn't know what to say, but he said, "They'll die."

"Yes, Captain, they probably will, but they buy us time."

For what? Lok thought. He looked over the barricade and was shocked to see that the Brothers had driven the horde a pace or two back from the wall. He never saw men fight like they did. They had spaced themselves evenly, close enough to reach defend each other. They moved independently, but each watched the other's side. Brigands flew off the pier. Bodies dropped with smashed knees and broken faces. Lok thought he recognized one of the young runners, but as he stared in awe, he saw the punishment the youth was taking. The young man was covered in cuts and bruises. Blood dripped from his body; spears and sword points punctured his skin even as he whirled and kicked men into unconsciousness. And then he went down, hit in the chest by a large iron mace. Tan cried out and tried to leap the wall, but Lok grabbed him in his huge arms and wouldn't let him go.

Tan screamed, "Let me go! Are we not men? Are we not Gardai?"

Lok would not ease his grip, and before Tan could utter another word of protest, V sent another Brother over the wall to take the place of the fallen youth. Lok wanted to cry. How could V spend them so carelessly? Would this be how the last of the Brothers would die? Sacrificing themselves to buy time? For what? There was no way they could fight their way out of this. He let Tan go, put his massive hands on his shoulders, and stared intensely into his eyes. "Our time will come soon enough. They do this because it is who they are. Give them the respect they deserve." Both men had tears in their eyes and watched another Brother leap into the battle. Lok and Rok-Tan, still Gardai to the bottom of their souls, stepped back from one another. Tan was right. Each drew his sword; Tan wielded a curved blade he had taken from a pirate years ago on the Inland Sea, and Lok held Vespex's cherished Gardai blade. They saluted each other and felt the cold battle rage take them, horrible to see, worse to stand against. They leapt the wall together. Telk Freem, less of a warrior, but no less a man, followed right behind, battle spear in hand.

The former Gardai moved to the center of the line and fought shoulder to shoulder. Telk stood behind them, wielding his darting spear, protecting their flanks, first one side, then the other. Neither Lok nor Tan were fully aware of his efforts, without which both men might have already been dead. For the first time, Lok realized the Brothers were singing as they fought. He couldn't make out the words, but the tune was low and forceful, measured, beautiful, even as they killed and were killed. Lok didn't know how many Brothers had died. With him and Tan in the battle line, they pushed the enemy back a few more paces and held. They fought and killed, and their passion screamed into the night. The unbelievable began to happen—the brigands, who weren't soldiers no matter how hard they tried, died by the score and began to break, retreating toward the quay, stumbling over those behind, away from flashing blades, deadly kicks, and powerful punches.

Lok felt hope; then all hope vanished as quickly as it had sprung to life. A terrible scream assaulted his ears. Everyone on the pier froze. The retreat halted; the charge stopped. Lok looked toward the quay and saw a huge shape in the smoke, backlit by fire. The creature's arms were raised to the heavens. In his right hand, he held a sword larger than a tall man; in his left, he carried a huge two-bladed battle ax. He began beating both on his chest armor, a rhythm punctuated by grunts and growls. The brigands were far more frightened of their leader than their quarry. They turned and began to advance against the thin line, only this time, the Giant joined the attack. Lok watched him wade through his troops. Lok could see the giant's red eyes blazing, as if the inside of his skull contained the fires of hell.

The giant reached the front line, no more than five paces from Lok, who stood before his men, feeling the monster's heat, ready for his last fight. But the abomination didn't attack. He hesitated, as if waiting for instructions, his head tilted at a strange angle. A few seconds passed, followed by an eerie voice that seemed to echo across the waterfront. "Who are you, little man? We do not know. Speak your name before death finds you."

Lok began to answer, but before he could, Telk Freem threw his spear with all of his heart and soul: his throw was good. The weapon pierced the giant's armor and stuck deeply in his chest. No one moved. All eyes were on the wounded creature, which had dropped to one knee. The brigands cried in dismay, as their champion went down. Lok knew better. No sound escaped the monster's mouth. It was not a killing blow. Even as the thought went through his mind, the giant stood and pulled the spear from his body. The spear tip was smoldering and he was laughing. "Well thrown, runt; my turn." He threw the spear at his assailant. No man could have avoided that throw because none could follow it flight. The spear hit Telk, lifted him off his feet, and pinned him to the barricade.

Lok and Tan were in shock. Everyone on the pier stood perfectly still. A loud, growling sound, perhaps, but hard to identify, because no one had ever heard a sound like it before, rumbled over the pier and quay. People snapped out of their trance. The giant shouted, "I am Sith-ast, one of the Mighty Twelve, servant of the Bas Croi, Soldier of Darkness, and you shall not stand against me."

Together, Lok and Tan screamed Gardai battle cries and attacked the giant. Lok went high, swinging Vespex's Gardai blade at Sith-ast's eyes, while Tan went low, aiming for the monster's knees. At the same time the Brothers launched themselves at the Ravers, and the bloody battle resumed in a red haze. Screams echoed and hot blood soaked the pier. Sith-ast blocked Lok's deadly strike, shouldering him away as if he were a child and nimbly sidestepped Tan's low slash. Once Lok went flying backwards, Sit-ast raised his mighty blade, and began a lightning vertical stroke to cleave Tan in two. Lok watched helplessly, his friend about to be killed. He got to his feet and charged again. He had only one thought: to reach the giant before Tan died. The blade began to flash through the night, both edges reflecting the red, poisonous light of Cala; Lok wasn't going to make it. Tan watched the blade descend, seeing death in Sith-ast's burning eyes.

But the blade stopped mid-stroke, as if invisible hands had locked onto the killer's deadly weapon. A bar of bright, sizzling light shot down the pier and hit Sith-ast in the eyes. Steam rose from his seared flesh. The inhuman warrior howled in pain, and began to swing his weapon wildly, trying to protect himself from threats imagined and no longer seen. Brigands who had the misfortune of standing close to Sith-ast died in large numbers. Lok and Tan knew what the life-saving light was, and their heads snapped out to sea, trying to pierce the illumination streaming from the end of the pier.

Lok shouted to the Brothers, "Back over the wall. Stay low." Five brothers made it; the sixth was hit in the back as he leapt, a throwing ax deeply embedded in his spine. He landed atop the wall, spread-eagled, beyond care. Lok gave another curt order: "Down on the deck!" And everyone lay flat on the pier boards. Just at that moment, four solid bars of light raked the pier. The incandescent heat cut through what was left of the barricade and scorched the giant and his minions. Flesh sizzled and fat sputtered. Badly burned outlaws roasted in place or jumped into the sea, desperately seeking relief from the living fire.

The *Ban Colm* had arrived. The beautiful crystals of secret Northland caves had done their deadly work. However, Lok knew the crystals would only last so long at night. He heard and then saw crew from the *Ban Colm* running down the pier, and they were led by KT. He shouted, "No, get back; get her back."

At the same time, Tan stuck his head over the wall to check on Sith-ast and his burning army. For the first time in his life, the battle-tested warrior cried out in fear. "Tor!" Lok twisted his head around and couldn't accept what he saw. Sith-ast was soaking up the power of the crystals. He was getting larger. His eyes, burnt out of his head during the first assault, were smoking, red pits of flame. Sith-ast grimaced or smiled; it was impossible to tell which. He walked forward, sword and ax in hand. He was ready to kill, and no one, neither Tan nor Lok, thought they could stand against him. The monster was beyond them. Tor finally understood V's words.

Lok shouted, "Run. Run to the *Ban Colm*. Everyone. KT, go back; get the men back to the ship. Now." Lok and Tan began to edge backward, but noticed the Brothers were not moving. Sith-ast had reached the wall. Lok called, "V, get your men out of here. Get out; get them to the ship." But the Brothers would not move. Instead, six more stood behind the wall in a defensive formation.

V shouted back, "What is different now, shipmaster? Evil is still before us. We must fight. Get back to your ship. When we see you are onboard we will leave."

Lok knew better than to argue. Sith-ast was at the wall. He hacked down with his sword and swung his mighty axe into the barricade. Wood splinters flew everywhere. A second strike demolished their last line of defense. While Lok and Tan scrambled down the pier, the six Brothers attacked. They moved as malevolent dancers. Lok could hear the thuds of their fists as he ran to the *Colm*. But the Brothers were dealing with another dimension. Every time they landed a punch, every time they connected with a deadly kick, their flesh was charred. Sith-ast had become a furnace of power, immune to the puny attacks of men.

The Brothers began to die, and Brother V fed more into the fire. Sith-ast reveled in the blood and gore. Brothers continued to fight with mangled hands and feet burned black, bare bone trying to inflict injury on a body incapable of feeling pain. Lok and Tan reached the *Ban Colm*. KT was standing on the wharf, waiting for them and the Brothers.

Lok shouted, "V, run!" Brother V whistled, and his men, those not crippled, broke off the battle and ran with him to the *Ban Colm*. The valiant warriors left behind burned, a funeral pyre honoring futility.

One Brother, his name Ri-an, was also eft behind. His wounds were slight. Early on, he realized the impossibility of a normal attack. Ri-an had taken a blow and feigned death, lying quietly behind Sith-ast, amidst the bodies of his brothers. As Sith-ast watched Lok and his people make their escape, Ri-an grabbed a cast aside spear, silently moved behind the giant, and, calling out the name of his god, jammed the spear blade into Sith-ast's mighty neck, cleanly separating the spinal column. He'd done it!

The demon warrior, however, was having none of it. He slowly turned his massive furnace of a body and grabbed Ri-an by the neck. Sith-ast lifted him effortlessly, and as he did, the young Brother burst into flames, which lit the gory wharf for all to see. There was nothing they could do. On board the *Colm*, Tor called, "Pole off. Oars in the water. Double time the beat. We need to get out to sea." KT was in shock. She didn't fully understand what had happened; she didn't know who these black-robed people were. She stood in the prow and stared at a being from hell who was burning people with his touch. In anguish, she shouted something unintelligible. Sith-ast threw Ri-an's broken and burned body into the sea, ripped the spear from his neck, and threw it at the ship. The burning missile became a star shooting through the night. One moment, KT was screaming in defiance, the next, she was lying on the white deck of the *Ban Colm*, her dark blood running into the scuppers. The spear tip sizzled in her young flesh.

Sith-ast rumbled, "We will meet again, little men. Leave your women at home; I have trouble telling your men from your women. Perhaps you will become better warriors in time."

The *Ban Colm* sped into the night. They still lived, but their escape didn't feel like victory.

Chapter 15:
Questions

Rok-Tan worked to stop KT's bleeding, and Seoult conned the *Ban Colm* out of the death trap called Cala. The second mate, a tall, wiry man named Restor, called the stroke, and Tor's men pulled for their lives. Cala burned in their wake as howling brigands shot fire arrows and snap-launched spears from the lower quay. All fell short. Lok watched the doomed city. He could hear screams from the shoreline—whether they were cries of anger or anguish, he couldn't tell. Perhaps both. Was this Athlan's fate? The sound of shuffling feet intruded on the tortured music of a disastrous night; he turned and saw KT being carried below.

"Take her to my cabin, Tan." Rok-Tan nodded and went down the companionway, carrying KT by himself. Two men followed. A third, their medical man, Antaneas, approached Lok. "How is she, Antaneas?"

"When she fell, she took a serious blow to her head, Captain. The spear itself passed through her left shoulder. She is unconscious, which is good in many ways. She can't feel the pain. I can fix her shoulder, but head wounds are difficult to read, and they always bleed heavily. I'll clean and stitch her head. The shoulder wound is massive. That will take a lot of work, but I've tended spear wounds for many years. We'll have to wait and see how she is when she wakes up. I'm sorry this had to happen, Sir. We all know....", but Lok wouldn't let him go on.

"Go, Antaneas, and stay with her. Tell Tan to set up a bed for you in my cabin. Let me know how she fares every so often, will you? I'll be down when I can."

"Sure, I'll stay with her. She's a tough woman. She has the heart of a lion. Have hope, Captain, I don't think our KT was meant to end her days like this."

Lok watched him walk away, and then turned his eyes back to the coast. The city was silhouetted in flame. All he could make out were black shapes against the hillsides, empty forms doomed to destruction. A grayish shadow of smoke crawled over the harbor, and he could smell the fires they narrowly escaped. "No, good Antaneas, terrible things, horrible things, happen to good people all the time." He had seen friends die early deaths in agony while serving in the Gardai. He had witnessed useless death, random death, almost whimsical death and he knew with absolute certainty that goodness had nothing to do with it. His plan had been a disaster. Dedicated men, friends, were killed, no real information gained, and KT's life was in jeopardy. What should he do? The nighttime offshore wind picked up. He could feel it on his face. Restor still called the stroke, but slower, the men tiring, and the *Ban Colm* safely made its way into the open ocean. Lok looked up into the night sky, which was cold and calm, his eyes sweeping over the bare masts and spiderweb rigging, insubstantial against the starlit night. He listened to the rhythmic sound of the sea, unchanging and unaffected by his latest folly.

Tor was reluctant to make a decision. His confidence was badly shaken: should he take his people to Arcasaid or flee the island to find a safe haven somewhere at sea? He should leave Athlan. He knew it. His hands gripped the wooden rail, and his fingers turned white under the pressure. He should leave. He should. But he could not leave the Gardai to face their fate. He could not leave Sighur before the last battle, if that was coming, not after the battle on the pier. Kon-r had to know what he was up against. Kee was absolutely right to be afraid.

Lok thought back many years to a time when the marine Gardai were camped at the mouth of a huge river for many weeks to the north and west of Athlan...

Pickets were out on the perimeter, and the men hunkered down around their fires. It was early spring. Ice mountains floated effortlessly down the mighty river to the sea. This had been nothing more than an exploratory mission. What could they find? Who might be living there? Could they develop trade? There were signs of a native culture, but no one showed themselves to the well-armed Gardai. The next day they would make their way up river, leaving a strong rear guard to protect the ship. Lok and Sighur were sitting by their own fire. Stars burned in the clear spring sky. Neither man had spoken for a long time, each content with his own thoughts and the silent company of the other. They were good friends and had fought together many times. People couldn't understand why they said so little to each other, but they knew. They understood that most things, the stuff that people complained about and whined over, were useless distractions. Kon-r and Lok were men of action, not talk. Besides, they saw most things the same way, and a few words went a long way.

Their fire crackled, and sparks shot into the night sky as Kon-r put more driftwood on the flames. There was one thing Tor wanted to discuss, and Kon-r was the only man he could talk to. "Kon-r, we've served together for many years. I've never asked you about those marks on your arms. I know they make you the Warrior, but what do they really mean? What's behind them, how do they happen? Who makes them happen? Why...?" Tor held his tongue. Kon-r smiled and firelight danced in his eyes. He had waited for *this conversation with his best, and maybe only, friend, but what could he tell him?*

Kon-r pulled back his tunic and held his arms to the fire. The Open Palm and Closed Fist could be seen in the flickering light. "I don't understand everything about these images, Tor. I have been tested, though, and I know that we are part of a struggle that extends far beyond our small earth." He looked up into the sky. "Those stars, Tor, on some of those stars are beings that live and die much as we do. They fight the same battle. There are beings marked as I am, or similarly, and they do the same job."

Tor was silent for a few seconds, and then asked, "And what job is that, Kon-r?"

"I stand and fight, Tor. Against the darkness that has always threatened us. People see me as the great Warrior of Athlan, leader of the famed Gardai, but even if there was no Gardai, even if Athlan sank into the sea and I still lived, my duty would still be to fight on, preserving what I have learned to be good, and defying what I have seen as evil. You've seen the same things as me, Tor. Your vision was just different than mine. You see things as a Gardai Commander. The best I have, while I see each event as being part of a larger battle, a battle I know very little about, other than it has to be won."

Tor thought that over and asked, *"Are we winning, Kon-r?"* There was no irony in Tor's question. That wasn't his style. His was a straightforward, honest question, and it deserved an honest answer.

"Tor, we win most of the battles we fight, and yet, I can't help but feel we are not as successful as we think. Whenever we prevail, another problem develops somewhere else. We sail there. We march there. We fight, we die, we prevail, and we sail away. We win the battles. I'm not sure we are winning the war. In the long run, what has been gained? The same threats rise again and again and have for thousands of years. Is this a coincidence, or is some intelligence directing these bloody activities? There are many in the world who hate us with a deep passion, Tor. You know this." Tor nodded. Kon-r hesitated and said, *"There will be a decisive battle on earth. I don't know where it will be, or when. My heart tells me the next great fight will be in our time, on our watch. How it will turn out, I can't say, Tor."* There was much more than Sighur knew, but explaining it to Lok would have stretched his friend's ability to comprehend the scope of the never-ending conflict.

Seoult called from the wheel, "What course, Captain?" Lok snapped back to the present. The entire crew paused, oars lifted from the water, top men and deck hands all listening for his decision. Lok couldn't afford to make another mistake. Athlan was closer to destruction than he thought. He needed time and convinced himself that KT needed time to heal. The Ban Castlean and Kon-r Sighur would have to wait.

He turned from the sea and walked slowly to the wheel. In a quiet voice he said, "Seoult, oars in, drop the foresail, and steer southeast through the night. In the morning, we'll employ the screws. When we hit the coast of Afrik, follow it south until we reach the Varangi River. We'll anchor in the bay just north of the river, take on water, and do what we can for KT. We need time, master. I need time. Sail us away from here, Seoult. I'm going below. Call me if anything changes during the night."

"Aye, sir." Seoult kept his gaze on the sea as Lok walked away. "Restor, oars in. Kell, drop the foresail." Seoult watched his men swarm to their tasks. *Never had he seen Torvyn Lok as he was this night—defeated and unsure. The world was surely changing if men like Torvyn Lok began to doubt themselves. Maybe the rising sun would bring better counsel.*

Chapter 16:
Retreat

The sun rose and the *Ban Colm* opened her hidden side panels; sluicing seawater began to turn the ingenious screws of Lok's unique propulsion system. Seoult still stood rock steady at the wheel, his feet braced wide, his massive hands controlling the spokes, feeling the sea through the keel, perfectly in tune with his ship. The *Ban Colm* began to cut through the water. The great advantage of the propulsion system was in straight-line sailing. The ship could easily reach twenty knots of speed, which made her the fastest ship afloat. The secondary advantage, and not by much, was its ability to turn. Sail-driven vessels played a demanding game of wind pressure and direction, and the captain had to have the skill to know his ship and master the angles created by wind and water. Turns were usually time consuming, covering large areas of sea. The *Ban Colm* could turn a hundred and eighty degrees within a hundred yards. A starboard turn required the right panel to be closed. A larboard turn required the left panel to be closed. Any greater angle would shut down the propulsion system due to lack of water passing through the screw mechanisms at speed. The keel, controlled by Seoult at the wheel, added another turning dimension. The *Ban Colm* could also out-dance any ship afloat.

The aft hatchway flew open and Seoult saw the first mate, Anders Farner, coming toward him in a rolling gate gained from forty years at sea. "Seoult, the captain wants you in his cabin. I'll take the wheel." Seoult nodded and stepped back as Enders slid into his place, both hands gripping the solid spokes.

"Steer south by southeast, Anders. What does the Captain want?"

Anders shook his head. "Don't know. He hasn't slept all night. He just sits outside his bedroom, waiting for word from Bones on KT." Seoult waited, but Anders said nothing more. "And....," asked Seoult.

"Nothing, Seoult, no word. Bones has been with her all night," Anders answered.

Seoult said, "Right—call me if there's any change in wind or weather. I should be back before long. If not, I'll send a relief for you."

The master made his way down the companionway and slowed to let his eyes adjust to the dim light. Lok's cabin encompassed the entire rear thirty feet of the *Ban Colm* on the second deck across the width of the ship. That made his cabin about thirty feet deep and fifty feet wide. When originally built, it was a huge open space, the largest on the ship, in fact, but necessity required the space to be divided, and so it was. Once through the main cabin door, Lok's secretary, aptly named Scrivaro, lived in a ten-by-ten space. In this room, Scrivaro had a hammock and a small desk and chair, the first built into the wall, the second bolted to the floor so it wouldn't careen wildly in rough seas. He had a large seaman's chest that contained spare clothes and the ship's books. One oil lamp was also bolted to the top of the desk, and it was by this light that Scrivaro wrote the captain's letters and kept his accounts. Scrivaro, who'd been to sea all his life in one capacity or another, considered himself very lucky to have a space of his own. Aboard a well-manned ship like the *Ban Colm*, men lived shoulder to shoulder, and hip to hip; only officers had the tiniest bit of privacy in cabins smaller than his.

Directly opposite Scrivaro's office there was a locker almost double in size. It was a small arms locker in which a large store of spears, swords, dirks, bows, arrows, and armor was kept safe. Oddly enough, this was also the captain's wine cellar, as it were. Torvyn Lok carried far less of these stores than most sailing men of his time. Instead, he used this room as a library that contained an expensive and varied collection that he had put together over his well-travelled lifetime. This is where he kept his sailing charts, any one of which was more valuable than a man's weight in gold, for without these charts, navigating the globe or entering harbors and passing through straits became a roll of the dice—a life-threatening gamble. The charts were kept in a multi-drawer brass chest about six feet long, five feet high, and four feet deep. It was heavily built, and each drawer had its own durable lock and key. Charts were divided into drawers by oceans and continents. Many were drawn by Lok himself, the painstaking work of a lifetime. Others had been purchased in faraway ports and were written in languages and symbols few could clearly understand. Lok constantly worked at the more difficult charts. He enjoyed the task, as he enjoyed being the captain.

Looking out from the rear of the ship, through the half wall of windows, the rest of the larboard side of the room was Tor's sleeping quarters. The starboard section of the space was Lok's living quarters. This area contained his desk and chair, both bolted to the floor, and a large dining table with eight chairs, one at each end and three per side. Under the windows, a long bench had been built, and the seat section of the bench could be lifted, so the bench could be used as another storage area. Above the windows, fitted into rails that ran along the ceiling, was a movable wall of thick wooden slats that could be lowered behind the windows during a battle. The glass could be shattered but it wouldn't fly into the room.

Finally, there was a large leather chair fitted into the corner with a small table nailed to the floor. This was Lok's favorite place to relax, a place where he could view the sea, read, and think about whatever required thought. This room, and chair, was his sanctuary from the constant demands of leadership. As he grew older and learned more of men and the world in general, he felt a need for this room's healing powers grow. Over the years, Lok was shocked to find out how demanding long-term decision making could be for two hundred people who put their lives in his hands. The weight of responsibility was heavy and, occasionally, like now, nerve-wracking.

Seoult opened the cabin door and walked into the captain's quarters. Scrivaro's door was closed. Seoult's eyes quickly readjusted to the light in the cabin, and he saw the Captain standing behind his desk, hunched over charts, moving his right forefinger over the precious map in front of him. Bones was lying on a cot placed before the door to Lok's bedroom, sleeping with a pillow over his head and his back towards the open room. Lok put his finger over his lips to signal silence, and Seoult walked over to the desk. Lok smiled and whispered, "No change in KT, Master Seoult. She is still asleep." Seoult nodded and leaned over the chart. Lok swung the large parchment around with the top toward the windows so they both could read it. Seoult recognized the area immediately. It was the large bay into which the Varangi River flowed from the heartland of wild Afrik. Seoult couldn't read the characters on the chart, but he knew the bay. Athlan had named it Half Moon Bay centuries ago for obvious reasons, and it ran from the northwest to the southeast. The bay was quite large and protected from the westerly winds. Within the bay, there were three large islands that acted as breakwaters against ocean waves whipped up by wind and tide. Two of the islands stretched across the mouth of the bay, and this created three channels into the bay itself, but the third island sat about a half mile behind the other two, directly between them. No ship could enter through the middle channel and sail directly into the bay. Nor could large ships use the side channels. They were too shallow at low tide. At high tide, the current ripped through these narrow openings toward the land and made navigation extremely difficult. A ship could, if the captain knew the depth and currents within the bay, anchor to the leeward of any of the islands and stay safe even in the worst storm. But the water around and between the islands varied in depth, some areas of the seabed clean, rippled sand and other places concealing sharp reefs that could tear the bottom from the stoutest ship.

Lok whispered, "Do you know this bay, Seoult?"

"Aye, Sir, I do. Years ago I made landfall here to replenish my ship's fresh water from the Varangi. We rowed up-river some ways before we got above the salt bracken. We were watched all the time, too, but we don't know who was doing the watchin'. We couldn't see a thing on shore, 'cause there was thick jungle all the way to the river's edge on both sides. Game trails here and there, but that was it. Didn't care to find out who was watching us either, so we got our water and rowed back as fast as we could. Always felt like an arrow or spear was aimed at the middle of my back. Probably was, too. Not lookin' to go back up that river, Sir. Is that what you have in mind?"

Lok shook his head, "No, Seoult. We'll anchor between the northern and middle island." He pointed to the spot on the map. "Right in here. No one will see us from the sea, and we'll be a safe distance from the shore. We'll be hidden from the river mouth, too. See how the river runs into the southern part of the bay? I bet you can't even see the river mouth from here." He pointed to a spot on the chart. Seoult tried to picture the bay in his mind. It had been many years, and maybe Lok was right.

"How long we stayin' there?"

"I'm not sure, Seoult. I guess that depends on KT. One, two, four, eight days, who knows?" This wasn't like Torvyn Lok. No matter what their feelings for KT, the men wouldn't put up with indecision.

Seoult waited a moment, then said, "Captain, no decision is still a decision; choosing to do nothing is still an action. We can't hide. We need—you need—the men need to know what is happening back home. We must sail to Athlan and learn our fate. You know this. We know it, too. Don't wait too long, Captain."

Chapter 17:
Ambushed

The *Ban Colm* approached Half Moon Bay cautiously in light winds, using only the foresail. Lok had shut down the propulsion system leagues ago. Speed was no longer required. While still a mile or so out to sea, he put two boats into the water with ten men each, one on the tiller, four rowers on each side, and one who would throw the lead to measure the depths through each side channel. Lok and Seoult estimated that by the time the boats got to the channels, the incoming tide would be at its highest. While anchored, they would send out the boats again to get readings at low tide. Lok was just being a good captain, and he really did want to add this information to his chart, but he was also feeling snake-bit and would take no chances. He smiled mirthlessly to himself. One never knew what bit of knowledge might save their lives one day.

As the boats rowed away and Seoult conned the ship towards the center passage, Tan drilled his men in repelling boarders. No one expected any trouble, but the Captain felt good about having Tan's men on deck ready for anything, and after the disaster at Cala, keeping the crew busy was very important. Entering the bay and getting to their anchorage would be tricky. The incoming tide, funneled through the center channel, created a fast current. The *Ban Colm* would shoot between the two islands, and Seoult would have to steer sharply to larboard, lose headway as fast as possible, and drop anchor quickly, while still in water deep enough to protect the ship at low tide.

As they entered the passage, Seoult ordered the right water vent opened as he quickly turned the wheel. The ship heeled over to larboard, her deck slightly underwater as Seoult steered hard and sharp. Once out of the current, he spun the wheel to starboard and shouted commands to close the right vent and open the left. The *Ban Colm* lost speed rapidly, and the propulsion system died off. With little wind behind the island, the ship lost all headway and ended up facing the way they had come in.

"Drop anchors fore and aft!" commanded Seoult. Both anchors dragged slightly, and the *Ban Colm* came to rest, her bow pointed toward the main channel. Lok smiled and the crew nodded in appreciation. Master Seoult was one of the best. The *Ban Colm* was safe.

"Well done, Master Seoult," said Lok as he clapped his sailing master on the shoulder. Night would come soon and fast. Lok called to the second lieutenant, "Mr. Brinn, keep an eye on the passages. Be sure we recover the boats as quickly as possible. I don't want those men on the water after dark. Hang lights from the mastheads and off the bow and stern. We'll look like a bawdy house of Cala, but better safe than sorry. When the men are back onboard, douse the lights. Understood?"

"Aye, sir. Understood," Brinn called from the deck.

"Mr. Seoult, dismiss the hands to dinner, you included. Set a night watch after the crew eats, I'll stay on deck. Get some rest, Seoult. You earned it."

"Aye, sir. I'll be back on deck at midnight." Seoult left the quarterdeck and Lok watched the crew finish securing the foresail, rigging, and the other moving parts of the great, white vessel. He marveled at how well these men worked together. Lok was so proud of them. He felt a giant weight on his chest—the weight of responsibility, and it got heavier every year. Except for lookouts fore, aft, and on top of the mainmast, the deck was empty. The ship moved very slightly under Lok's feet. They had found a fine anchorage. He stood amidships at the rail, looking into the heavily jungled coast. He couldn't see anything. Darkness had fallen. He was lost in thought. Seoult was right. The men expected better of him. This was no time to crawl into a hole. He'd give KT tomorrow; they'd sail to Arcasaid the next day. What they did after that would depend on what they found. Lok's stomach churned; excitement and fear were battling for control. He realized he was a mess, but couldn't shake the feeling that something was waiting for them and, either way, it wasn't good.

The boats sent out to map the channel depths hadn't returned. By this time, some of the crew had come on deck to enjoy the warm night and the blaze of stars above. No one stood anywhere near the Captain—an old sea custom. "Mr. Sixt, bring the mirrors topside, now." Sixt ran to the hatch, calling three men to go with him, and a few minutes later they returned with three metal mirrors about the size of a man's chest. They were slightly concave, like very shallow bowls, with handles on each side. "Sixt, one fore, aft, and one up the main mast, please."

"Aye, aye sir." Three men sprinted away, each with a mirror, one climbing the ratlines to the top, as if they were simple stairs. The men placed the mirrors behind lamps, and highly magnified beams of light shot into the darkness, lighting the placid surface of the sea. Only small areas were illuminated by the beams, and it took a long time to find anything. Lok became increasingly worried as the search wore on.

Finally, a seaman in the bow shouted, "There, off the starboard bow, about sixty yards out." The mirror wielder swept the area again, back and forth, and then steadied his beam on a dark mass floating slowly with the current.

Lok, who had moved into the fore rigging, shouted, "Lower a boat and bring it in." A third boat was lowered and ten more men went to retrieve whatever was in the water. Lok watched them row away, and the beam of light stayed in front of the ship's boat. He watched as the boat's crew threw a grappling line into the dark shape and began to pull it close. The 3rd boat turned and began to tow the dark shape back. As they got closer, Lok could see by the concentrated beam of mirrored lamplight that their burden was the wreckage of one of the ship's boats.

Men had brought more lamps to the ship's side. The boat crew tied the wreckage to the side of the ship, and Lok dropped down into the destroyed vessel. Rok-Tan dropped beside him. Lamps were lowered and they studied the inside of the ravaged boat. Deep gashes were cut into the bow and stern plate. *Axes*, he thought. Dark stains were everywhere on exposed wooden surfaces. The oars were gone. Rope, rags, crushed and torn clothing, and gear floated in the bottom of the ruined craft. There was no sign of the men. The stains told the story, such as it was. They were dead or captive. Ten good men were gone. Maybe twenty if the western channel boat had met the same fate.

Then the masthead cried out, "Captain, the other boat, drifting aft with the current, sir!"

Lok and Tan jumped into the rescue boat and began to row. Both masthead and aft shafts of light were locked onto the second boat. As they approached, Lok could see that the boat was in better condition than the first, but no men could be seen. They rowed, lifted oars on the larboard side, and drifted into the derelict with a muted thud. Lok leapt into the channel boat and cried out, "Bring water and bandages!" Tan and one of his men brought the water and rags. Lok dropped to the bottom of the boat and lifted a man's head and shoulders into his lap. Rok-Tan knelt and placed the water jug against his lips. The sailor, who they all knew as Padric, gulped the liquid. Lok saw a deep cut through Padric's stomach, and there was little hope that he would live. "What happened, Padric? What happened to the others?" He was trying his best to answer, but he was fading fast.

Tan gave him more water. "Ambushed...." he gasped. "Natives, canoes—too many, too fast. Captain, we couldn't....couldn't...," and he was gone.

Lok ordered, "Tie a line to this boat and let's get back to the ship. Take care of Padric. We'll bury him in the morning. As soon as we get on board, rig for repel boarders. Stay on duty all night. Change shifts every four hours. Keep the lamps and mirrors on deck. They know we're here;

let's make sure they stay away." Tan barely nodded. He knew his job. They rowed back quickly. Both boats were lifted out of the water and stored.

Within seconds, Tan ordered, "Repel boarders!" The netting went up and his men lined the ship's rails, ready for battle. The lamps were shielded, making sure the beams of light played across the sea, preserving the crew's night vision as well as they could. More lamps were lit, and more mirrors brought on deck. Lok was taking no chances. He'd already lost twenty men. Twenty good men and that was a serious blow to the *Ban Colm*. He thought of V's Brothers. They would have to learn fast. They would leave with the morning tide and hope for better luck.

Lok turned to Seoult. "I'll be with Antaneas and KT for a while. Call me if anything changes. We leave on the morning tide." He left the deck without hearing Seoult's answer.

Chapter 18:

A New Life

Cean Mak-Scaire woke up and had no idea where he was. Trying not to move, he could feel the stone slab beneath him. A soft pillow cushioned his head. A rough woolen blanket covered his body from the waist down. He was naked, which was a big surprise. Head still, his eyes took in the simple room, which consisted of bare stone walls with one heavy, wooden plank door, a plain wooden table, and an empty wooden shelf hanging on the far wall. Dropping his eyes, he saw a smooth, white stone floor. The ceiling was smooth stone, identical to the walls. He had the strange feeling he was inside an egg. Where were his clothes? Where were his weapons? Sunlight came through a small, open window, heating an equally small square on his bare chest. The heat felt good. He was afraid to move; he was more comfortable than he had been in a long time, and he didn't want to lose that feeling. He took stock of his body, gently moving muscles, trying to find what worked and what didn't. He was surprised—nothing seemed broken; he couldn't even feel anything bruised. How long had he been lying here? Cean closed his eyes and remembered what had happened over the last few weeks. The fires, the death of his parents, the battles he fought in the Ban Castlean, and then his test and everything that followed. *Heaven help me*, he thought. *Am I even human anymore? What's next?*

A single knock on the door broke his train of thought, and before he could say anything, a man entered. He was old, with pure white hair. His arms and legs were stick thin, and his skin was almost translucent. He carried a white tunic, leather sandals, and a black cloth sash. He put the clothes atop the table and, without looking at Cean, said in a quiet, but surprisingly strong voice, "You are required at the practice arena. Kon-r Sighur waits for you." The name Kon-r Sighur brought the whole thing crashing back. Comfort time was over. The old man walked to the door without saying another word, and would have left, but Cean leapt from his bed and wrapped his blanket around his waist.

"Wait, wait. Please!" He had a thousand questions. The old man stopped and turned. His eyes were clear and gray, but he didn't look at Cean's face. He stared at Cean's forearms. His gaze seemed to make Cean's tattoos burn.

Slowly, the old man said, "I didn't believe the stories, but they seem to be true. Are those marks real?"

Cean nodded. "Yes, apparently they are."

The ancient warrior stepped toward Cean and snapped a lightning fast straight kick into Cean's forehead. Cean stumbled across the room and collided with the outside wall. The old man was right on him and threw two punches into his chest, followed by a deadly kick to his groin. The punches landed, but Cean blocked the kick at the last second and trapped the man's right ankle. He grabbed the ankle and twisted and flipped the leg into the air, thinking the fight would be over once the old man crashed to the floor. Not so. His ancient opponent somersaulted through the air and landed with knees bent, balance perfect, and hands raised, ready for more.

Not again, thought Cean. He moved into a defensive stance, saw the blanket on the floor, and realized he was standing naked, facing an old maniac. *What in the name of the Four is happening to me?*

Cean sensed the old man tensing for another rush, and before the attack began, an unusual sound rang within the castle. He could feel the deep vibration in the floor and the massive percussion in his ears. His adversary stopped dead in his tracks, relaxed, and, once the echoes had died, said, "Come, we are late." The old man turned on his heel and walked out the door. Cean began to follow, realized he wasn't dressed, grabbed the clothes from the table, and threw them on as he ran out the door and down the corridor, trying to keep his dangerous guide in sight.

Cean lost his way through the endless mountain halls. He couldn't estimate how many doorways he'd passed, and he didn't have the time to wonder what might be behind them. *Maybe one day*, he thought, *I can walk through these rooms… find treasures…* He had been following the old man at a quick pace, and they had dropped many levels within the castle. He lost sight of the man as he turned a corner. Cean followed and found himself in bright sunlight. His was blinded, and he had to stand for a few seconds with his arms over his eyes, waiting for them to adjust. During that time, he was helpless, blind, and he didn't think he could afford to be defenseless again. There was no sound around him; he dropped his arms and squinted through the light. He could see shapes all around him, but none were moving, as if they were all waiting for him. He saw a dark form walking out of the sun. He shaded his eyes and made out the features of Kon-r Sighur, whose face was now inches from his own. "Welcome to the Ban Castlean, Cean Mak-Scaire, Warrior of Athlan."

Kon-r's words were a slap in the face. The reality of his initiation almost brought him to his knees. "Walk with me, Cean. You slept for almost two days. Do you remember anything?"

"Unfortunately, I do, Kon-r."

"Good, then I won't have to go over it all with you. Do you understand everything?"

"I'm really not sure I do. I have questions."

"I'm sure you do. Maybe I can answer some of them, but I'll tell you right now, I won't answer all of them, because I probably have the same questions." Cean didn't know whether he felt better or worse after Kon-r's answer. He was hoping the Warrior could fill in all the blanks, and now it didn't look like that was going to happen.

Cean realized he was in a large open space that seemed to be against the outer castle wall. The area was covered in white sand and groups of men were spread across the yard. It appeared that each group had an instructor and the rest were students. Kon-r and Cean stopped walking and watched the action. The "students" were not young; they were men, Gardai probably, and they were taking instruction in the killing arts. Each group worked in a different style—some with weapons and others without. Cean found the action fascinating. One group worked with three-foot sticks, one in each hand, and they attacked with such speed that the fighting sticks became a blur, while the clacking of stick on stick got faster and louder, occasionally punctuated by the sharp slap of stick on flesh. Another group worked without weapons, but they leaped from the sand to incredible heights, and kicks flew out at impossible angles, as men crossed paths in the air. Instinctively, he moved his muscles with the men he watched. He felt their strength, and he knew without doubt why they moved that way. He saw Dana Fear in each man. He became entranced by the instructors. They were old, frail-looking, but incredibly fast, and it was obvious they were the best of the best. They all seemed to glide over the sand with strength and grace, so assured, so fluid in their movements. He saw his guide, the man who'd attacked him earlier, leading one of the cadres through a stylized exercise at an excruciatingly slow pace. He taught his charges to move with precision and control. Thirty men moved as one across the white, hot sand. Cean understood that each move represented a punch, kick, or block normally executed at speed, and he was mesmerized. He'd never seen anything like it, and, while he instinctively appreciated the pressures put on bone, muscle, and sinew, it was the mental discipline that amazed him, the concentration, the calm, the intense energy held in check. Cean thought he had never seen anything so beautiful. Compared to the bloody chaos outside the walls of the Ban Castlean, these classes offered a quiet, intense stability missing from life on Athlan.

Kon-r noticed Cean was no longer by his side. He walked back to the young Warrior, figured out which group he was watching, and nodded: Master Kane's cadre. Kon-r wondered if Cean understood the importance of Kane's work, the importance of control. Cean broke the silence. "Who are those men?"

"All of them, or one particular group?"

"Well, all of them, I guess, but them, the ones moving so slowly, what are they doing?"

"These men, Cean, are all Gardai officers and non-coms. They train in various martial disciplines, and, once proficient, they teach the rank and file Gardai troopers. Every group is led by a master who carries on the martial tradition as it should be taught, who has spent a lifetime becoming one with his art."

"The one led by the man who brought clothes to my room—what group is that?"

"The man is Kane, and he teaches what is called the Fuar Tine."

"What does it mean?" asked Cean.

"The words are ancient, and usually translate as cold fire."

Cean closed his eyes and murmured the words to himself. "*Fuar tine*, cold fire, *fuar tine*, cold fire." He opened his eyes. "I see it, Kon-r, cold fire, passion and control. I understand, but Kane attacked me in my room earlier. He saw my arms and came at me. Why did he do that? What kind of control was that?"

Sighur began to chuckle. "Oh, Cean, what Master Kane did was completely logical from his point of view. You see, there can only be one Warrior. Two Warriors at the same time means chaos. From a certain perspective, chaos is uncontrolled power, and, when people are involved, uncontrolled passion. To him, you represent uncontrolled power and passion, and for Master Kane, high priest of the Fuar Tine, nothing could be worse. You, Cean, are his worst nightmare!"

Cean didn't know what to say. He leaned back against the cool stone of the castle wall, and while he continued to watch Kane and his acolytes, all the old questions filled his head. What was his purpose? He was the Warrior, wasn't he? He had passed the test. He gave his oath. His thought was interrupted by Kon-r. "Not here, Cean. I can see the wheels grinding in your head. After we leave the sand, you and I will climb to a special place. There we can try to answer the questions that haunt us both."

Cean nodded. "Will I ever have a chance to work with Master Kane?"

Kon-r let out a deep sigh. "Normally, every Warrior learns all of the disciplines taught by our masters. The last form and most difficult to master is the Fuar Tine. Kane will tell you when your instruction begins. The Fuar Tine can never be mastered because passion and aggression lurk within each of us, and they never sleep, always looking for a way to the surface, for the chance to erupt into destructive action. As humans, this aptitude for destruction is part of our nature. So far in our long history, practicing the Fuar Tine has proven to be the most effective shield against our own destructive tendencies. Now, back to your question, Cean, I'm not sure whether you will work with Kane, because I'm not sure if Kane will agree to work with you. Let's walk."

Chapter 19:

New Threat

The rising sun found the *Ban Colm* ready for departure. High tide wasn't for two more hours, and the offshore breeze hadn't begun yet. Even so, they raised the aft anchor, and topmen were in the rigging waiting for orders to drop sail. Each masthead had a lookout, and Rok-Tan's combat team was armed and ready. Seoult had been on deck well before dawn and had already set his course for Arcasaid. No danger was evident, but these were veteran sailors and former marines. Appearances meant nothing. Even as Seoult and Tan quietly talked about making a quick and easy passage out of the bay, the foremast lookout shouted down to the deck, "Ships in the east channel!"

While all eyes turned to the east, the aft lookout shouted, "Ships in the west channel!" Worried heads then swiveled to the west. Large canoes and slab-sided rafts filled with dark warriors paddled into the bay from each channel.

Seoult grabbed a sailor and whispered, "Get the captain." The man ran as fast as he could. The canoes and rafts began to inch closer to the *Ban Colm* but were still more than a thousand yards away in both directions. Tor, who had spent the night in his cabin with Bones and KT, charged up the stairs and onto the deck. He checked both channels, estimated a force of approximately two hundred and fifty warriors coming from each direction, and ordered Rok to bring up the crystal weapons and mount them on their swivels. Archers were stationed on the fighting platforms high on each mast, each armed with a variety of personal weapons, ranging from heavy mallets to war clubs to double-sided dirks, hook spears, and just about everything in between.

Once he was sure the ship was battle ready, Lok switched his attention to the canoes and rafts and the men in them. Something was strange, and then he realized that each boat was a dark black color, making the warriors hard to see, as they were dressed in black and had dark skin. *Paint?* he wondered? Who had an organized army or navy in this part of the world? Who would take the trouble to paint so many small craft the same color? Even Athlan's image-conscious admirals wouldn't do such a thing. "Seoult, up anchor. We need to get to the main channel before they do." He pointed to the flotilla coming from the east. Neither Lok nor Seoult would have worried about these small craft, no matter how many there were, if the *Ban Colm* was sailing at speed—but it was not. Men would die, his as well as theirs. His crew was already twenty men light.

The morning land breeze was sketchy. From the bow, a voice called, "Anchor in, sir!"

"Mr. Seoult, set all sail, please." Seoult gave the order. The crew sensed the urgency in Seoult's voice as well as Lok's. To someone unfamiliar with large ships, so many men running and climbing, shouting and lifting, would look like utter confusion, but both Tor and Seoult watched in complete satisfaction. This crew was a marvel, and they both knew it. Sails dropped and began to fill. Lines tightened. Masts and yards creaked as they began to take the strain. The *Ban Colm* slowly gained headway, and the sound of water bubbled below the bow.

The black craft began to close the gap from both directions. Lok figured his ship would make it to the center channel, catch the rising tide, and shoot out of the bay like a cork from a bottle. He relaxed just a little. He should have known better. Just then, as they cleared the center island, the main mast lookout called, "Two ships off the larboard beam!"

Lok's head whipped left toward the Varangi river, and sure enough, two giant warships were under full sail, quickly covering the distance to the Colm. His mind went into overdrive, and a hundred thoughts went through his head in seconds. Those ships were far larger than his. And they were black, just like the channel canoes. Both monsters were four-masted and the amount of sail and rigging they carried was mind-boggling, but that wasn't all. From this distance it looked like they could also be propelled by at least a double bank of oars. This would give them the ability to move up and down windless rivers or enclosed bays with great speed and agility. They would never become becalmed. And what was that black wood?

Still, Lok thought they could escape. The *Ban Colm* was sailing well. "Mr. Seoult, open the propulsion doors, if you will." Seoult issued the order, and it was echoed through the ship. They could hear the doors slide open and the screws begin to turn. *Yes*, Lok thought, *we'll make it through now*. Again, he was caught off guard when the foremast lookout called out, "Ship off the starboard bow!" *What is going on?* Tor stared past the easternmost island and saw a third large four-masted ship sailing out to cut off his escape. What force was he fighting? He could see no markings on any craft, but obviously this was a coordinated attack, and the *Ban Colm* was in real trouble. Lok's options had narrowed very quickly. He had to take on the ship blocking the middle channel and couldn't take very long getting past her. His was a great ship, but she was greatly overmatched.

"Seoult, raise all sails! Tan, train every crystal as she bears on the ship trying to block our way out of here. As soon as we are in range, fire everything we can!"

"Yes, sir," answered the battle master. Rok-Tan walked up and down the larboard rail and gave instructions to each of the crystal weapon crews, because on their present course that side of the ship would fire first, which meant eighteen weapons would discharge as they came to bear. Lok figured that when Tan unleashed the crystals that would take care of the ship trying to block the main channel and they could still make it out of the harbor unscathed.

Seoult gave the order to partially close the starboard intake, and the *Ban Colm* healed to starboard just as she hit the mid-channel current. Lok stood shoulder-to-shoulder with his sailing master and watched the crew work. Rok-Tan shouted, "Steady, now, no one fires until I give the order. Then fire as she bears." The black warship was closing fast. Tor checked the other two ships and was surprised to see how close they were. Both vessels had their oars out of the water and their sails set. He estimated that within fifteen minutes at most, they would gain the mid-channel current—not a good thing. The *Ban Colm* still had a chance. Just as he was beginning to feel confident again, a tremendous crash shook the ship and the foremast , from about halfway up, and all the attached rigging began to lurch toward the sea over the starboard side. Unlucky topmen were thrown to their deaths, and even those who came to the surface were left behind. The black warship off the bow had launched a large, rounded stone from over five hundred yards away. The missile had made a direct hit on the mast. The ratlines held the broken mast out of the water, but that wouldn't last.

Lok began shouting orders. "Seoult, shut down the water drive, but stay on course and drop sail. Rok, fire, and make it count. Argon, cut those lines and get the mast over the side." He hated closing the intake vents, but once the mast was cut loose and the rigging went over the side, there was no doubt that wood splinters or rigging would be sucked into intakes and that would destroy or damage the mechanisms.

The crew worked like madmen with axes to cut the lines and get the wreckage over the side. Lok was everywhere, directing his men and cutting lines himself. Seoult kept the ship on course as well as he could. The *Ban Colm* was pulling to the right and would until the wreckage was cut away. No one paid any attention to the other warships or canoes, which were all steadily gaining on the *Colm*. Rok-Tan's crystals were all in service. Each one concentrated its fire on the hull of the enemy warship. Crew captains waited to see the telltale wisps of smoke that told them the beams of light were doing their job. But nothing was happening. There was neither smoke nor flame. Lok shouted, "Concentrate all beams on one part of the hull, Rok!" And Tan did. They waited for what seemed a lifetime, but they saw no fires or explosions on the enemy ship. The men of the *Ban Colm* could hear cheering from the enemy boats. *Why isn't the black wood burning?* Lok issued another order. "Tan, aim for the sails." Rok-Tan gave the order and the gunners moved their beams up to the sails and rigging. Results were immediate. The blood-red sails of the huge black warship burst into flames, and fire began running down the rigging, falling on the warriors who crowded the deck below. Cheers turned to screams as men began to burn.

    Lok turned his attention to the remaining warships. They had already furled their sails and all oars were already out; their speed decreased, but not by much. They were in the middle of the current and closing in fast. The foremast wreckage finally went over the side, and the *Colm* shot ahead without the dead weight. Lok knew there were men in the water, but he couldn't stop, couldn't save them. Standing amidships, he shouted to the quarterdeck, "Seoult, open the vents; get the drive system working again." The master didn't answer but shouted the order. Sails were raised once more. The vents slid open, and water rushed over the screws. The *Colm* leaped ahead. They left behind canoes and rafts, but the two warships began a heavy fire of stones from their forward catapults. The warships couldn't get an angle to fire broadsides into the *Colm*. Each ship had only two catapults in their bows that could be brought to bear. As for the enemy ship now off the larboard side, they were still putting out fires and would be out of this action for a little while. The *Colm* was rocked twice in quick succession. Two large stones, one from each ship aft, had hit her. The first, launched by the ship directly behind, had smashed through the stern glass of the captain's quarters. The second boulder, shot from the other enemy ship, behind and to the larboard side, smashed through the rail on the quarterdeck, skipped across the deck, and smashed through the rail on the other side. Lok saw Seoult sag at the wheel, and then he saw the blood sheeting down his face. Lok ran down the deck and up to the quarterdeck wheel. He caught Seoult before he collapsed. Splinters had cut him to shreds, and one had gashed his forehead and knocked him senseless. The wheel spun free, and the *Ban Colm* slowed as the amount of water going through the vents lessened.

Lok laid Seoult down on the deck and sprang to the wheel. With all his strength, he wrenched the wheel around. He put the ship back on course and prayed that they had retained enough speed to keep the propulsion system working. Seoult was covered in blood, but he would have to wait. Boulders continued to fall around the *Colm*, but Tan had managed to ignite furled sails on the pursuing warships, and those fires had slowed them. Lok felt the water drive kick in, and the *Ban Colm* began to put some distance between her and her mysterious foes. "Mr. Harad, get up here and take Master Seoult down to his cabin. Get Antaneas to tend to him." When this was done, he called out for the carpenter. "Fin, see what you can do about strapping a yard onto the foremast, so we can rig sail."

"Aye, sir." He marveled at his men. Nothing seemed to faze them. Lok checked aft. The Ban Colm was gaining ground, but his enemies were not turning back. It was clear they would follow him out of the harbor and give chase. The *Ban Colm* would be fine if nothing broke down. Once darkness fell, he would change course, veering southwest to pick up the ocean current and then run at full speed through the night. They would make Arcasaid in a few days—if they had a few days.

He began to review the battle in his head. *How extraordinary*, he thought, *a fully equipped navy, obviously led by a competent commander, here in Afrik*. He'd sailed this coast and these rivers before. Nothing like this had ever happened. He had fought against only a few advanced navies as a Gardai Marine officer, and he'd sailed everywhere. Who were these people? In his mind's eye, he saw the giant warships—four masts superbly rigged with clouds of red sails stretched taut from bow to stern. A flag? Yes, there was a flag flying from the tallest mast... He closed his eyes and strained to see it—black with something red in the center, that was all he could recall. A shiver ran down his spine. And what were their ships made of? His crystals could burn every type of wood known. These ships showed no sign of damage. There existed, then, a native Afrik hardwood that Athlan wasn't aware of, which meant the wood came from deep in the Afrik jungle. That superior materials and perhaps technology existed in the world outside Athlan was a shock. That he could be outmaneuvered after all these years was a rude awakening. He had been bested every step of the way from the time the *Ban Colm* entered the bay until the water drive had kicked in and gotten them to safety. If they had stayed anchored even ten minutes longer, they'd probably be captives or dead. The water drive had saved them. Speed, speed, and more speed. If those ships had what he had, the battle would have been over before it began. If one of those boulders had hit the Colm at the waterline or just below, the drive would have been smashed and things would have been very different. Lok looked aft again; they were still coming. He checked the sun and was surprised to see that it was still early. Time changed in battle—sometimes it moved slowly and sometimes it seemed to run faster. He was tired, but he'd stay on the wheel. He'd check on KT and Seoult later. The world was changing in more ways than one and good people were paying the price of change.

Chapter 20:

Just Liam

The Outcasts walked quickly from the massive earthen ring of death. They headed west by south, hoping to catch the river. Scouts were out front, and flankers protected both sides of the shaken group. They walked as fast as they could. The Raver troops were still behind them, and who knew whether they would, or could, resume the hunt. Liam took chances and he walked with the rear guard. He pushed his people hard through the dark. They would walk until dawn, then hide and rest. He could sense their exhaustion. Could their flight have begun only ten hours ago? Liam had many things to consider, but his mind was a confused mess of inexplicable information and emotions. Being attacked by the Ravers he could understand. Ravers attacked everyone and everything. But why would they circle back out of their way to attack his small group of wanderers? Tomas's severed head kept appearing in Liam's mind—he was having flashbacks. He'd thought it was a message, a warning to the group, but maybe not. Maybe it was a warning to *him*. Li couldn't ignore what had happened in the circle, what he'd seen, who he'd seen. He couldn't remain blind to the green fire erupting from the brand over his heart or the stone that flared when he was in danger. His people had seen the fire and the light and they couldn't ignore what he did. He saw them casting quick glances at him, wondering what he was. He was no longer just Liam. In the eyes of the Outcasts, he was the creature who had fought and resisted a Raver commander as well as the two supernatural beings who built the massive earth wall with little observable effort. Surely they were not human, but Liam had bested them, fought them to a standstill. So, *what* was their leader? *What am I?* he wondered. He'd always felt different. The stone he wore on his neck and the brand cut into his skin had set him apart. No one else seemed to think much of these things as he grew up on Athlan. That he had kept the stone, that someone hadn't taken it from him, was a minor miracle. Any discussion about the two things was limited to something like *What is that stone, Li, and that mark over your heart?* To which he always answered, truthfully, "I don't really know. I've had them since I can remember."

Liam listened to his small group stumble through the night. The temperature had dropped, and he shivered along with his fleeing friends. What made the stone and brand fire with white and green light up when he was attacked? When did they fire? Nothing happened when the Ravers had cornered them and began their attack. No light burned while he heard the screams of those who had caused a diversion, so he and the others might live. When they were caught again by the Ravers and were close to complete extermination, nothing flared, nothing burned. Liam ran the night over and over in his head as he hiked with his men. Celine. The key was Celine. No, that wasn't right. The stone and brand had flared three times. Each time he'd been attacked—first by Celine, once by the Raver Captain, and a third by Celine. Each attack was like none he had ever experienced. His attackers tried to take him over...what did he mean? They had tried to capture his mind and body, to make him something else.... They had each tried to kill him by stealing his mind and heart, maybe even his soul. And he'd resisted. Liam fought each of them and remained Liam. He knew his passionate act of resistance had surprised them. Where did he get the power? He had no idea, and he couldn't remember asking the power to flare into being. When did it happen? Liam thought back over each battle. He felt their power again along with the hopelessness that began to engulf him. Like he was disintegrating under the force of their wills. His mind began to scream one loud, long syllable: *Nooooooo!* And then it happened: he resisted. He gritted his teeth, bunched up his muscles, steeled his will, and drove them from his mind.

It worked each time. He had pushed their thoughts out of his mind and thrown them back into themselves. He began sweating at the memories. He had been so scared. He started to feel good about himself, about his resistance, about his strength. Then he shivered, suddenly remembering that he had, for a time, wanted to give in to Celine. She was so warm, so comforting. He wanted to surrender as she worked her way through his body, trying to absorb his mind, his soul. She felt so right as she sang a soft, sweet song of surrender. It would be good to lay down his responsibilities, his pain and his doubts. Let her make the decisions. Put his fate into her wonderful, capable hands. So much peace, so warm and safe.... Liam realized she was the most dangerous person he had ever met—if she was a person, because part of him wanted what she offered: oblivion. *Never again,* he thought. He no longer knew whether he loved her or whether he'd simply fallen under her spell. It didn't matter: never again. No surrender. No enslavement by man or god ever again.

Chapter 21:

Walking Away

Celine snapped out of her reverie. The Sisters had never been asked to change. They had always been responsible for preserving the basics of civilization within their families. Sisterhood meant love, nurturing the young, helping them to grow tall and straight. Without the Sisterhood, life would have turned barbaric thousands of years ago. To ask them to give up their families, and their humanity to join Celine in a battle they could not conceive wasn't fair. She knew that and she could hear the Sisters arguing about her last remarks. *If they knew even half what I know about the sacrifice I'm asking of them, they would all run away horrified*, she thought. *But was it so terrible?* She really didn't know, and more importantly, she didn't care. Celine had moved on. Her new life left little time for doubt or even self-reflection, because she was a new being, a unique creation, a part of the whole, no longer essentially alone, like all humans. She was more than they could imagine, but less also, and that made her pause. She thought of Liam, recalled her deep emotional reaction to him, and saw her weakness. He was human—at least she thought so—and she cared about him, and that was a mistake. She understood why Mother warned her: he was a threat. Nonetheless, she couldn't ignore her feelings, which she should have left behind, must leave behind. She must eliminate emotional attachment; she would ask her sisters to do the same. Celine wondered how much she could tell. Could she explain the battle for earth and their upcoming role? No, she realized. It had taken her a long time to grasp the enormity of the change, and her metamorphosis was still incomplete. Liam's existence had made sure of that.

Ironically, they would have to accept her offer on faith, as if she promised some type of religious salvation or membership in a secret, radical society. She felt a twinge of guilt over the critical deception, but there was no way to fully explain what was required of them. They would learn the truth soon enough. She stood up and drew strength from the earth beneath her feet and walked back into the glade to confront her one-time sisters.

The noise dropped until the enclave was completely silent as Celine approached. It was warm. Anger seemed to radiate from the women as they waited in the sun. "You are upset. I have asked the impossible—to leave the ones you love and leave your humanity behind. Indeed, who but a madwoman would accept those conditions? As members of the sisterhood, you have preserved the best of Athlanean life. You've nurtured ideas of fairness, family, manners, and love. Over the centuries, Athlan has degenerated around you. We have seen the growth of greed and the spread of slavery. Closer to home, how many have witnessed your husbands, sons, or daughters toughen under your eyes until they are no longer recognizable?" Women were nodding in agreement. All had suffered in that manner. Athlan grabbed their families and tore them apart in the name of money and power. "What I am about to ask is not for all of you. You are kind. Your strength shows itself in the love you lavish on those around you. You uphold the world and are unappreciated. But there are some here carrying the terrible burden of red anger. There are women in this green glade who yearn to strike back at the invisible forces that destroy families and all that the sisterhood has long tried to preserve. There are women who recognize how they have been denied and tortured, diminished by the society in which they live. How often have we felt powerless to change what needed to be changed, to save what needed to be saved? Is there anyone among us who hasn't known despair at some point in her life?"

Powers Revealed

She had them now, or more accurately, she had the ones she wanted. "You know the truth of my words. Am I not one of you? Have I not suffered as you have? What I ask is beyond reason. Most of you need to be with those you love. So be it. Those of you who accept my challenge; those who wish to strike back at the powers destroying what we hold dear, powers that constantly try to put us in a place of dependency, step forward and stand with me." For a long moment, no one moved. Their heads swiveled, looking for the first sister to accept Celine's appalling proposition. A murmur arose at the back of the crowd. A small woman with red hair was making her way to the front.

Celine could hear the sisters saying, "No, sister, don't go!" and "What about your family?" and other sentiments that would break one's heart, but she pressed on, and soon broke from the crowd and proudly stood before Celine.

"I accept your offer, sister." And that was all she said as she circled Celine and stood behind her. In the end, three more women walked away from everything they had held dear, and they were enough. Celine watched the faces in the crowd before her. The sisters looked so sad. Four of their kind had given up all the sisterhood stood for. Who would take care of their families, their now motherless children? Many of them felt varying degrees of guilt, as if they thought less of themselves for not volunteering; yet each one felt relieved, as if death, or something worse, had passed them by.

Celine admired these women and their sacrifices over the years. She had no wish to cause them any further pain. "Sisters, I thank you for answering my summons. Go back to your families. They need you now more than ever. Think not harshly of these who go with me to an unknown fate. They know not what lies before them, only what they have given up to serve. Remember them, and me, in your prayers." An awkward silence settled in. No one wanted to be the first to leave. Eventually one sister began to walk away, head down, and her retreat broke the spell. Celine and her charges stood silently under the oaks. No one spoke to them; few glanced their way. The sisters went back to their homes, and the thought occurred to Celine that they appeared to be marching in a funeral procession. Maybe they were.

Once the clearing was empty, Celine faced her new charges. They met her gaze unflinchingly, and she was impressed. "I will not ask who you are or why you have volunteered. Your former lives are over. The future will be like nothing you can imagine. We have a short journey before us, and I will begin your instruction as we travel. Your questions will be answered shortly by the one who we serve. Once we leave this sacred grove, there will be no turning back. This is your last chance to return to your past lives. Who would not go on?" Each remained steadfast in her silence and her choice. "Then follow me, sisters, follow me to a new life of power and determination."

Chapter 22:

Hope and Faith

Thirty men sailed a small wooden ship into the unknown. One mast, one sail, and a tiller manned by strong men, they sailed on courage, on faith. Known in the northern seas as Na Gael, each was marked with a small green tattoo just above his heart. No one remembered why the Na Gael marked every newborn boy in this fashion. An old tale was told around fires at night about green fire marking them as a special people, but who believed an old man's tale? Prophecy drove them south, always south, away from the Lode Star, seeking a man known only in dreams. Their captain, Dermid Andar, and their holy man, Ar Altair, had experienced the same dream. Years ago, a boy came to them in their sleep, but strangely enough, he also appeared as a large, shimmering stone, and his form passed from one to the other, as if the two were one. His message to them was brief: "Find me; find the rock; find yourselves." Before the dream disappeared, an intense green light burned through the boy's chest. The Na Gael debated the meaning of the message for years. Everyone thought it was important, but no one could decipher the code. Andar and Altair spoke often, many times in heated discussion, about meaning. Even if they knew who they were looking for, no one had a clue where to look. And what rock was he talking about? He was a rock from what they remembered. Was he saying the same thing twice? And the blinding circle of green light, small and intense—what was that supposed to be?

The years passed and the Na Gael became a restless people. Something was not right, although no one could put their finger on the cause of their discontent. Ar Altair, as high priest, intuitively sensed the tension in his people and prayed for enlightenment, but no direction came. Discontent continued to grow. Walking through a dark forest one spring day, contemplating the gods and their failure to help, he was drawn to a sparkling stream, fresh mountain run-off, flowing freely down a wooded slope. The water seemed to dance in the air as it fell a short distance into a small, sandy-bottomed pool. It was the kind of spot one finds by accident and never wants to leave. Ar Altair felt the pull exerted by the small grotto and the musical cascade of sparkling water. Soon he found himself standing in the pool, gazing at a small mote of light resting on the sandy bottom. He reached down and grabbed the shining object. His hand felt warm as it closed around what appeared to be a bright, white, flat stone the size of his palm. His gaze was drawn into the stone, and he knew this thing was connected to the great dream of the Na Gael. For a long time, he tried to unlock the secret of his find, but illumination evaded him. Finally, he realized his legs were freezing, and he stepped out of the pool. He would take the stone back to the village and talk with Andar. Perhaps, together, they could make sense of the newest part of the mystery.

Once back in the village, Altair learned Andar had gone to the southern end of the island with a band of hunters. The hunting camp was well known to all Na Gael and was a three-day walk in good weather. Ar Altair packed food, rope, and extra clothing, and he picked his favorite walking stick to begin the journey south. He relished the idea of three days alone, walking the land, letting his thoughts fly. While he enjoyed his role as high priest, he occasionally needed to get away from listening to everyone's problems, both personal and spiritual. "Why don't the gods bless my flocks?" had begun to wear on his patience, but that was alright. People just needed someone to talk to, someone who would actually listen. Over the years he'd learned a valuable lesson: most people didn't really want him to tell them what to do, or learn why the gods did or didn't do something. In the end, they wanted to talk about themselves and their families, their hopes, dreams, and fears. With a bit of compassion and a little common sense from his advice, they would come up with their own solutions and in doing so, they would feel better about themselves and their priest. His teacher, the previous high priest, was roundly despised as a strict disciplinarian with little concern for people. For him it was all about power and control and Ar Altair had clearly learned what not to do.

He took comfort in his memories, wandering the hunting paths of his ancestors. He looked forward to doing the basic tasks a man on the road had to perform, finding shelter, reading signs, building a fire, and cooking simple food that always seemed to taste better under the stars. But the sky had clouded and he knew it would rain soon. He found a rock face, an overhang, and built a simple lean-to into the rock surface. Altair stepped back to inspect his work. *Not bad for an old man*, he thought. *It should hold for the night.* He still needed to get a fire going before the rain came. It would be good to have hot food. With hot food in his belly and a dry shelter out of the wind, he could enjoy the storm when it came.

He began gathering wood and returned to camp with a large load and dropped it next to where the firepit would be. Then he took out his knife and scraped a shallow hole about two feet across and three inches deep into the earth. Altair had spotted some perfect rocks earlier and now brought them to his camp. He ringed the pit with stones and laid a fire of dried moss and twigs, made sparks with his flint, and blew gently on the smoldering moss. He slowly fed small twigs into the flame until the fire was going well, and then began to add larger branches until a steady blaze filled the rock ring. As he sat in front of his campfire, he took out the stone and held it before the fire. He marveled at its smoothness and the warm heat that never disappeared. He had felt the heat against his stomach for the entire trip. Staring into the white stone held up against the red background of fire, he gasped. His eyes focused on the luminescent mineral, and he saw a man walking toward him. He seemed to be moving through flame and over his head hung a brilliant white star and vivid green leaf. Ar Altair waited breathlessly for the man's face to become clearer, but just as that seemed to be happening, the astonishing vision vanished. He was left staring into an empty, smoky, white stone.

Altair sat in shock, clutching the rock in his shaking hand. He completely forgot his food. Rain began to fall. He lowered his arm and slipped the stone into his robe. He stared into the sizzling fire. Had the gods answered him? Was he being shown the answer to the dream? As to the second question, he thought, *Yes, this is the boy we must find.* He had a strange feeling as he watched the man walk through fire: it was a feeling of pride. Somehow, he was proud of the man and the gods. Well, he knew the gods really had nothing to do with it. How could that be?

How could he feel so good about someone he didn't know? Yet, he did, the gods be damned. The star, he thought, was the burning stone in his hand, or maybe it represented the boy himself. And clearly, he was one of their own—the leaf was a symbol of their people. Wasn't every Na Gael child marked with green?

Altair broke camp early the next morning and hastened to find Andar. They met in a forest glade. Andar was returning. The leaders sat down and Altair told his tale. They went home, and the tribe gathered and agreed on a course of action. Andar and Altair would sail with a crew as soon as possible. Questions remained, though: where were they sailing to, and how would they know who they were searching for? After much debate, Altair silenced the Na Gael, and spoke the only words that made sense. "We must have faith in the power of the stone. There is no other answer. If the vision shown to me was true, it will show us the way. If it was false, we may perish. Does anyone here think we have any choice in the matter? Search your hearts. See the truth of my words. Is there any disagreement?" No one spoke and the matter was settled.

They sailed south because the white stone embedded in the carven prow of the ship shone brighter when they sailed directly south and dimmed when they strayed from that course. No one questioned the stone; no one questioned the dream. They sailed on, into the dangerous

C. T. Fitzgerald

unknown, believing in a vision. They sailed on indeterminate winds of courage and hope.

Chapter 23:

Sailing Away

Lok listened to the sea running through the water drive as it sped through the gears, faster and faster. Looking aft, he saw the three, black warships reach the mouth of the bay. One moved with oars alone while the other two had new sails set and were pulling ahead, leading the pursuit. He spared a small smile. That would teach them to come in range of his weapons with sails set. But the oars bothered him; so did wood that didn't burn. That was technology he didn't have, and it was a very rare day when Athlaneans found themselves at a technological disadvantage. The world was changing, but he knew that already. Lok checked his own sails, waiting for the critical moment when the billowing cloth actually became an impediment to the speed of the Colm generated by the drive. He watched as the canvas, tight and stiff, full of wind, suddenly shivered, and the speed of the Ban Colm, pushed by the water drive, equaled and then surpassed the speed generated by the wind.

"Raise sail!" Lok shouted, and the topmen, already ordered aloft by their officers, began to pull the sails up, where they would be lashed to the spars. Top men were the elite in the ship when it came to matters of the sea. Lok had admired them from the first time he shipped out as a Marfach Gardai. In the roughest seas, those men would climb one hundred feet above the deck, dance out along spars less than twelve inches wide, and pull seventy feet of heavy, rough, wet, sometimes icy sails up by the strength of their bodies, tie them off, descend to the deck, and go back up an hour later to reset the same sails as conditions demanded. Top men would do that all day and all night if the captain ordered and they took great pride in their ability to do so. They were the best.

Today the sea was easy, and the Ban Colm was flying. Lok looked back one more time. The mystery vessels were falling behind. The ship he had attacked was rigging new lines and sails and continued to row out to sea. The second warship had moved ahead, trying to keep the Colm in sight, sails drawing full. The third ship was trying to keep a middle station between the two. By dusk they would be hull down and by nightfall, the Colm would be leagues ahead into the limitless ocean. Lok felt lucky. His escape could have gone much differently had he been in any ship other than the Colm. In fact, without the water drive, there would have been no escape.

Lok joined Seoult at the wheel. The sailing master, with a large bandage wrapped around his wounded head, was his usual reserved self, but he knew Lok had a lot on his mind, and needed to think certain things through.

"What course, Captain?" Seoult asked.

Lok wasn't used to the formality in Seoult's voice. He also knew that Seoult often spoke to him as an unofficial representative of the crew. It wasn't that he was elected by them, so much as he was the ultimate crew member himself, and any question that ran through his mind would, eventually, run through theirs.

"What's the problem Mr. Seoult?" he asked.

"No problem, Captain, but we almost ended up at the bottom of that cursed bay just now, and I was wondering if you might happen to know by the thirteen hells of Krastos what just happened to us and who were the blood-thirsty devils that almost made it happen?"

Lok silently nodded. That was the question, wasn't it? He closed his eyes and felt the wind on his face, smelled the salt sea, and took a deep breath. So many questions, he thought. And for the first time in his life, so many near disasters in a row. Were they waiting for him, or did he blunder into something no one was supposed to know about? Who were they? Where were they going; what was their mission? Why was all of this happening now, when Athlan was crumbling? Maybe that was the answer. As Athlan fell, other kingdoms began to rise in the world. People would step in and grab whatever they could.

Were they waiting for him? He didn't think so. If events had gone well at Cala, he would have sailed directly to Arcasaid. Half-moon Bay was a reflex reaction to KT's injury. A moment of panic on his part, he realized. No one could have predicted his path. Lookouts along the coast of Afrik must have sent messages ahead of him. Half-moon Bay was a logical place for any ship to drop anchor along that stretch of coastline, and, therefore, a logical setting for an ambush. He was a prize—nothing less, but nothing more, either, and that was good.

Still, something was going on in that bay; something was being put together up the Varangi River, and whatever it was, it was following them right now. Or was it? Were those ships actually tracking the Ban Colm, or were they following their own course, carrying out their own plans? Could he have accidentally blundered into something significant, some power making its first move on the world stage? Whoever this group was, they certainly had the men and ships to make an impression wherever they went. Only the Colm could have escaped their net, and only the Colm could outrun them on the open sea. Lok knew his ship fought well because of the large number of former Gardai in his crew.

They made everyone who fought next to them better warriors, better men. But the Ban Colm was unique. Lok couldn't think of a single ship, or any pair of ships, no matter who crewed or captained them, that could stand up to the threat now sailing in his wake.

Lok began to get the old feeling when action was on the horizon. He owed no allegiance to anyone. Yet, could he simply sail into the darkness, leaving the tremendous threat behind to do whatever they wished? The people in charge of those warships were killers, and it was obvious they had a plan. Every instinct he possessed screamed at him to get away, get to Arcasaid as fast as possible; save the crew, a captain's imperative. It was no good. He couldn't run from the threat. "Mr. Seoult, please close the drive doors a little and steer a course west-southwest."

Seoult thought he must have fallen asleep at the wheel. Close the drive doors? That couldn't be right. "Sir, could you please repeat the order, I don't think I heard you correctly."

"You heard me, alright. Close the drive doors a little and steer west by southwest. Slow us down, Sir."

Seoult, to his credit, gave the orders immediately, and spun the wheel to put them on the right heading. Lok could feel the ship slow as the drive doors closed. The effect on their speed was immediate. Without looking at him, Lok said, "Go ahead, Mr. Seoult, ask away."

"Sir, meaning no disrespect, could you please tell me why we just cut our speed—which may cause us some difficulties with those heathens behind us—and picked a course that would take us away from Athlan, any help we might need, and send us into the emptiness of the deep? With, as I say, all due respect, sir."

"Good questions, Sailing Master. I would expect nothing less from you. We hurt their feelings this morning, Mr. Seoult. We spit in their face and probably ruined their day. I would like to rebuild their confidence by letting them creep up on us. Please make sure we do not lose sight of them. When they do begin to close the gap, open the doors again, but try to keep the distance between us steady." Lok stopped talking and Seoult's mouth opened, but no words came out. He was stunned.

Finally, "You want to rebuild their confidence, then, as if they were harmless children just learning to walk, is it? Captain, did you take a blow to the head I didn't see earlier today?"

Lok laughed, really laughed, at his trusted friend. "Aye, Seoult, perhaps I did. It's like this: I need to know if they are following us, or sailing their own course. If we lose them in the night, I'll never know. If we keep them close and they follow while we sail into the middle of nowhere, we'll know they really are after us."

"It's a dangerous game of cat and mouse you're playing with a very large and hungry cat, I think. Why are we playing at all?"

"We're playing, Mr. Seoult, because these are very bad lads, and they have something on their mind. We're playing because they tried to kill us, and I don't like that one little bit. We're playing, Mr. Seoult, because my gut tells me we are involved in something we can't walk away from, and those black ships that can't be burned and the Ban Castlean are now part of a story we must see through to the end. In short, my old friend, we are caught in a web not of our own choosing."

Chapter 24:

Slaughter

They were tired and beat up. Liam had pushed them hard for two long nights through rough country. Turned ankles, skinned knees, and deep scratches from thorn bushes passed in the dark were commonplace. Their food was almost gone. Just before dawn they had found the river, although no one was sure where they were along the watercourse. At least they now had water, and Liam sent a party down to fill canteens, instead of sending the whole group to drink their fill. He wanted to run down and soak in the cold water himself, but with the sun about to rise, they would be terribly exposed, and Liam didn't want any more surprises. They would follow their original plan: hide during the day and travel at night. He would have to send out a few hunters, because everyone was hungry, and scouts had to be sent out up river. Guards had to be posted. Liam moved through the brush offering words of encouragement. He listened to his people, offering advice on everything from blisters to headaches, as the Outcasts settled themselves in the thick brush that lined the river. There would be no fires until Liam said they could cook whatever the hunters brought in, and he would do that only if the scouts reported the area free from danger.

Liam walked out of the bush to the top of the bank. Columns of smoke rose far to the north, the sky obscured by red haze and dark cloud. He watched a weak and watery sun come up in the east, oozing like blood through the dark smoke. This dawn would not cheer men's hearts. More than ever Liam had the feeling that time was running out for Athlan and everyone on that doomed island. None of the scouts had cut across the trail of Rat or Ka-an and they should have by now. Liam's spirit dropped even further. Where were they? He shook his head. They had to be alive. He would stay positive. He lifted his water skin and drained it. Doubt: there was always doubt about everything. Nothing was clear. He felt like he was wading through mud, trying to think his way through a morass. He could feel in his heart that their time was running out, as if every pulse of his blood marked another second of his life lost to inaction or indecision. Liam wanted to stand and scream, to shake his fists at the darkened sky: what was happening to Athlan, to himself? His strings were being pulled and this fact drove him mad. Living like this wasn't freedom, it was just a different form of slavery because he wasn't in control of his own life. Somehow, he was being pushed or pulled, as were all the Outcasts, and he hated his inability to control events.

He couldn't sit here for another day, waiting for darkness. He had to do something, learn something, and find Rat's tracks. Do anything, as long as he was moving. He paced up and down the bank, checking to make sure the guards were in place. He tried to pick out his people in the bush and was happy to find it a difficult task.

Should he leave or shouldn't he? Liam shut off this line of thought and smiled. Caution and the need for safety demanded that he stay with his people. But he could not accept inactivity! Still, Liam knew he couldn't go alone, as much as he liked the idea. He might need a messenger to send back if he found anything along the river or a change in plans was necessary on the fly. In fact, Onex alone would do; he was a good man in a fight and his bow could be very useful. He walked down into the bush and softly called for Onex and Sentar, another of his best men. He found them sitting together near the front of the relaxed and hidden column.

"I'm going ahead to scout the river," Liam told them. "Onex, you come with me. Sentar, you're in charge. Have the people rested and ready to pull out at dusk. When the hunters come in, light the fires and cook food as late and as fast as you can. Have everyone fed and ready to go. If we aren't back by the time the hunters come back, stay on this side of the river and walk until dawn. We'll meet you. I don't expect any problems. Onex: water, food, weapons, and make sure you have your bow ready. We leave in fifteen minutes."

Li wasn't sure what he would find. He had an uneasy feeling in the pit of his stomach, and he just had to move. He refilled his water skin, made sure he still had a heel of bread in his pouch, and grabbed his weapons—sword, dagger and spear. Though he would be prepared, he wasn't looking for combat and hoped to avoid any trouble. He wanted to move quickly and find his friends. Time...time was their enemy. Liam again walked up the bank and crouched down, presenting a smaller silhouette against the river. Onex found him and they began a steady lope along the water, running low to the ground. Li moved at a controlled pace and Onex, once a farrier's slave, had no trouble keeping up. They stopped at regular intervals, crouched, watched and listened to the land around them. Neither could see, hear, nor sense danger or anything out of the ordinary. It was a hot day, muggy, and both men soon became wet with sweat. They looked at each other and actually grinned. Running free felt good. Their young bodies responded well to the country and the exertion. Before long, Liam realized they were eating up the miles quickly, and it was still morning. He held up his hand and they slowed and then stopped, kneeling together on a lush band of green grass. The land had changed; it was more rugged and they were going uphill. Were they entering the foothills of the Westron Mountains already? Bush and scrub had been replaced by larger trees: oak, chestnut, and stands of white birch grew down to the water's edge. The river was a shimmering length of fractured glass blinking brightly through the dense, green-shadowed forest.

Liam looked into Onex's eyes and saw that his partner sensed the same thing he did: danger. No birds sang; no animals moved through the trees. The heat was suddenly oppressive. Li made a hand signal to follow him, and he moved off along the green pathway, skirting the edge of the trees. They moved silently, as escaped slaves had to learn to do. Onex nocked an arrow and Liam nodded his approval. He drew his own sword with his right hand and adjusted his grip on the spear in his left. They moved slowly in a hunter's gait, then stopped, listened, their eyes wide, mouths open, hoping to improve their hearing as they crept along what Liam now realized was a man-made path. Stone markers, some broken, others tipped over or half buried, lined both sides of the path. All were much worn and old. Liam couldn't even guess their age. Were they a thousand years, two, three? Did it matter? Edges were rounded and though there had been images engraved on them, the details were blurred.

He got the impression of small bodies, distended, and ugly somehow. He bent down to pick one of the markers out of the grass, but stayed his hand just above it. He felt something pass between his hand and the stone. Something—he didn't know what—heat maybe, a quick tingling in his palm. Whatever it was, it didn't feel right to him. His heart began to beat faster and his blood buzzed in his ears. He pulled his hand back quickly, looked at Onex, jerked his head forward, and they continued the hunt. Something about the stones, about the path, about the forest wasn't right and both men could feel it in their gut.

  They moved forward low and slow, Liam in the lead, Onex three paces behind. After a few hundred yards that seemed to take forever to cover, Liam noticed that the grass before them was bent and, as they moved forward, he began to pick out footprints; clearly, men and women had run down this path, which moved into the trees and narrowed. Everything became darker. Li raised his eyes from the path and couldn't see the river. He checked on Onex's position and moved on. Not far along he came upon a woman's shoe, then more pieces of clothing, and supply bags, weapons, and then the first body—an older man. Liam recognized the face but couldn't remember his name. He had a long gash cut into his back, which was covered in dried blood. Flies buzzed around the body.

Onex came up. "Gontar," he said. "He wandered in one night with a young boy and said he was his grandson; they were a farmer's slaves."

Liam, heart pounding, nodded, and they moved on. More bodies littered the path and now they knew what happened to the rest of the Outcasts. Sixty, seventy bodies sprawled over the ground in a hundred-yard stretch of pathway. They checked each body. Small darts stuck out from many of the dead. Neither Li nor Onex had ever seen anything like them before. If there was anything good about the death of his people, it was that neither Rat nor Ka-an was among the slain.

Men, women and children; it must not have mattered to the killers. His first thought was "Ravers," but Ravers would have stripped the bodies of supplies and weapons, and nothing was taken from the dead but their lives. Liam and Onex split up, each taking a side of the path, walking into the trees, searching for signs of the attackers, anything that might explain what happened. Both men took their time, but in the end, they met back on the path, each shaking their head.

Li asked, "Anything, Onex?"

"Men were hidden deep in the woods. They waited. They were good."

Liam agreed. "They got by Rat and Ka-an. That says a lot right there. This is their land and our people were herded like sheep into the killing ground." The same thought passed between them almost instantly: "We're standing in the middle of the same trap."

They moved into the trees as fast as they could. Liam's mind raced. "Onex, go back. Have Sentar lead everyone away from the river, but continue north. Bring back a dozen well-armed men as fast as you can. I don't know what's ahead, but I have to believe Rat and Ka-an are alive. If they are, we have to get them back. Bring your men through the trees, right? Not on the path. I'll mark my trail—three lines up and down. You'll have to make up your own mind what to do as you follow. Good?"

Onex nodded and said, "Be careful, Li. We can't lose you, too." They clasped arms, and Onex was gone, sprinting low through the trees. He was soon lost in the darkness.

Liam took a deep breath. Even so far off the path he could smell the corpses of his people. Their faith in him was, in the end, misplaced. He couldn't protect them. Could he save his friends, or was he making another mistake by risking his life and those that would follow? Living had become one decision after another and people seemed to die no matter what he chose. He fell to his knees and grabbed the stone around his neck. It felt cool. He breathed through his mouth, again and again, trying to avoid the stench. He felt himself grow calm, even as a terrible sadness filled him. Liam gathered himself in the shadows and summoned his will to go forward. He couldn't leave his friends. Anger began to displace sadness. Someone was going to pay for these deaths and he would collect the debt. Liam checked his weapons and began to run through the trees, an angry shade moving through indifferent shadows. He never looked up as he ran, like many animals never look up, and he should have.

CHAPTER 25:

TAKEN

Liam felt the pressure of time as he tried to balance speed and stealth. He worked his way through the dark wood, expecting the path to wind down to the river, which he could no longer see or hear. While his hyperactive mind registered these facts as strange, he was more intent upon following the trail towards his friends. The path itself had narrowed considerably, becoming more like a very old and worn deer trail than a walkway. Old oaks hung low, blocking most of the light from above. It was cool now, almost damp. Mosquitoes whined in his ears.

In effect, Liam was walking in the dark. His skin tingled, sensing more than he could see. He was brought up short when the trail simply ran out. He stood before a solid wall of moss-covered stone with nowhere to go. He was mystified but moved towards the wall and put both hands on the damp rock surface, hoping pressure might open some hidden doorway to Rat and Ka-an. Nothing happened.

He stepped back and stared at the wall. He walked to his left, but found nothing on the surface, so he went back to his right and found noth—.

He stared, head thrust out, eyes opened wide to use every bit of light. Was there something along the edge? Yes? No? No. But wait. He closed one eye and looked, then opened it and closed the other and examined what appeared to be a shadowy edge. He stepped to the wall and extended his hand, trying to touch the shadow line, but failed. There was nothing there. He retracted his arm, as if his fingers were burned.

Tentatively stepping forward again, he pushed his arm past the edge of stone, and found that the flat, solid wall was an illusion. He saw a space between the front slab and a rear slab, like two walls overlapping one another. A narrow gap separated the two flat surfaces. As he moved into the gap, he wondered if it was a man-made illusion or a natural feature.

As soon as he did, he felt a sting in the back of his neck. It wasn't painful; perhaps an overly large mosquito or some other flying pest. He had other things to worry about. The space was cramped. He pulled himself to his full height, sucked in his stomach, and began to slide through the stone gate sideways.

Liam held his spear over his head with both hands as he shuffled along. His chest and back scraped against the rock faces, and for a moment he experienced a sense of panic. If the rocks moved ever so slightly, he would be caught and crushed. He kept moving. *If this is man-made*, he thought, *They must have been small men.*

His right knee scraped an outcropping of rock, and he winced. He felt a small trickle of blood begin to run down his leg. He came to a spot where the rock face in front of his eyes bulged, making passage impossible unless he lowered his head. He bent at the knees, but found he didn't have much room to move. The walls at knee level had also subtly drawn closer to each other. Liam was forced to contort his body down and to the left, so the spear point in his hands now pointed to the sky. He began an awkward shuffle in this position, and began to experience some dizziness as he did. It was nothing. Blood rushed to his head. He pushed on.

The space became tighter. His breathing grew more rapid. The stone walls ground against his exposed skin, scraping away large pieces in exquisitely thin slices. He was meeting real resistance now. The passage was narrow. Not made for someone like him. He felt trapped, suffocated. There was another sharp prick in his right thigh, but he couldn't turn his head to look behind. Besides, compared to his other scrapes, cuts, and bruises, it was minor.

Liam was breathing hard and fast, and that proved very difficult to do. He stopped, his face rubbing against the wet, slimy surface of the rock. He felt tired and weak. He needed to get out of this passage. Gathering his energy, he made one final push with everything he had. Skin tore away from his face, arms, legs—it didn't matter. He had to get out. Keep going, got to keep going…

Liam found himself on his hands and knees, breathing deep draughts of air into his beaten and bruised body. He had popped out of the crevice like a newborn babe. He found it impossible to raise his head or to get his feet underneath him. He stayed on all fours, panting like a dog. He couldn't think, couldn't move; didn't want to, really. He felt confused but totally calm, as if all his worries had disappeared. He couldn't recall why he was there. He waited contentedly on hands and knees, head down, blood streaming from dozens of shallow scrapes and cuts.

A small figure moved easily through the passageway and came to a halt behind Liam. No more than five feet tall, he was solidly built with long black hair and brown/blackish skin that rippled in the light, as sunlight glistens off a snake's scales. His eyes were almond slits with vertical black irises. What appeared to be a ceremonial horned hat was, in fact, not. Two small horns grew from his forehead, one on each side, barely protruding from his thick hair.

His clothing was difficult to describe because it matched the rock walls and forest colors. Other than his exposed skin, which would never be identified as human skin by even the dullest eyes, one would not be able to see the stranger against the backdrop of forest and stone, unless he moved.

He had picked up Liam and Onex in the forest. He was a much-honored sentry left behind to see if anyone came to investigate following the great slaughter. Sitting high in the trees, he had watched Liam and Onex search the dead and the area around the bodies. He never worried. No one ever looked up, and even if they did, he was well hidden.

Once Onex left, Axtol—for that was his name—decided he would take the large one who stayed behind and bring him before the elders. His fame would grow enormously. The capture would be simple: one dart, maybe two and there would be no chance for his quarry.

In one hand, Axtol held a short knife with a black, obsidian blade, but in the other he held a long, collapsible tube that, when extended, was about as long as he was tall. Now, he sheathed his knife; his darts had done their work.

Barefoot, he stood next to Liam, put a small dart into the tube, and blew. The dart shot through the tube into Liam's right side. With such large game, one could never be too careful.

Liam never even twitched. He didn't know it, but he now had three darts in him, and the chemicals that had entered his body rendered him completely docile. The small man waited a few seconds, then delivered a powerful kick to Liam's ribs. Li toppled over onto his left side but showed no pain, no emotion, for he felt none. Axtol removed Li's knife, sword, and spear and tied them together with a length of leather. He slung them over his shoulder and helped Liam regain his hands and knees, offering soft words, as he would to any stupid animal, and looped a length of braided leather cord around Li's neck. Axtol, now master, began to walk the winding path with a small smile on his cruel lips, as if he was walking a dog that had just been well disciplined. The path began to descend into darkness. Liam crawled without a word of protest, completely unaware of his capture and humiliation.

Chapter 26:
A Dangerous Gift

For perhaps a quarter mile, Axtol led Liam down a narrow defile roofed over by short, thick branched trees. There was very little light in the tunnel. Axtol's eyes gleamed as he walked over and around rock shards that had accumulated on the tunnel floor over the ages, but Liam crawled straight through the sharp-edged debris, leaving a trail of blood that flowed from his severely lacerated hands and knees.

Axtol kept the leather leash tight, taking no chances with his captive. Soon they would break free of the World Door and begin to descend into the Valley of the Mel'an—the People. Axtol wasn't one for deep emotions or an appreciation of anything other than fine weapons and the strength to use them, but entering the valley always left him speechless. Coming to the end of the Door, he stood upon a large slab of stone cut who knew how long ago. Drawings on temples in the valley suggested the People came to this world many, many generations ago from a land far towards the setting sun, but no one could offer any other information.

    The valley ran for miles through the Westron mountains, but it didn't open up to the sky. In fact, the opposite was true. The home of the Mel'an had been cut from the mountain rock by a once mighty river, now known by the People as the *Beathe'uuis,* The Birthwater. The base of the valley stretched for miles across at its widest point, while the valley walls lifted and curved towards each other, so that the space between eastern and western half-domes was not wider than a few hundred yards and ran the entire length of the valley. This unique feature created a very fertile area that was hidden from above by a continuous rock dome on both sides of the valley. These half domes had acquired plant life over their long lives, and if one could see from the air, the valley would appear to be a gently sloping mountain crowned with greenery, with a river running across the surface. The difference between what one would see from the air and what actually existed was approximately five hundred feet, which was the height of the split dome over the valley floor directly over the Birthwater.

    The river fell from the face of the southern rock wall, and crashed almost three hundred feet to a deep pool created over centuries. From there, it flowed through the center of the vale before finally disappearing under the northern mountain face five miles away. The waterway was cold and clear and had become a completely enclosed system.

The center of the valley, extending significantly on each side of the river, was the only area in the vale to receive direct sunlight. Irrigation ditches ran from the river outwards into the shaded areas of the kingdom, creating extremely fertile farmland that produced two crops per year of every vegetable the Mel'an needed. An ingenious system of mirrors created from highly polished, water-washed quartz allowed the people to direct reflected sunlight to any part of the valley whenever the sun shone. Still, lamps burned in the darker, far reaches of the isolated world of the People at all hours of the day.

Axtol stood on the rocky platform taking in the beauty of his country. He could hear and feel the water thunder beneath his feet. Cool mist rose in clouds from below and dampened his skin. He licked the water from his dark lips, felt the moisture bead on his scaly skin and run towards the ground. He checked his captive, grabbing his hair and tilting his head up so he could see into his eyes—still docile. Good. Three was the right number of darts. Perhaps four would have killed him. This trip down the five hundred stairs and behind the falling water to the valley floor would be difficult for his slave, but what did it really matter? He would be dead soon enough.

Axtol took the first stair. He tugged on the leather, and Liam followed. Guard platforms were set up every four flights of stairs, as the stone stairway wove back and forth across the face of the Southern Rock cliff. Each platform had been cut into the rock so objects thrown from above could be avoided. Each platform had a very low opening cut into the stone, which made each traveler stoop to enter the platform. This feature alone made the platforms easy to defend. An invader would have a difficult time working their way down the snaking staircase, finding a dangerous bottleneck every sixty stairs or so. The stairs themselves we not deep, nor were they wide. They were also always wet, and there was no outer rail for support. The People had long ago learned to navigate this treacherous passage with speed and agility, but no one else had ever conquered the stair.

Axtol moved at a measured pace, not wanting to see his captive tumble down or over the edge. The trip would take longer, very much so, but delivering a live prisoner from the outside world was worth the trouble of a slow descent. Half way down Liam was leaving a bloody trail that was getting worse. Axtol didn't care, really, but he checked Li's hands and knees as he would any valuable animal. His prisoner needed a break. Each guard platform had a ring drilled into the stone for just such an occasion. Axtol lead Liam down two more flights of stairs and looped the leather cord through the ring, tying a knot that Liam couldn't undo in his present condition. He then tied Liam's hands behind his back for good measure and lightly ran down two more levels to where a manned sentry station was stocked with food and drink. There were also medical supplies of a simple nature: strips of cloth for bandages and a fiery alcohol the Mel'an made from grain grown in the valley. He also picked up a few pieces of dried meat, unsure of what kind, and returned to his animal.

Axtol sat down and leaned against the wall. He threw a few strips of meat in Liam's general direction and looked out over the valley. His thoughts drifted back to the attack: how Axtol and his men used their darts to freeze the intruders before calmly walking up to them, slashing their throats, and removing their heads. Except for two who they could not pierce with dart or spear, two who fought back to back and had killed five of the People before a net was used to bring them down. They were warriors, and had to be respected, but they would pay a heavy price for killing members of the People nonetheless. They fought much better than this prisoner, who turned out to be easy prey.

Axtol studied Liam. This one was larger than the others and more muscular. He was ugly, like all of his kind, and Axtol wasn't very impressed. Hopefully, he would die well. Axtol studied the man's weapons. The edges were sharp, and all seemed to be in good condition, although there was evidence of heavy use. He studied the man again, as Liam leaned back against the rock and chewed his food in a slow, methodical manner. Nothing special, nothing...

Axtol's eyes almost bugged out of his head. Why hadn't he noticed before? How could he be so blind? His prisoner had a sky star around his neck. It was small, granted, but there could be no mistake.

Axtol moved to take the star, but as his hand approached the small white stone, it began to tingle with pain. He made a final effort to grab the gem, but the pain became too great, and he snatched back his hand in frustration. How did this animal come to possess such an awesome power, and why couldn't he use it as it should be used? Why did he fall so easily to Axtol's darts? A sky star. Power of the heavens. There were stories about the stars, old tales the People told to their children at night, about stars being planted over the entire earth. But none had been found, except the one worn by King Vardar, the mightiest of the Mel'an.

Axtol sat back. He had to think. Maybe his prisoner was more than he bargained for. Maybe the King wouldn't want another star in the valley, unless, of course, it was his. That thought grabbed Axtol by the throat. How could he, Axtol, own an animal who wore a Sky Star? It was impossible as he himself owning a star. The only answer was to give his animal and the precious stone to his ruler. A gift unasked for, a gift given before it cost him his life. Axtol shivered. King Vardar was different from the rest of the People. Everything about him was huge, completely out of proportion to the rest of his nation. No, that wasn't quite right. The proportions were correct, but the size of everything else was easily one and a half times larger than he himself. And he was much darker than the rest of the People, black on black, almost blue in the sunlight. The King exaggerated all of the physical details of the Mel'an, but the frightening thing wasn't his size; it was his mind. Vardar was always three steps ahead of everyone else. He ruled the Valley and had done so for hundreds of years with absolute and unchallenged authority, and the Mel'an were better off for it. Vardar had been and still was a good King.

Axtol was deep in thought as he stood to resume the journey. So deep, in fact, that he never noticed the change in Liam's eyes.

"Come on, you scum" Axtol shouted angrily, yanking the leather cord around Liam's neck. "The King will decide your fate, and the gods help you."

Liam crawled on as before, hands and knees a bloody mess, head down, but his eyes were bright behind lowered lids.

Chapter 27:
Command

Millions of stars burned brightly in the limitless, night sky. Torvyn Lok held the wheel of the Ban Colm steady. Their course remained west by southwest. The water propulsion system had been shut off with the coming of night. The Ban Colm moved under a full press of sails. Not usual at night, but Tor could not slow down, not with the red-sailed ships still in his wake.

Tor had also sailed these waters before and knew there was nothing to fear in terms of shallow water shoals. They were sailing into the deep; no one knew how deep. Sailors would murmur some invocation to gods major or minor whenever they sailed these seas. Superstition. Lok thought about his adversaries. The same questions kept repeating themselves again and again: Who were they? Where were they going? Was it chance that caused their combat? Were they following Lok now, or just following their own course, which also happened to be his for the next few hours?

Anteneaus, the ship's doctor, came on deck and made his way to The Captain. His face was partially lit by the binnacle light. Even in the shadows Lok could see how tired he was. Lok wanted to ask, wanted an answer, but decided to wait. Anteneaus would get around to it in his own way.

"Quiet", Anteneaus said. "Stars everywhere. Right there, as if you could grab one, or sail into the sky." He became quiet again, then added, "Lok, KT isn't coming around. She isn't getting any worse, but she surely isn't getting any better. I've never seen anything like this. She just lies there. Her breathing is steady but slow. She doesn't have a fever—if anything, she's colder than she should be."

"Well, that can't be all bad, Doc. How are her wounds?"

"Wounds are fine, as far as I can tell. I cleaned and stitched them. Put a good bandage on her. No, nothing is wrong with her wounds."

Lok took it all in and said, "What's wrong then, Doc? What has you so worried?"

Anteneaus dropped his head, as if he were studying the wooden deck, and said, "Captain, when I checked her eyes, thinking she may have a head injury, I noticed, or thought I did, a very slight red tinge. I didn't think much about it. She hit her head, or maybe her eyes were just bloodshot from the smoke. I had other things to worry about. That was almost eight hours ago." The doc became silent once again.

Lok waited as long as he could. Finally, he said, "And?"

Doc looked up into Lok's eyes, the binnacle candle making a grotesque mask of his craggy face. "Now…now her eyes are completely red. Her beautiful blue eyes are gone, and I don't know why."

Antenaeus' last words came out as a fearful wail. The deck crew all looked aft to where their captain stood with the doc. Lok wished his medical man had kept his voice down. His crew was jumpy enough. Everything was uncertain. They looked to him for calm strength. Doc wasn't helping.

"Anteneaus, go below and stay with her. I'll come down around sunrise. Keep her comfortable. If anything else strange happens, let me know immediately. Can you do that?"

Doc was nodding his head even before he answered. "Yes, yes, that I can do. Sorry, Captain. I know better."

"There's nothing to forgive. I know how close you two are. Go ahead. Take care of her for us." Old Anteneaus shuffled away and disappeared below deck.

Lok watched the men returning to their work. He didn't know what to think. The ship moved under full sail in a steady breeze. She handled beautifully. But he couldn't concentrate on his greatest achievement, his one true love. There were people chasing him; they had already tried once to kill him. And now there was something wrong with KT's eyes? What did that mean? Why would her eyes turn red? Blood? He wasn't a doctor. He was a ship's captain. And all his decisions were going bad. Red eyes? Who had red eyes? No...But there was someone or something that had red eyes: the monster on the quay. The thing that cut KT with an impossible spear cast. It had red eyes. But there couldn't be a connection, just couldn't be, but in his heart, he knew there was.

The night was shattered by a call from the masthead lookout. "Ships aft! Veering away north by northwest."

Lok swiveled his head around. He saw the lanterns hanging from the yard arms like small stars in the dark, but the ships themselves were vague shapes in the dark. Sure enough, the three mystery warships were peeling off to the north.

So they did have their own course to follow, he thought. *We stumbled into them as they assembled for departure. Bad luck.* Or was it? Where were they going? Their present course would take them up the western coast of Athlan. There was nothing there except a few ill-protected fishing villages and then Arcasaid, the port of the Ban Castlean, the only deep-water port on the western shore. But no, these war ships had no business at Arcasaid, unless...unless their business was war.

Lok had another decision to make. Really, there was no decision to make, he thought, his hands tightening on the wheel. He had to sail the Ban Colm to Arcasaid. He had to find Kon-r. He had to save his crew. He had to save KT. He had to do all of these things, and he had no idea how he was going to do so.

Lok rubbed his hand over his face, as if he could rub away his responsibilities. *Command: that's what I always wanted*, he thought. *And I've done a good job over the years. I've led a good life and provided a good living for my crew. But now, now command doesn't seem so appealing. Their trust, for the first time, may be misplaced. My needs and theirs are in conflict. We should sail away. But I can't. What does that make me? What if I get them all killed?*

Lok wasn't used to self-doubt. He was a strong man and always had been. He was thinking himself into a dark hole with no way out. He raised his head and took a long, deep draught of sea air. He checked the stars for his position. Act, he told himself. Do something. He would. He would wait until the lanterns disappeared completely. Then, he would sail to Arcasaid. KT would have to wait. His crew would have to trust him a little longer. He would believe in himself until...until... He would believe in himself until the end, and that was all he could ask of himself.

"Bosun," he called, "dowse all lanterns. We sail to Arcasaid."

Chapter 28:

Axtol the Great

They stayed that night on the platform. Axtol fed Liam a green, leafy plant called ananaba along with the scraps of meat he had brought back from the guard platform two levels down.

Liam, now fully awake and aware of his situation, had eaten the plant, trying to make Axtol think he was still drugged by the narcotic found on the tips of Axtol's darts. Shortly after eating the leafy substance, Liam found himself drifting off, once again losing any sense of self. He was quite unaware of the fact that ananaba was the source of Axtol's mind numbing drug. Liam, whether he knew it or not, was now on a maintenance program. He could be kept as a senseless slave forever, as long as he continued to eat the plant on a regular basis, and he would, as long as he was fed while still under the influence.

Axtol settled back against a low stone wall and considered his future. He stared at the Sky Star, desperately trying to figure a way to get it off the slave's neck. But what if he did? He couldn't touch it. It burned like a hot coal. He also noticed something strange: the longer he stared at the Star, the more he coveted the power and the more frightened he became of it. The Star was beyond him, simple as that. He lay his head on his pack and went to sleep.

In the morning Axtol once again leashed Liam and yanked him awake. Getting behind him, Axtol kicked his prisoner to make sure he was still docile and moving in the right direction. He was and he did. They passed the lower guard platform after a short time and the guards, the shift having changed since last night, clapped and whistled in admiration of Axtol as the diminutive warrior led his massive captive down the stairs with a minimum of fuss and bother. Occasionally, Axtol would sit on Liam's back and ride him like a small pony to the delight of the guards. Liam could have cared less. His mind was gone. He was a contented pack animal.

After an hour or so, the two came to the base of the stairway, the final platform. This one was far more formal than the guard platforms above. An officer ruled here, and his men were well-uniformed and appeared very well-disciplined. Axtol recognized the officer. His name was Xtlotl. He was larger than Axtol and came from a wealthier family. He left his guard post and approached Axtol and his slave. Xtlotl didn't say anything. He circled Axotl and Liam, left hand behind his back, right hand stroking his square chin. The laws of the Mel'an were clear. The prisoner was Axotl's, and no rich-boy officer could take him. Nonetheless...

"Axotl, what do you have here?" Xtotl asked.

Axotl knew he had to keep his answers short. Short answers were the only way to handle officers. "Prisoner, sir. I caught him trying to enter the World Door after the great Slaughter."

"Very good work, soldier. I will take him to the King from here. Return to your post."

Axotl had to think fast, and that wasn't his strong suit. "I have made this slave a gift to the King. I have already sent word to him I come bearing a great gift. This slave is not yours to have. I need transportation and I need it quickly". As he said these words, he fed small leaves of ananaba to Liam, who ate them automatically.

Xtlotl instantly became furious. He closed to within spitting distance of Axotl. "Who do you think you are, you runt, you worm? You bandy-legged, short horned, dim-witted lizard! Stand at attention when I talk to you!" Xtlotl was now literally frothing at the mouth. His black snake eyes glittered with malice. He clenched and unclenched his scaly hands, trying to regain control of himself.

He called to his men. "Guards, seize these two. The prisoner is harmless—Axtol needs to be taught a lesson."

There were six guards, and all of them understood what this meant. Axotl was to receive a severe beating but was to be kept alive.

Axtol also understood what was coming, but he was in no mood for games. He let the guards get as close as he dared, then drew two throwing knives and launched them at Xtlotl's throat. Both knives connected. Blood spurted from the wounds. Xtlotl's hand grabbed his throat, but he was rapidly losing strength. He pawed at the bloody knife handles, but couldn't get a grip on either of them. Gurgling sounds escaped with his green blood. Suddenly, his eyes rolled up into his head and he pitched forward onto his face. Dead.

Xtlotl was no one's favorite, but he was an officer, and he had just been murdered. The other guards were in shock, but Axtol was a warrior, and he didn't waste time. He drew his sword before Xtlotl had hit the ground, and as Xtlol died, Axotl was into the guards, slashing and stabbing for all he was worth. He killed three before the remainder could draw their swords from their scabbards.

A fourth guard was more alert. He grabbed a spear, and as Axotl dispatched the third guard with a wicked slash across the neck, the fourth guard jabbed the spear at Axtol's chest.

Axtol, sensing the weapon's approach, twisted away just in time to avoid a vicious skewering. The blade, however, did slice though his jerkin and gash Axtol's ribs. The cut wasn't deep, but it was painful and bled profusely. Axtol trapped the spear haft beneath his left arm and body, grabbed his sword by the hilt and threw it like a short spear. The blade penetrated the guard's throat and came out the back of the neck, neatly severing his head, except for a few strands of skin and sinew that kept it from falling to the floor.

Axtol didn't stop. He grabbed the spear and reversed the bloody blade towards the remaining two guards, bellowing a hideous war cry as he charged, a message of death in his eyes. Being good readers of violence themselves, one guard turned his thoughts to the future, hopped the railing, and jumped into the swiftly flowing Birthwater. Panicked by Axtol's charge, he forgot he could not swim.

The second guard, remembering that he couldn't swim, made a dash for the steps going up to the next level. As he ran, he pulled the sash connected to the alarm bell. The bell chimed and echoed up the stone walls and steps.

Axtol ran to the bottom of the stairway and unleashed a massive throw. The spear hurtled up one flight of stairs and passed through the fleeing guard's back and chest. He stood still for a moment on the top step, in shock, then, clutching the protruding blade, fell backwards down the steps. He landed at Axtol's feet.

Axtol ripped the spear through the guard's back and leaned over the rail, looking to spear the guard in the water like a fish, but the guard never came up for air.

Axtol spit into the river. Cowards, he thought. He put his hand over his bleeding ribs. The pain was getting worse now that he had time to think about it. He pulled his sword from the dead guard's neck, wiped the crimson blade on the guard's chest and sheathed it.

He walked over to check on his slave. Axtol looked into Liam's eyes and saw nothing but oblivious contentment. One part of his mind wished his prisoner could have seen him in action- one officer and six guards- not a bad morning's work. Of course, the other part of his mind was grateful the prisoner remained so docile. The leaves were working, as usual, and that meant that the invader was one less thing he had to worry about.

Axtol pulled his throwing knives from Xtlot's throat and put one away. With the other he cut strips of cloth from Xtlotl's tunic. He took the strips, and poured water on them from his canteen. He wrapped the strips around his ribs. His blood tinted the bandages a light green. He and his captive had to go. The alarm bell had sounded. No one would understand why so many of the People and their officer were dead. Axtol shook his head. What in the three hells of Delos had just happened?

Axtol sheathed his knife, grabbed a spear, leashed Liam, and walked as quickly as he could to the dock along the river. Axtol looked up and down the dock for a boat. They would use the river to get to the King.

He found a small row boat hidden behind a larger craft not far down the quay. He pulled Liam as hard as he could, and the stupid beast ambled along behind him. Axtol untied the bow and stern lines, kicked Liam down into the craft, jumped in, and used an oar to push away from the dock. He would have to row himself. As he moved out into the current, he turned and gave Liam a staggering blow to his head with an oar. Axtol couldn't afford to have his slave regain his senses while Axtol was rowing for his life.

Liam dropped to the floor of the bow like a sack full of rocks, his head bouncing off a side strake. Axtol settled in, got the two oars in place, and began to row. The current moved them along, and Axtol began to feel good about the entire episode. The sun was high in the sky, and sunlight burned through the dome opening, shining brightly on the Birthwater River and Axtol in his tiny naval command. He began to smile, then he giggled, then he began a great belly laugh! He rowed and began to sing. Oh, what stories would be told about Axtol the Great and the Battle of—

He never finished his thought. He stared stupidly at a black-shafted arrow with grey goose feathers that stuck in his chest, loosed by a guard alerted by the alarm. His hands dropped from the oars and hung loosely to the floor of the small craft. His mighty little head, held so high just seconds ago, fell forward, his chin resting on his chest. The malicious sparkle in his reptilian eyes faded away. Axtol, the famous Hunter, Axtol the renowned warrior, was dead.

In the front of the small craft, Liam lay in the bottom of the boat, head bashed, dreaming the dreams of the drugged and stupid. The ship moved along with the current, conned by a dead captain, oars secure in the pintels, oar blades cutting through the clear, cold water, completely useless.

Chapter 29:

Awakening

The Birthwater gently guided the small fishing boat westward, its deceased captain resting at the oars. The river width varied, but this stretch was about four bow shots wide. From either shoreline an observer would have come to the conclusion that the rower was taking a break, allowing the river to do the work. No one would know there was a second passenger in the craft.

That second passenger was finally coming to his senses after an unconscious hour on the water. He tried to open his eyes. He had to squint because he was looking straight up into the sky, and the sun was bright. He tried looking off to the side, figuring the brightness would be less, but he was wrong. The underside of the dome rippled with light from the inverted bowl. He lay in confusion, watching the light show and unable to figure out what was happening. He couldn't quite figure out where he was, either, or, for that matter, who he was. One thing he did know was that his head was killing him. He rubbed his hand over his forehead and felt a wet stickiness there. He moved his hand away from his face and saw his fingers covered in red. Blood—his blood. What the hell happened to him?

He tried to relax, letting his weight fall back to the bottom of the boat. The roof of the dome drew his attention. Light continued to move in waves across the dome. How was this happening? He shifted his gaze to the back of the being who should, but was not, rowing the boat. Who was he?

"Hey! Hey! Wake up! Hey, little man! Wake up!"

There was no movement, no response. Liam looked around the bottom of the boat. Within reach of his left hand was a mesh loop on a long handle, used to net fish. He grabbed the net and shoved it into the back of the mysterious rower. No response. He did it again, harder. Nothing. This "thing" wasn't asleep. It was dead.

From the back it looked like a black lizard dressed as a soldier. He noticed the short tail, no more than a hand-length, and then he saw the horns, scales, and claws at the ends of its fingers. He wanted to scream. He began to draw large draughts of air into his lungs as he tried to fight off the panic. He needed to find…Who? He was looking for someone? The wall…He had found the wall… tight, so tight…so tired, then nothing.

He closed his eyes. Calm down. Breathe. Calm. He lay in the bottom of the boat and listened to the water slide by. Who am I? He felt something warm lying in the center of his chest, just below the hollow of his neck. He raised his hand and found the leather cord, then the stone. He looked down. White and…warm. His stone; and to the left of the stone a green leaf on his chest. Stone and leaf; stone and leaf; stone and lea…Li.

"Liam! My name is Liam. A slave—no; no more—a free man. An Outcast. Yes! Ka-an, Rat—my friends. I'm looking for my friends." He said the words out loud in his excitement, and then he remembered his dead and the light above suddenly dimmed.

Li had tears in his eyes. He was back, but where was "back?" He struggled to get his legs under him and slowly raised his head above the side of the boat. He knew he was on a river, and the river ran under a high dome of rock with the center removed. Something was strange about the roof of the dome. As he scanned the roof from side to side, he also saw tilled fields on each side of the river, some planted with crops, others lying fallow. Every inch of ground was part of the farming system. Irrigation canals ran from the river and crisscrossed the fertile plain. Beyond the fields and in the walls of the canyon he saw buildings carved into the rock face. They were far away. He couldn't tell how big or how many there were. From this distance they seemed to be crammed together.

He turned his head to study the other side but found much the same. The buildings reached to the curved ceiling along the far walls. Roads seemed to be carved into the stone surfaces, but he really couldn't tell.

What was this place? Who was his dead ferryman? Was Liam captured trying to sneak behind the wall? Did this thing and things like him kill his people? Liam couldn't think of any other explanation. He studied his companion again. If all of the people in this valley looked like this thing, Liam had to stay hidden. Staying as low as he could, Liam worked his way around the body, so he could see him from the front. This meant that he was now lying in the stern of the boat looking downstream. First he saw the arrow in the beast's chest; so much for the cause of death. But why was he dead? If this was his land, who shot him? Why didn't Liam have an arrow in his own chest? Too many questions with too few answers and no one to supply them. Liam reached up and snapped the arrow. As they got closer to the shore, an arrow sticking out of this reptile's chest would not be easy to explain.

He examined the body. He was an extraordinarily ugly creature: half man, half reptile. Skin replaced by scales, snake eyes, taloned fingers, taloned feet. He was muscular and compact. In the light Liam couldn't decide if the creature was dark brown or black. As the river gently rocked the boat, the dead warrior's scales shimmered in the sunlight. When the sun hit the scales just right, he was actually hard to look at. In fact, with his brown and green jerkin, this creature would have been almost invisible in the forest. Hidden high in the trees, he would have been completely invisible.

Now a warrior by necessity, Liam checked the little man's equipment. He had two knives and a short sword on his person. A spear lay in the bottom of the boat. A small water skin was looped over his right shoulder. Liam took one of the knives and cut the skin's leather cord. He opened the stopper and sniffed. It seemed good. He took a small, tentative swallow, and then eagerly drank most of the rest. It was clean water. Nothing ever tasted better. He put the stopper back in and laid the skin down in the boat.

Liam tilted his head around the body and looked downstream. He looked back upstream and thought he could see a waterfall through the mist a few miles back. He looked downstream again and saw the black spires and towers of a city on both sides of the river. He couldn't tell how much further down the river the city was. The river flowed slower here but maintained a steady pace. The entire area under the dome was remarkably flat. If he just remained hidden, he would probably reach the city by nightfall, but should he want to reach the city? What did he know? Nothing! Who were these people? Were Ka-an and Rat even here? Maybe they were and maybe not. Would people be searching for him? He didn't know, but to be safe, he had to assume they were. After all, someone had shot and killed this little monster in front of him.

Liam examined his hands and knees in the light. He was beat to hell. His skin was raw. He must have been crawling. He felt around his neck. The skin was lacerated, painful to the touch. So, he had worn a collar and had been led around on his hands and knees. He didn't remember any of it and that scared him. He had been a slave once and, apparently, he had been a slave again. No, worse, they had stolen his mind and his soul, and he had surrendered without a fight.

Even in the heat, a cold shiver ran down his spine. Whoever or whatever could do that to a man was evil incarnate. His decision was made. He had to get off the river and hide. He studied the shore, searching for a sheltered cove or reedy area where he could hide himself, his deceased passenger, and the boat until dark. He would sneak into the city. He would learn what he could. He would search for his friends. If he could save them, he would. If not, he had to find a way out. He remembered ordering Onex to return to the Outcasts and bring them to the wall. Li knew he, himself, wouldn't make it back to the wall; it was under heavy guard. He would need to find another way out. He hoped Sentar would continue to lead the rest of the Outcasts to the western ocean. Who knew—perhaps he might meet them there, someday.

Chapter 30:

Catching a Ride

The lights on the dome began to flicker, disappearing as dusk settled on the river. Liam found it difficult to see the stone gardens falling from each cliff face. He took a chance and pushed the body of his captor into the front of the boat, cautiously moved onto the bench, grabbed both oars, and began to pull for the larboard shore, which was covered in thick reeds.

He had to get rid of the body. He'd seen an anchor in the bow of the boat earlier. He stopped rowing, reached back around the reptile-thing, grabbed the anchor and line, and began to wrap the body. It was a gruesome task, but Li never hesitated. Once he had the body wrapped tight, he got as low as he could in the boat and pushed the corpse up and over the side. There wasn't much of a splash. He got back on the bench, grabbed the oars, and began stroking hard. With the oar in his right hand, he guided the boat towards the shore. Finally, he shipped oars and glided into the reeds, the bow of the fishing boat sliding through them with a soft hiss, nosing onto semi-solid, sandy ground. Liam slid off the bench and wriggled to the front of the boat, put his head against the thwart, and closed his eyes. Tired, confused, and worried, he fell asleep.

He awoke to a narrow band of stars overhead, as small insects buzzed and hummed around his head. It took him a few seconds to remember where he was. The boat rocked gently as everything came back in a rush. He squeezed his eyes shut once more but too late. Awake now, Li thought about his situation. He had to get to the city downstream. He would search for Ka-an and Rat, although he had no idea how he was going to do this. His hand closed around the white stone. Warm, as always, he wondered for the thousandth time what the stone was and what it meant, if anything. Somehow, he had a feeling that he would learn something about the stone, maybe something about himself, before this journey came to an end.

Liam poled his boat through the shallows and reeds with an oar. As he broke through the wall of slender stems, he jammed the oar into the mud and brought the craft to a halt. He sat stunned as he studied the far wall. After a few moments he realized both cliff walls of the domed canyon had come alive with flares or hanging lanterns, and beams of sharp light projected from those cliff walls and slashed through the night, playing out in circular forms on the river surface in random patterns, making the darkness come alive. The beams were focused and bright. How did they do that? What kind of power or magic did these people possess? And how in the name Hepspida's Virgins was he going to row down the river unnoticed? Shafts of light crisscrossed through the night air. Liam imagined each beam was searching for him with deadly intent.

The only thing he could do was to move down the river while trying to stay in the reeds. Pushing the boat through the shallows was hard work. He couldn't really row, so he had to grab the reeds with his hands and pull himself along the banks. This was difficult; his hands had been badly cut and the slender reeds, so innocent to look at, left almost invisible cuts on his already battered fingers and palms. He soon realized this method of movement was futile. At this speed, he'd still be in the reeds when the dome roof sparkled from the reflected river light come morning.

He stopped to rest and think, and just as he did so, the boat thunked into something solid. Liam didn't know what it was, and couldn't see in the dark. He jumped over the side and walked around the boat, knee deep in mud. As he got to the back of the boat on the land side, he ran into the problem and yelped in pain. A large log was caught by the reeds and the boat happened to bump into it. Could have been much worse, he thought, rubbing his bruised knee. He began to pull the boat away when he had a sudden thought: could he float down to the city by holding onto the log? Would that be better than pulling himself and the boat through the shallows? He realized he had no choice. He had to move faster. Perhaps, if he stayed low in the water, he would remain unnoticed. Who would pay any attention to a log?

Liam checked the boat. Was there anything he could use? He spotted the canteen, picked it up and drank what was left, then tossed the canteen back into the boat. Seeing nothing more of value, he pushed the boat back onto the muddy shore so it wouldn't drift and call attention to itself. Then he grabbed the log, pushed off into the river, and kicked hard to get into the current.

The water was cold. He tried desperately to keep the log and himself out of the streaming light, but he was now at the mercy of the current and soon found himself under the roving lights. Sometimes he was brightly lit, and sometimes he floated in darkness. He reached under the log, looking for a handhold that would get his arms under water, or at least below the top level of the log. No good—nothing. He grabbed the dead man's dirk, let most of the log slip by, and threw both arms over the end. First with his right hand, then with his left, he cut hand holds into the soft wood. Once cut, he slipped the knife back into its sheath, grabbed the end of the log with both hands, and rested his head against the flat edge. This was as good as it was going to get, so he just hung on and floated downstream.

Stars wheeled across the narrow sky. Body numb, his mind wandered. How strange his life had been. Images flickered in his cold brain. A woman who took care of him but disappeared. Red hair was all he really remembered. Running around the village with the dogs—a wild boy no one really cared for. Then someone noticed the stone around his neck and the small grouping of green leaves tattooed on his chubby chest. Funny, no one ever tried to take the stone and cheap leather string. But the tattoo, or birthmark, or whatever it was—that eventually drew attention, and his wild days were soon over. He found himself living with other boys larger than he, all working for a man who continually hammered metal bars and stuck them in a never-ending fire. Years later he learned the name "blacksmith." Liam remembered liking the heat of the forge, the sound of hammer on steel, and the hiss of red-hot iron sliding, steaming, into cold water.

His reverie was broken by sounds coming from upstream. He turned his head, his neck stiff. He pulled himself up on the log a little, so he could see, and then he ducked his head as quickly as he could. A large river boat, many oars per side, open-decked with a high prow, was sculling at great speed right towards his rustic, little craft. He had to get out of the way or get run down. Liam strained to turn the log towards the shore as he kicked like mad. He heard the stroke being called on the ship, although he had no idea what language was being used. He kicked harder, but saw it was no good. This was it. At the last moment he let go of the log, took a deep breath, and dived down as deep as he could.

He had assumed the river was deep, but it was surprisingly shallow. He reached bottom and grabbed a handful of weeds, which allowed him to stay down, even though his hands burned with pain. He heard, felt, and saw the great ship pass overhead. Just as he was forming a small victory smile, the weeds broke in his hands, and he shot to the surface, sucked up by the passing ship. He screamed as he rocketed upwards. And then he saw his chance: a ship's boat being towed behind. He kicked, arms stretched towards the surface. Liam broke the water just as the boat passed his outstretched arms. He lunged and grabbed the stern of the small boat with his right hand. His shoulder screamed in pain but he wouldn't let go. Slowly, so slowly, he pulled himself up and over the transom.

He fell into the boat breathing heavily, beat up and exhausted. Li tried to find something he could hide under, but there was nothing. He slid his cold, shivering body partially under the bench seat and pretended he was a small, invisible boy.

He was awakened by a jolt. He sat up quickly and realized the ship had stopped, and his boat, tied with a painter, had bumped into the ship. He quickly dropped to the floor again; he was worried that someone would look over the side after hearing the thud. No one did. Liam had to make a move. He couldn't stay in the boat. He went over the side and swam underwater, making for the shore. He held his breath as long as he could and slowly broke the surface. He was close to land, but there were no reeds. The river here had been developed into a harbor, with quays and steps leading down to the surface of the river. Treading water, he turned to look at the ship. Creatures like the one who'd held him captive, were working the ship into a berth for the night. No one was paying any attention to him. Liam began to swim towards the steps, thinking he could get to land and begin his search.

Chapter 31:

FORCED TO FIGHT

Cean was exhausted. He had lost count of the days and nights; he had been worked mercilessly by the masters of the Marfach Gardai in hand to hand and weapons combat. He had gotten his wish to train with the Gardai, and Master Kane had turned him into a quivering mass of jelly. When one master finished with him, another would call him out onto the sand. He fought with weapons he hadn't known existed. His knuckles were bruised and raw. His elbows and knees were nothing but swollen, purple welts. His ribs were difficult to see through the array of blacks, blues, and yellows. He had been drilled in tactics and strategy. He had been confined in the Great Library with a master of indeterminate age, who pounded Athlanean and Warrior history into his head throughout long, long nights. His body was bruised and his mind was mush, but now, leaning against a parapet overlooking the great plain before the Ban Castlean, he stared at the night time sky in wonder. Never

Powers Revealed

before had he looked into the deep night possessing such knowledge. He knew the stars, knew their stories. He could navigate by them, if he had to. He knew about the stone he stood on; he knew almost as much as any man alive. This knowledge made him feel vibrant, strong...no, no, something more. He felt special, because he knew he was truly different. Not because of the markings on his arms—although that should have been enough—but because he knew he was part of something extra-ordinary. He had attained real knowledge. He was no longer ignorant. Or, as Master Pau-li would say, he was no longer *as ignorant*. He was a Warrior. He was an integral part of the history of Athlan. And he knew, just as surely as he stood upon the ramparts of this magnificent castle, that his kind, other than Kon-r, existed nowhere else on the planet.

And yet, there were so many questions. In fact, he realized that the more he knew, the more questions there were. He had said as much to his nighttime archival tormentor. "Nex, it seems the more you teach me, the more questions I have. I mean, the more I know, the less I know I know. How can that be?"

The old man had stared at Cean for what seemed to be a long time. "Yes, young Warrior. You are correct. The more you learn in life, the more you will understand how much you do not know. Perhaps you are not completely useless after all."

Cean remembered the conversation, but aside from constant teaching, those words were the only words of a personal nature the Master had said to him.

Now he understood. Learning never ended, and, perhaps, there were some things he would never know or understand. Why did his parents have to die? Why was he tortured by the Cath Angeal? Who was the Cath Angeal? Who directed her? What…

"Thinking so late?" a voice whispered in his ear.

Cean almost jumped over the parapet. He spun around and reached for his dagger. A hand gripped his arm and curtailed his panic.

"Cean, it is only me."

Cean looked into the shadowed face of Kon-r Sighur, Warrior of the Marfach Gardai, Defender of Athlan. Kon-r wore a black robe with a hood pulled up over his head, his scabbard barely visible on his hip. Cean didn't know what to say. He was still in shock. How could he not have heard Kon-r's approach? Was this something else he had to learn?

Kon-r read his mind. "A simple trick, really, Cean. All hunters learn to move quietly. I took my sandals off. They lie by the keep door. Stealth is often more effective that brute strength. Remember that, Cean. You will find yourself outnumbered many times in battle. Victory does not always come to the strongest. A good commander wins battles. A great commander avoids them whenever he can."

He smiled. Cean saw the bright, white teeth.

"You scared me, Kon-r. I was hoping I was beyond that kind of thing."

Kon-r nodded. 'One never gets over fear, Cean. What were you thinking of out here all by yourself? I'm surprised one of the masters isn't forcefully improving your body or mind in some way." He laughed, a clear, honest laugh that made Cean feel better.

"I escaped for a few moments, Kon-r. Some master I didn't recognize was calling to me with a strange piece of metal he wanted to teach me about, but I ran away before he could get his hands on me. So, here I am, trying to figure things out."

"How are you doing?" Kon-r asked.

"Not well," answered Cean.

"And the problem is?" asked Kon-r.

"The problem is what it always has been. What will happen here? What will happen to us?"

"Don't be a stupid boy, Cean. You know the answers to these questions. Everyone knows the answers to these questions."

"Oh, really, everyone knows the answers, and now I'm stupid to boot?"

Kon-r turned serious. "Yes, if that's your attitude, you are stupid. Would you like me to tell you the answers so you don't have to think so hard?"

"Yes, if it isn't too much trouble," Cean snapped. "If you actually know anything, yes. Tell me the blasted answers."

Kon-r got into Cean's face, grabbed his tunic, pulled him as close as he could, and hissed: "There are no damned answers, you ignorant fish boy." Kon-r shoved Cean away, and Cean had to struggle to keep his balance as he bent out over the parapet. He recovered and took an aggressive step towards Kon-r, who put out his hand, palm outwards, and said, simply but forcefully, "No." Cean stopped. "Think about what I just told you, Mak-Scaire," Kon-r said. "Think before you act, son."

Cean did just that. He thought. No answers? Didn't anyone know more than he did? But that was insane, impossible; didn't anybody know what was going on?

Cean took a short step towards Kon-r: "Tell me you know more than I do. Tell me we aren't blundering about in the dark. Tell me you have a plan, or there is a plan."

Kon-r heard the anguish in Cean's voice. He thought they had covered this before. Kon-r himself was tired of having this particular conversation because he had been having it since he became the Warrior so long ago. The Four- Priest, Warrior, Scientor and Poet- constantly discussed "the plan" or lack thereof. The best answer the Four had ever come up with was the wheels within wheels within wheels concept, which argued that the universe operated on many levels, and seemingly independent plans could be made on one level that were really cogs of greater plans, which were cogs of a still larger plan, and no one was capable of seeing the "Last Plan" or the "Last Planner." In other words, there were no final answers to the bigger questions. There were only beliefs. There was only faith or lack thereof.

If, on the other hand, one was concerned only with the here and now, the answers were fairly simple: good people had to fight bad people. Period. If the good people didn't fight, bad people would dominate, and life would not be worth living. But this story wouldn't satisfy Cean. He had seen the Cath Angeal. He knew there was more to life than the simple view. He had an inkling of the complexity of the universe, as did every Warrior, and simple answers would no longer do. Knowledge was a blessing, but knowledge was also a curse, particularly for a Warrior like Cean, who was unlike any other Warrior, including Kon-r. Cean resisted.

Cean questioned. Cean was independent of the Cath Angeal, and she knew it. Kon-r may have been a transitional commander, but Cean was something new altogether. He demanded more.

"Cean, we have gone over this. There are some things I know, but you know them, too. You are a Warrior—same as me. You have seen the same things I have seen. You know there are forces at work beyond our control. We are part of a larger battle. How it all turns out? We have no idea. Are you happy with those answers?"

Cean fired his back: "No I'm not happy with those answers. We are being played for fools. Trapped here on this island, we must fight a battle not of our choosing. People will suffer; people will die. Why?"

Cean's refusal wasn't unexpected because Kon-r had said the same things a lifetime ago. The difference between Kon-r and Cean was that Kon-r had accepted his role, as laid down by the Cath Angeal, while Cean was not accepting her story. "Cean, if you knew nothing about the Cath Angeal; if you knew nothing about the Warrior history; if you were a simple fisherman's son and vagrants attacked your village, putting your mother and father in danger, what would you do?"

Cean answered immediately, "I'd fight them. What else could I do?"

"Exactly, you would fight them. You wouldn't fight because it was part of some universal plan; you wouldn't fight because some unearthly creature told you to fight; you would fight because it was the right thing to do. Am I correct?"

Cean thought about Kon-r's words, searching for the trap, but could not find one. "Correct" he said, and as he said the words, he understood the real trap Kon-r and he were in: they would do the work of the Cath Angeal because they had to, because on a very basic level, they had to fight. They would have to fight the Bas Croi even if there was no universal battle because the Bas Croi was a fact of this world and he threatened their very existence: he was going to kill them if he could. They had no choice, and in the end it was this fact alone that drove Cean mad with anger. They had no real choice. They would fight and by fighting, however reluctantly, they *would* serve. The rules of the game—set by the Cath Angeal and the Angeal Dorada—had been made by others and Cean and Kon-r could not withdraw from the game because the game controlled their lives; indeed, was their life..

Chapter 32:

Lost and Found

Liam swam through the cold river, sometimes kicking, sometimes treading water. The large ship had dropped anchors fore and aft and had tied up at the dock. The current pulled at the ship. Liam continued to inspect the docks directly above the weed-slick stairway. Where there had only been small pools of light cast by well-spaced torches before, now there were long lines of bright firelight approaching the ship from all directions. Liam treaded water and watched.

They're going to unload the ship, he thought. He was right. Monsters, for that is how he thought of these strange, dark creatures, began to shout at each other from land to ship and back; the gangplank was lowered to the dock, and goods began to be off-loaded. Smaller loads were walked down the gangplank by small, squat workers, while heavier and larger loads were lifted to the dock by ingenious contraptions that swung over the ship's rail, grabbed a bale or wooden crate and swung back onto the dock. These wooden machines looked like gigantic cranes in the flickering firelight, and for a moment Liam forgot about his precarious situation.

Not for long, however. He couldn't remember the last time he ate, and the cold water was sapping his strength. He had to get out of the river. Liam took a deep breath and went underwater, kicking and stroking towards the stone jetty. The steps formed a pyramid from the water to dock's edge. A boat could tie up on either side, and crew could climb stairs to the stone jetty. Liam swam to the shadowed right side and slowly emerged, making sure to exhale as softly as possible. His right arm looped over the lowest stair, followed by his left as he pulled himself partially out of the water so a good portion of his weight hung on the lowest step. He rested and looked back at the cargo ship. The work seemed to be finishing. Many monsters had left with their loads, while a large mix of bales, boxes and coils sat on the dock, waiting for transport.

Liam turned away from the ship, closed his eyes and rested his head on his arms. He was tired. He was hungry and cold. What was he going to do? No ideas were coming. Unthinking, he put his hand around the small white stone. It was still warm, as if life existed within the rock itself. His thoughts wandered. He didn't fall asleep, but he wasn't fully awake, either. His mind was a jumble of disconnected images and sounds when a ship appeared in his thoughts, fuzzy, indefinable, following a small bright light that burned away a heavy blanket of fog. No details, no clarity—a disconnected image...

He came to with a start as his head slipped off his arms and hit the rough, stone stair. Liam immediately checked on the ship, wondering about the craft in his—what? Dream? Was it this boat or another ship? He was dazed and threw some water on his face.

Then he saw something that galvanized his whole being. Two figures were walking down the gangway carrying heavy loads on their backs. They were different, taller, more typically proportioned; they were not monsters. He watched them drop their loads by a cart, turn, and go back up the planking for another load. As they turned, Liam could clearly see their faces. Ka-an and Rat. There was no doubt about it. His friends were working as slaves, but something was wrong, terribly wrong. Both Outcasts walked with a heavy gait and they never raised their heads, never talked to each other, never even looked side to side. He watched and ground his teeth as Ka-an and Rat continued to work. At one point a monster stopped them and gave them something to eat. His friends took what appeared to be loose leaves and eagerly stuffed them into their mouths. Chewing steadily, they resumed their work without a word, without a gesture of any kind.

A warning bell went off in Liam's head. Watching his friends eat, he had a flash of memory and he knew his one-time master, now sitting at the bottom of the river, had fed him in the same manner. Were they the same leaves? He didn't know, but he knew that if they were, his friends were mindless animals who would do anything they were told to do without the least bit of resistance. He shuddered. Liam couldn't be sure if it was from the cold or from the thought of what had happened to him and was also happening to his friends: slavery. Seeing them like this was a shock. But then he began to get angry. Slaves. These people had turned himself and his friends into mindless, soulless slaves. "Never again," the Outcasts had sworn. Never again would they submit; yet here they were: completely submissive, completely dominated. Animals.

Liam knew he had to get close to his brothers. That was what they were, really, brothers more than friends. He couldn't let them out of his sight. He had two choices: he could go up the steps and try to skirt along the dock, staying in whatever shadow he could find, or he could swim to the ship and try to get up onto the deck somehow. Neither was a good choice. He thought the dock would be too exposed, and who was to say more people wouldn't come down to or leave the ship? On the other hand, swimming to the river boat offered no immediate access to the deck above. He decided to swim. If he stayed in the water, he was unlikely to be spotted, and if he couldn't find any way up, he could always return to the jetty and try walking the dock.

Liam slipped back into the water and began a slow breast stroke over to the ship. As he approached, he heard gravelly voices above, along with their heavy tread down the gangplank and the creaking of the giant machines as they swung back and forth. He knew no one would be aware of him.

He reached the keel and grabbed it, steadying himself in the slight current. He saw the stone wall of the dock, saw the stern lines holding the ship in place. The anchor line ran from a hole in the ship's larboard side down into the river. The line was very taught and knotted at regular intervals. Liam had been to the ocean before. As a blacksmith, he had made parts for ships and had delivered them, sometimes installing them. He had seen ships. He knew the line was knotted so men could easily gain purchase as they pulled the anchor up; he also knew the knots would tell the captain how deep the water was where they anchored, the distance between each knot being exactly the same.

Studying the cable, he realized he could climb that rope; the knots would make it relatively easy. But what then? He would stick out like a diamond surrounded by lumps of coal. Yet, what other choice did he have? None. Liam swam to the anchor cable, grabbed the line a little above his head. His feet found a knot just below the surface of the water. Slowly, carefully, he pulled with his arms and pushed up with his legs. He emerged, dripping with water. He continued his climb, all the time wrapped in shadow. No rodent ever climbed a boat's line quieter than Liam did that night. When he reached the top, he eased his head over the side. The deck was still covered with goods, but he saw through small openings and watched the men work. He decided. He quickly slithered over the rail, fell to the deck with a soft thud, and scurried behind a few large boxes, soon to be off-loaded.

Li, you idiot, now what, he thought, silently doubting his own sanity. He peeked around one of the boxes and saw Rat being loaded like a mule. Rat stood docile as the load was strapped none too gently to his back by one of the monsters who seemed to be in charge.

Once loaded, the mate, or whatever he was, kicked Rat from behind to help him down the gangway. Rat stumbled, fell hard to one knee under his heavy pack, struggled to get up, and slowly trudged off the ship. No sound. No emotion. No life. Rat was no more. A sound like grinding glass and stones came out of the mate's mouth—laughter, maybe—and Liam saw red. He wanted to sprint across the deck and choke the life from that squat monster, and he could have made it, too, but then the game would have been over. Instead, he sunk to the deck, back resting against the box, knees drawn up to his chest and took a few deep breaths. *What to do?*

Chapter 33:

I Am a Cow

Liam knew he had to come up with a plan fast. The deck would be emptied of cargo soon and he could hide no longer. Pushing himself up against the tall crate, he heard a commotion towards the bow of the ship. Looking around the corner, he saw that one of the giant transport machines had collapsed and a large pallet of boxes and bales had crashed to the deck, spilling cargo everywhere. Liam saw the mate run over to the shattered goods, screaming at the crew, which stood dumbly, staring at the ruined valuables. Quick as a flash, Liam ran out onto the gangplank while everyone's attention was on the disaster in the bow. Lowering his head like Ka-an and Rat, he trundled up the gangplank behind Rat and waited to be loaded like his friends.

The mate returned after soundly berating his crew and resumed loading carriers with backpacks. As Liam approached the front of the line, he became as still as he could. He pictured himself as a cow: dumb and placid. He was a cow; he was a cow; he was—The mate grabbed him by the shoulder and roughly turned him around. His talons dug into Li's shoulder. The pain was considerable. *I am a cow*, He felt the frame tied to his body, then the bales were tied to the frame. The weight was staggering. He stood there, back to the mate, unmoving. *I am a cow...* The kick came, and he was launched down the gangplank, stumbling heavily, skinning his hands and knees again, as he fell. He wanted to scream in anger. Twice now he wanted to kill that pig. *I am a cow*, he thought. *A stupid, dull cow.*

Painfully and slowly, Liam raised himself off the old wood. His hands were filled with jagged splinters, his pack askew. He shrugged the pack into place and lumbered down onto the docks and followed the other slaves to a series of wagons where, he assumed, he would drop his load and go back for another. He was partially correct. He did drop his load, but he was immediately grabbed by another monster, almost identical to the mate, and was pushed in front of a very large wagon that was already heavily loaded. He stood with his head hanging down, but he saw that Ka-an and Rat stood directly in front of him in a single file line. In fact, there were six beings in his line: himself, Rat, and Ka, plus three small but very powerful looking monsters. A second line stood next to Liam's, completely made up of rough looking monster workers.

Liam stood looking as stupid as possible, trying to figure out what was going on, when a stiff, circular collar was dropped over his head from behind. Monsters proceeded to drop collars over the heads of each person in both lines. More monsters came along and threaded bright chains through the collars. By now, Liam knew he and his friends, as well as the collared monsters, had been harnessed to pull the wagon. This wasn't good.

Just as he had that thought, a whip whistled through the air and cracked into the flesh of the lead monster on the right. The whip flashed again and bit into the shoulder of the left line's leader. Greenish blood ran down both scaly backs as the leaders began to pull. Everyone got the message. The newly assembled slave team began to strain and pull, their bare feet slipping on the ancient dock stones. Some went to their knees; most kept their feet as they pulled and the whip continued to crack and slice into flesh.

Two monsters sat on the wagon's seat: the driver, who held the reigns, and the whip man. The whip man was very good, very thorough. His metal tipped lash tickled each and every slave as they struggled to move the heavily laden wagon uphill. The paving stones had become slick in the night air. Their progress up the slight slope to the road was minimal. More workers began to slip and slide, but the whip man wanted to show his mastery of his tool. He began picking out body parts—a head here, an ear there—as he doubled his output of pain and encouragement. The whip sang and cracked, cracked, cracked. The monsters screamed in pain, but Ka-an and Rat made no sound. Liam bit his lips, clenched his jaw. He couldn't make a sound, couldn't flinch. He felt the whip curl around his shoulder and retreat- his skin split open and blood sprayed over the ground.

This went on for a good while as they struggled up the path. Finally, with one convulsive heave, they made it onto a hard-packed dirt road and headed towards the black city. Liam raised his eyes to check on his friends. They were shredded; their backs were in bloody tatters. Skin hung in loose strips. Their shirts were a memory, and what cloth remained was stuck to their skin in ribbons of blood. He suspected he looked much the same. While they could survive another lashing due to the effects of the drug, he couldn't. They were numb to everything. Their actions meant nothing to them. They could fall, dead in place, without another thought or emotion. All he could think about was the bloody pain and how he was going to get them out of this valley.

They pulled for what seemed to be miles. Liam was exhausted. He became just like his friends, another dumb animal incapable of thought. His first concern was putting one foot in front of the other. His second and only other thought was to avoid the whip. After another slight rise in the road, the driver screamed something, and Liam's collar was jerked backward with tremendous force.

All of the slaves were yanked off their feet and fell hard into the dust. Liam was stunned and, as he lay on the ground, he heard that gnashing sound again, the ugly laughter made by the mate when he had kicked Ka-an onboard the cargo vessel. He felt like lying in the dust forever. Whatever plans he had were gone. They would all die here. For an instant he wished he had the mysterious plant to eat; he could forget everything and say goodbye to pain forever.

As his eyes began to close, the collar jerked him up as a team of monsters grabbed the reigns and pulled forward. They wanted the slaves on their feet. Liam struggled to rise. He saw Ka-an and Rat were already standing, as were all of the other monsters. He was too late. The whip whistled and cracked into his back. He stifled a scream. He did not flinch. He lowered his head, but raised his eyes to study where they were. Directly in front of the wagon was a gigantic jumble of stone. A moat had been dug around a building that reminded Li of a castle, or what he thought a castle should look like, and it was filled with river water. A bridge extended from the road to the other side of the moat.

As Liam watched, a large wooden gate began to open. No one moved. Even the wagon master and his whip man, now off the wagon, where mesmerized by the opening of the massive portal.

Liam didn't know what was going on, but he had a feeling that whatever was behind the gate was not good. The monsters began removing the slaves' collars. Liam stood with his head bowed as the collar was roughly pulled up and over his head. He knew it was now or never. He shuffled to stand directly behind Rat and Ka-an. No one was watching. The whip man's attention was on the opening gates. Liam grabbed Rat's right arm and Ka's left. He squeezed as hard as he could, trying to shock them out of their trances. No good. They acted as if he wasn't even there. Liam began to panic. He had to do something. Now. What? He had to get into their heads, through their stupor. He had to…

Oh no. No. Not that. No. Liam knew what he had to do and he was horrified. Ever since he had battled Celine, the earth guardian, over the possession of his soul, he had been frightened by his power and he hadn't tried to use it. But now, what choice did he have? He had to violate his friends or abandon them to whatever was behind the opening gate. This was wrong, and yet, a choice had to be made. Control their minds or abandon them.

He grabbed their arms again and concentrated. He tried to move into both at the same time. He made no progress. Something was wrong. He tried again, only he let Ka-an go and concentrated on Rat. His mind moved along his arm and he found he had moved into Rat, immediately grabbing his brain. Liam was shocked. There was nothing: no response, no feelings, nothing. No real life. Rat was breathing, but he was a husk of a human being. Liam became scared. He got angry. He started to shout at Rat in his head, and he pictured himself grabbing Rat's brain and shaking it with all his strength. *Wake up! Wake up, Rat! Now. Please! Rat! Please, wake up!*

Liam couldn't explain what happened next. He felt as if something had slithered under a pile of wet leaves. Liam was startled. Wanting to withdraw from Rat's head, he couldn't. He held on and forced his mind into Rat. He began to whisper his name: "Rat, Rat, Rat, Rat..." Slowly, oh so slowly, the wet leaves fell aside and that squirming being began to grow in Liam's mind. He felt as if his own skull was being filled with some kind of mush, lit with a dull, but growing, light. "Rat, Rat, Rat..." He continued to apply the pressure. Rat began to shake his head like a wet dog. After a few confused seconds, Rat found himself looking into Liam's blue eyes. Recognition came slowly. Before he could speak, Li covered Rat's mouth with his hand and whispered: "Quiet. Don't move. Watch."

Rat nodded slightly. Liam went through the same process with Ka-an with the same results. When both men were completely lucid, aware of their surroundings, Liam told them to remain still while he began to whisper his plan to escape, but before he got very far, the whip man began cracking his weapon over their heads. Others began herding them to the back of the wagon. Liam caught both men's eyes and they understood: continue to play dumb. Their lives depended upon it.

Powers Revealed

Chapter 34: Showdown

Cean continued to work on his martial skills. Not surprisingly, he was a quick study. What was surprising was his capacity to learn and remember the history and culture of Athlan and the Gardai. Yet he was not accepted by the Gardai nor the Masters. They respected him for his ability and accomplishments, but they did not accept him as an equal. He was a threat to their way of life. He was a Warrior and an outsider, but there could be only one Warrior. They could not bring themselves to trust him. Cean understood. He was different. He was a threat. even so, they talked to him occasionally. Some even liked him.

Rumor circulated throughout the stronghold: conditions outside of the Ban Castlean were becoming desperate. People were collecting at the base of the castle walls, begging for food, for protection, for salvation. Some of the displaced people were brought inside for questioning. Their tales were sketchy, some incoherent, but a pattern eventually emerged. There was a force driving people towards the castle, strange warriors who preached nothing but hate. If you resisted their call, you died. There was no appeal. Join or die, and most joined. They were coming and would be at the castle soon.

Cean had witnessed a few of the interrogations- tales of torture and death. He listened and learned. His time must be coming and coming fast because Athlan was falling apart and, logically, he, the 2nd Warrior, would play his part soon. He just didn't know what it would be. While listening to one bedraggled woman, he felt someone behind him. Turning, he found Kon-r.

"Terrible, isn't it?" Kon-r said.

"Yes, and getting worse," answered Cean.

"Walk with me, Cean."

They strolled across the arena, men working hard all around them. "Cean, how are you being accepted by the Gardai and by the Masters?" Kon-r asked.

Was Kon-r reading his mind? "Not as well as I had hoped, Kon-r. They can't get over the fact of two Warriors existing at the same time. I don't know what to do about that."

Kon-r nodded. "Yes, it is a paradox beyond their comprehension. They will not accept it, unless..." He stopped speaking.

"Unless what, Kon-r?"

"Unless they see that you and I are the same. Unless they believe they can trust you like they trust me. Unless they believe you can protect them as I protect them."

Cean shrugged and said, "But how am I going to do that? You've guarded these people for years. They know you. Their parents knew you. Their grandparents knew you. We may have a few days left, maybe more, but how am I supposed to gain their trust in such a short time? I don't think it can be done, Kon-r."

Kon-r didn't say anything. Instead, he simply walked over to one of the groups practicing with battle mace and short swords, took a sword from a smiling Gardai officer, and approached Cean. Kon-r's eyes were bright. He walked like a panther on the hunt.

The hair on the back of Cean's neck came up. "What are you doing?" he asked.

Kon-r circled him. "The only way I can think of to convince our people of your ability is to fight you in front of them."

Kon-r made a short rush towards Cean and swiped at his legs. Cean had to jump over the blade. He knew that cut would have crippled him. Kon-r was not playing. Gardai had seen Kon-r's attack and formed a ring around the pair. Cean skipped away from Kon-r, who continued to stalk him.

"Give the boy a weapon", Kon-r commanded, and a short sword was thrown into what was now a combat ring. Cean picked it up and Kon-r was on him in a flash. *Was this how it was to end?* Cean thought, as he blocked Kon-r's overhand chop and spun away.

"Is this really what you want, Kon-r?" Cean asked.

Kon-r hissed, as his sandaled feet slid over the sand, "Fight for your life, boy, or I will take it from you."

Fire raged in Cean's eyes as he jumped to the attack. He was fast in every way. His sword moved in a shimmering arc of steel, occasionally darting out at Kon-r's eyes, throat or heart. But Kon-r was just as fast, and their swords rang like the bells of death. The battle circle was filled with the sound of combat: men's heavy breathing, grunts of effort, small cries of pain. Primordial growls escaped from parched throats. The Gardai watching this unexpected spectacle were shocked by the violence, by the deadly skill, by the fact that no one was dead yet. The combatants threw themselves into the battle as if they were absolutely sure of their own deaths and didn't care.

After what seemed to be a long time but wasn't, the Warriors separated. Both bled from multiple cuts, but neither was daunted. Cean had found a new respect for himself. He knew he could go toe to toe with Kon-r Sighur, Warrior of the realm.

Kon-r, for his part, had expected nothing less. In fact, he would have been surprised if Cean had not performed as well as he did. The Masters had reported Cean's progress to him; those reports were the basis for Kon-r's decision to fight. The fight had to be convincing; the fight had to be vicious; the fight had to be real. Short swords weren't enough. They would have to battle hand-to-hand.

Kon-r tossed his sword out of the ring and assumed an ancient fighting stance. Cean, recognizing the form, threw his sword away and adopted an opposing combat posture. Two styles would be showcased. Both men charged at the same time. Even the soldiers of the Gardai, the best troops on earth, held their breath.

The collision was massive. Both men moved in a blur of punches, holds, and kicks. Fists and feet thudded into unprotected flesh. They fought in silence, neither man giving evidence of the massive damage being done to both. Gashes appeared on Cean's face, as if an invisible knife had cut him. Kon-r threw a punch at Cean's chest that would have easily killed a normal man, but instead, where once he had a fine aquiline nose, Kon-r retreated with a bloody mess. Blood exploded onto his chest. No quarter was asked and none was given.

Every Master in the circle saw their techniques used perfectly. Strike and counterstrike went on and on. Neither Warrior would quit because both were incapable of quitting. The conclusion was obvious: both were Warriors and both would die in that bloody ring before either surrendered.

An old man, master of many forms, stepped into the circle. His voice, a sandy rasp, was incredibly powerful as he shouted: "Enough! Stand down."

Neither man wanted to stop. Their blood was up and they wanted to fight. They eyed each other warily, but stepped away, both wanting the other man to make a move so the fight could continue. Honor and discipline won the day. They withdrew from each other.

The old man spoke again: "You do the Masters much honor. Never before has something like this been witnessed. Age old arguments on what style is better have been answered. No style is better, only men are better. But you two are equal, and we must stop you from harming yourselves any further. Kon-r Sighur, I see your purpose and you have succeeded. Cean Mak-Scaire, you have proven yourself to us. We do not know why, but you are a true Warrior, and so, at the end of days, something new has happened which we must accept; and I do."

The old man bowed low, went to his knees, head and palms resting in the sand. Without a word the circle of Gardai did the same. Kon-r and Cean walked to each other. Both had tears in their eyes. Both were hurt and bleeding. Both knew with certainty they would have fought to the death. Clasping each other's forearms, feeling the marks that had changed their lives irrevocably, two Warriors of Athlan walked out of the circle, their heads high. They had a battle to plan.

Chapter 35:

A King Comes Forth

Liam, Ka-an, and Rat were shoved to the back of the heavily laden wagon. The whip cracked constantly. Strange lights glowed atop poles set at regular intervals along the path to the castle; Liam could see the small lights within what looked to him like large crystal globes. The light seemed to be magnified as it lit the loading and unloading area. Bales and packs of all sizes were carried through heavy shadows on the dark side of the wagon. Everything needed to be offloaded.

The whip cracked as the slaves were lined up. Liam, Rat, and Ka-an followed each other as closely as they could without drawing attention to themselves. Their backs were to the castle gate, and they were afraid to turn their heads towards the commotion. Something was happening, but they had to play dumb; they would have to let events play out.

Liam, leading their little band, was the first to be loaded. He was slow to answer the wagon master's command to step forward and for his tardiness, he was rewarded with a bash to the side of his head. He went down hard. Rat and Ka-an could do nothing. Liam picked himself up, showing no emotion, and presented his back to be loaded. The straps were tightened horribly by the master and Liam was pushed away from the wagon towards the castle with an extremely heavy load digging into his back. Stumbling along a well-worn path, Liam raised his head after a few steps and stopped in his tracks. His mouth fell open in surprise. He couldn't move. The bearer behind him, Rat, his own head down, bumped into him and both stumbled forward. Ka-an was right behind and all three stared in wonder and horror at what they saw. It was impossible.

While they were being loaded, a company of monsters, armed and armored, had left the castle, marched down the lit path to the unloading area, and surrounded the wagon and the slave porters. Liam was used to seeing these people; a hundred or more in military garb was not much of a surprise to him. What came after the armed company, however, was nightmare vision from hell.

Another monster came behind the procession, but he was of a different magnitude altogether. He had the same black scaled skin, taloned hands and feet and horned head. He was powerfully built. But this monster was well over twice Liam's size. A large tail with a three-headed barb swung lazily from his backside. Liam thought he could actually feel the earth vibrate as the huge monster approached.

He wore a gigantic, black blade that seemed to shimmer in the refracted light on his back, and two huge daggers that would have served normal men as swords hung from his hips. Liam couldn't imagine anyone challenging this brute. He continued to study what had to be the king of the river vale, but suddenly he was looking up at the dome, Rat and Kaan lying beside him. In fact, every monster was prostrate on the ground before their lord. The three Outcasts had moved too slowly and had paid the price for their insolence. Blood dripped from Liam's right ear. Checking his friends, he saw blood on their faces also. The wagon master had just impressed respect onto them with his fists.

Rat whispered to Liam, "Put your ear to the ground."

Liam turned his good ear to the dusty ground and listened. After a while he heard something, though he wasn't sure what. Perhaps it was the giant monster walking towards them. No, wait. Thunder? Thunder was rumbling underground and the earth quivered slightly, then it was gone. Before he could consider the noise further, there was a booming, grinding sound that stunned everyone in the area. Everyone was thrown to the ground. Liam felt sure the giant was speaking but he couldn't understand what was being said. The monsters around him began to stand, and the Outcasts did the same.

The wagon master issued a command in the same fractured tongue, and the slaves began to shuffle forward, towards the castle gate. The armed company of guards separated to let them through. In this manner each porter had to walk directly in front of the monster king.

Liam watched the slaves in front of him. None raised their faces to their ruler. They walked with heads down in abject servility. Liam, Ka-an, and Rat did their best to imitate them. Just as the Outcasts were about to pass the giant, his voice boomed, and Liam, Rat and Ka-an were once again knocked to the ground. Almost senseless and not in his right mind, Liam made the mistake of reacting to the violence. He struggled to his feet, shrugged off his pack, and checked his friends. His behavior was automatic, but a serious mistake.

Liam heard an audible intake of breath from the surrounding soldiers. Slaves felt nothing. Slaves did nothing. Something was seriously wrong. One hundred swords were drawn from their scabbards with a sound like hissing, deadly snakes. The guards advanced on the Outcasts.

There was nothing Liam could do for his friends, still lying defenseless. Nonetheless, Liam stood over his brothers and would defend them with his life. His right hand unconsciously stole to his chest, rubbing the green tattoo. His white amulet hung down, forgotten. He had no weapon and was fresh out of ideas. Slowly, he helped his friends to their feet. At least they would die together.

The native slaves scurried away. Liam, Rat, and Ka-an were left alone in the center of the ring of guards, whose swords were drawn and pointed at the Outcasts. They stood in a tight triangle, facing outwards, waiting for the inevitable charge, which would be followed by their quick deaths. None flinched. There were no tears or cries for mercy. Three more ex-slaves were soon to be dead. Who would care? Who would miss them? No one.

The charge began, but before the guards took two steps, the king's hateful voice boomed once again and the killing blades froze in mid-stroke, creating what must have looked like some strange flower with sharp, silvery petals. Another harsh command, and the guards moved back to their original positions, this time creating a pathway between Liam and the king.

Liam raised his head and looked directly into the monster's yellow, reptilian eyes. Two beings with nothing in common were locked in each other's gaze. Liam felt a strange connection with this beast, but also a deep revulsion. He had experienced it twice before: when Celine and the Mother had tried to gain control of his mind and body.

Without warning, he felt the creature trying to enter his head. The pressure was enormous. Liam broke eye contact as he tried to rally his own defenses, his own mysterious power. Dropping his gaze to the king's chest, he was startled to see a familiar object: a white stone hanging from a metal necklace. He had to react quickly. He exerted every bit of his own being. He remembered the lessons taught by Celine and by her master. Concentrating completely, Liam pushed the brute out of his mind. He tried to go farther. He tried to grab the king's mind. He failed. The door was shut.

Rat and Ka stood behind him now, both men facing the brutish monarch. They didn't really know what was happening, but they could see Liam straining. Sweat beaded Liam's forehead and his body shook almost imperceptibly. Rat noticed the guards quietly inching towards them. He realized that whatever was happening, these soldiers wouldn't let their king be harmed if they could help it.

Liam took a step towards the king, and the king took a much larger step towards Liam.

Rat shouted to Liam, "No, Li. You can't beat this thing. Stay back."

But Liam didn't hear Rat. He didn't hear the rumble in the ground. He didn't feel the earth shiver. All Liam desired was to close with this giant and finish him. He didn't think about dying.

Liam noticed the king's face. Was that his version of a smile? As they approached each other, the massive Ruler reached back and drew his mammoth sword, fully Liam's own height if not more. The king held the pommel with two taloned hands, the blade pointing directly at the green tattoo on Liam's chest.

Liam exerted his power once more. He strained; he pushed; he tried to grab the brute's mind. He was angry. He was determined. He wanted to crush this monster, and for a second, he entered that alien brain. Liam saw strange sights: images of flying machines, a red planet, many other images that made absolutely no sense. The Monarch froze where he stood. The sword point did not waver, but the king could not move forward. For the first time in his long life he had been challenged by strength as great as his own, another being carrying a sky star of heaven. He had often wondered whether there was more than one stone bearer, and now he knew.

The king concentrated his own power. He began to growl in a grinding, menacing, horrible way, and he hurled his psychic might, invisible and deadly, against Liam.

Liam staggered mentally and physically. Rat and Ka-an rushed to his side. If they hadn't, Liam would have collapsed to the ground. As it was, he felt weak, worn out, but he couldn't surrender. He gathered himself once more and exerted his will. For the first time Liam noticed how bright the area was. He wondered if it was really that bright or if the light was some kind of side effect of his battle with the king. He pushed, but nothing came. He started to panic. He was tiring, but was the king also wearing down? Liam was sure he couldn't break the monster—he only wondered how long he could resist the king's onslaught.

Just as Liam was about to launch another power surge, the ground shook. It was as if everything solid turned to mud. He went down to one knee, trying to stabilize himself. Rat and Ka-an steadied themselves by putting their arms around him. Liam checked his opponent. The king stood tall, his powerful legs spread wide, taloned feet dug in. But his guard was not so fortunate. They lay sprawled everywhere along the path and around the wagons.

Liam tried to stand, but the earth shook again, and this time the terrible sound of an avalanche filled the valley. Liam recognized the sound and knew what was happening. The plains of Athlan had been shaking, burning, and erupting for a long time. He thought it was quite likely that those events had skipped this protected valley.

He turned towards the king again. They locked eyes. Liam felt the hatred and, looking into the giant monarch's mind, saw that his name was Vardar. Vardar knew what was happening, even if his subjects did not, for he was a being of vast experience and memory. He knew the end was near. All those years, all those accomplishments—all about to disappear. He gathered his mind for one final effort. He would crush this outsider and his friends. He would kill them if it was the last thing he did. He knew he had almost beaten the other star wielder on his last attempt. This time...

Vardar never got the chance. A tremendous cacophony of sound echoed through the valley. Everyone looked up. It was difficult to see, but Liam thought he saw the dome covered in spiderweb cracks where there were none earlier. The ground rumbled again, more severely, and the earth split into a wide chasm between the Outcasts and the king. Most of the guard perished into the depths, as molten earth began to surge towards the surface. Vardar Mel'an bellowed in anger. He realized he could leap the chasm and so come upon his foes. There was no other choice. He moved incredibly quickly, a gigantic black shadow leaping through the dust filled air.

Liam, Ka-an and Rat stood in awe as the huge nightmare flew through the air, bringing certain death. And they would have died. They were no match for Vardar. Not on this world or any other.

But no one controls chance. No one is invulnerable. Vardar's mighty, taloned feet landed on the edge of the chasm, and like the natural athlete he was, he immediately leaned forward to shift his weight to solid ground. But the earth failed to cooperate, and just as he took his first step away from the rumbling fissure, the ground shook more violently than it had before. The king slipped back toward the fiery chasm. He dug his talons into the shifting earth, but his slide continued.

Liam couldn't stand and watch. He staggered over to the monster and actually grabbed his massive hand. But to no avail; Vardar was far too heavy for Liam to hold. He saw the smile again on Vardar's face. The magnificent king ripped the white stone from his neck and just as he offered the stone to Liam, the ground shifted, and the king of the River Vale, Vardar, son of Var-ar, son of Van-ar, a family going back to the depths of time, silently vanished into the fire and smoke of his dying kingdom, taking his sky star with him.

Liam stared into the fire, mesmerized. He felt the heat on his face. Hairs smoked on his head. He couldn't move. Vardar had filled Liam's head with his lineage, with his pride, with mysterious connections to time and space unknown to Liam. More importantly, Vardar knew, he knew what the stones were, but that piece of information he had taken with him to his death.

"Li, come on. We have to go. This place is falling apart."

Rat snapped Liam out of his reverie. So much to know; so much lost. Who was the king? Someone great, that was for sure. But Rat was right. Liam could think about this later. He got to his feet and looked around. The sides of the valley, once covered with terraces, plants, and dwellings, exploded into the night, rivers of magma flowing down the ruined walls. The land heaved continually, writhing, convulsing in pain. The river steamed, and the once-beautiful dome cracked further, large chunks of stone beginning to fall.

Liam said, "Come on, we have to get to the river."

Liam led and his brothers followed. Footing was difficult; sight was difficult. It became tougher to breath as Sulphur replaced air. Liam saw the river ahead and picked up his pace. A large chunk of dome landed just behind them, and they all went down on their hands and knees. They couldn't stop. Liam kept them going and, after what seemed an eternity, they reached the water. The river was filled with refuse.

"Now what?" asked Ka-an.

There were only two choices: Go back along the river and try to get out the way they came in or go down river and find an exit. He felt certain there had to be one. The river had to lead somewhere.

"Get into the water," Liam said. "We'll go downstream. We can't go back. There are plenty of monsters still alive, and we can't fight them all. Let's try to find something to hold on to and float down together."

Finding a large spar wasn't difficult. Ships were being smashed by falling boulders all along the river. Selecting a piece they could wrap their arms around, the three outcasts pushed off into the current, desperately hoping for a way out...

Chapter 36:

Ship and Crew

The dome crumbled. Canyon walls exploded into the valley, torrents of magma flowing down in beautiful red, deadly falls. The river hissed and steamed as lava met water. The temperature rose alarmingly. The earth rumbled and groaned. The world of the People was coming to an end. Liam felt an overwhelming sadness. He didn't owe these creatures anything. They had caused him and his friends considerable pain and thought nothing of it. Yet, they had made a life for themselves, a good life it seemed, and they had for the most part left the world alone, asking the world to leave them alone. And by chance Liam ends up captured and before their ruler kills him, he kills their magnificent king. Their strength, the symbol of their own greatness gone, their world collapses. Was it his doing? Was he the catalyst or was it all chance? Liam closed his eyes and hung on to the raft. This was all too much. How could he decide what had really happened? If this was madness, life was madness.

He, Rat, and Ka-an continued to kick down the river. They kept their heads low and their eyes open. It seemed like the river was filling up with flotsam and refugees, People who didn't have anywhere else to go, People who had just lost everything, People who had no hope and no future outside of their dome. And yet, they continued to struggle for survival. The life force in them was as strong as it was in Liam, Rat and Ka-an. In this there was no difference between the Outcasts and the People. They just wanted to live. But to live, how would they get out of here?

Rat wondered the same thing, but Rat was a Shadowman, the elite guards of the Outcasts, and his instincts for survival, for maneuver, were sharper than both Liam and Ka-an's. "Li, this river has to go somewhere," he said. "Otherwise, this place would be underwater. It has to drop under the Western wall. Where else could it go?"

Liam thought about that. Rat was probably right. They would have to watch as they approached the wall, paddle to shore, and study the situation before they made a move. They couldn't go in blind. That would be stupid.

Their raft continued to move in the middle of the stream. They had to watch for pieces of wood colliding with them as it seemed everything in the valley was being sucked into the river and everything that could float was now floating alongside of them. They could see others holding on to anything that would float. Some kept their heads above water; some did not and died.

Liam held onto the rear of the raft, while Ka-an had the side facing the north shore and Rat the south. Above, the dome rumbled and shook. Chunks of the roof fell everywhere. Dust and steam filled the air. The smell of Sulphur was becoming stronger. Liam noticed that it was getting very difficult to see the canyon walls and breathing was more difficult than it had been. The Vale was deteriorating at an alarming rate.

Li could no longer see the Lord's castle. While looking backward, he heard Ka-an shout. Liam turned to his friend and saw him point to the northern shore. A small boat with a vaguely military look was pushing off from a partially destroyed dock. People fought to get on it, but those already on board were trying to break away.

Six archers stood in the boat and loosed six arrows into the crowd. Six bodies fell. In rapid succession three more flights of arrows flew; eighteen more bodies dropped. The archers couldn't miss. Those deaths created separation from the pack, and the ship pushed off, leaving a massive, angry crowd screaming for help, for life, for salvation.

Liam tried to count the warriors in the ship, which wasn't large. Each side had eight oars from what he could see, and all were manned. Men stood between the rowers' benches, and there were lookouts fore and aft. Liam estimated the ship carried no less than twenty-five armed, alert men, all ready to repulse boarders. He would like to keep up with them. He was certain they would know where to go, how to get out.

He screamed as loud as he could, in order to be heard above the roar of the crumbling dome. "Kick, kick hard—keep up with that ship."

Rat and Ka-an got the message. The raft moved faster, but in the end their efforts did not suffice. The sleek craft began to pull away, archers loosing shafts at any who tried to approach. It was hopeless. Their pace slackened as Liam, Rat, and Ka-an rested their heads against the waterlogged wood.

They were discouraged, but they had no choice. They began to kick again, occasionally warding off large pieces of wood that came to close to their fragile craft. The valley was almost dark now, obscured with steam and smoke. Li couldn't see the walls, could barely see the shore on either side of the river. The black cruiser was almost out of sight. Li strained to see the western wall up ahead but couldn't. A tremendous crack filled the valley, followed by a loud and deep rumble. The dome, eternally open to the sky, was collapsing. The pressures of the earth had overcome the natural strength of the ancient rock formation. Large chunks of stone began to fall from the eastern end of the gigantic cavern. The opening in the dome became larger. The earth shook harder than it ever had before. Liam, Rat, and Ka-an felt themselves rise as the river seemed to leap out of its bed, propelling everything in it upwards and outwards towards each shore—or, more accurately, what was left of each shore.

The geography of the valley was now unrecognizable from only a few hours before. The city behind was a collapsed memory. The dome continued caving in, the smooth sides now falling in towards the river. Liam, Rat, and Ka-an hung on desperately, trying to anticipate their next move. Liam saw the warship ahead on the northern shore, where it had been driven up onto the land. It lay on its side, half of the oars smashed, the other half pointing up into the air, like a wounded centipede.

Liam yelled and pointed to it, and Rat and Ka-an began to kick and paddle towards the upended cruiser. Before they had gone far, Liam yelled, "Wait," as if they could stop moving on the convulsing river. He pointed again, and all three witnessed one of the strangest sites they had seen yet.

The small war craft and the warriors that remained with it were being attacked by another small group of ragged beings. In this chaos, such an attack wasn't that strange, but the attacking group was made up of people, real, human people. It came to Liam that he should have realized there would be other prisoners like them in this small, reclusive kingdom.

Others had to have approached the hidden doors and been taken down with the same narcotic darts. *Here was proof*, he thought.

They began kicking once more, hurrying to reach their fellow humans. The battle seemed to be favoring the dark warriors, who fought professionally with martial weapons and stayed in battle formation. The freed slaves made weapons of whatever they got their hands on, which in most cases were nothing more than rocks and improvised clubs of some kind.

Rat didn't need any direction from Liam. He knew what they had to do. He pushed off from the raft and began to swim as fast as he could toward shore. Liam and Ka-an did the same. They all saw what Rat had in mind. He swam to the far side of the ship, the side with the oars pointing towards the sky. From that side they could come up behind the enemy warriors and be on them before they knew what was happening. Finding weapons, however, would be a challenge.

A few more strokes brought them all to the river's edge. Rat was already standing there when Li and Ka-an dragged themselves out of the water. He had two large rocks in his hands, and Liam and Ka-an understood what he intended. They scrambled around the beach and found rocks, too. Once ready, they ran as quickly and quietly as they could to the fight. They closed the distance and hurled their rough weapons at the unaware warriors. Their attack might not have been deadly, but a number of soldiers went down and didn't get up. The slaves saw the soldiers fall and fought back with renewed spirit and vigor. Liam, Ka-an, and Rat picked up the weapons of their disabled opponents, each taking a spear and sword, and that turned the tide. With weapons, the Outcasts made short work of their enemies, remembering in anger their own shame and pain of their recent enslavement, while the remaining slaves finished off the rest. When the fight came to an end, there were only a few dozen slaves left alive, all men of varying ages.

Liam faced them with Rat and Ka-an standing on each side. Their spear points and swords dripped red. The slaves, carrying their rough clubs, knelt in the sand. They were thin and haggard, exhausted. Some had the vacant eyes of those still affected by the People's leafy drug. The ground shook as the dome continued to collapse.

"We can't stay here," Liam shouted. "Do any of you know the way out?"

One man, sturdier than the others, spoke up. "There are two ways out of this cursed place. Both go through the western wall. I don't know where they lead, but I once worked on a farm at that end of the valley, and I saw small ships disappear through the wall."

Disappear through the wall? Was this one still addled by drugs? Liam couldn't wait to find out.

"We need to get out of here, now. We need this ship. Drop your weapons, get to your feet, and do what we ask of you. There is always hope." Most of the slaves staggered upright and gave a ragged cheer. Rat directed the effort to right the ship while Ka-an worked his way through the slaves, doing whatever he could for the injured. Liam watched the effort and considered what they would do once back on the river. The slaves worked hard of their own volition. They worked to escape with their lives. Liam understood their mindset and wondered if any of them would make it.

Chapter 37:

Treasure

The first problem was moving the ship. When the killer wave had deposited the craft on shore, the starboard oars all snapped as the ship crashed onto its side. But the oars were stout and more than a few inches of the thick wooden shafts plunged into the soft shoreline. These broken shafts acted like pegs, pinning the side of the craft to the muddy earth. Rat, trying to move the ship, didn't know about the pegs. He couldn't figure out why the ship wouldn't move. He felt certain they had enough men and strength to move the craft. Maybe there was a heavy cargo inside? Rat hopped the rail and found a hatch that led into the ship. Opening it, he disappeared into the darkness of the shallow hull.

On shore Liam had gathered the oldest men who could still move, and gave them orders. "Don't go too far away, because we will leave as soon as the ship is ready, but scavenge for supplies. Whatever you think might be useful: rope, food, weapons, clothes. Bring them back here as fast as you can. Go in two-man teams—no one searches alone. It's still dangerous out there. Questions?"

There were none. The men picked partners and went inland as fast as they could. Liam told the remaining men, "Gather all of the weapons from these warriors. Strip them of all valuables and armor, and make sure you gather their bows and arrows. I have a feeling we will need them before long."

Ka-an approached Liam with an older man in tow. "Li, we need medicine for these people. Some have suffered here for years and are in poor condition. This man says he knows where some things can be found, if the building still stands."

Liam didn't answer right away. He didn't want to lose Ka-an, but he knew he didn't have much chance of stopping him, either; Ka-an would take care of those who needed help. "Go ahead," he said. "Arm yourselves before you leave, and take two younger men with you in case of trouble. And Ka-an, be back as fast as you can. We don't have much time."

Ka-an nodded and grabbed weapons. He shouted, "Were any of you soldiers or hunters?"

Two youths, tall and thin with straw colored hair, stepped forward. "We're brothers, sir. Our father taught us to hunt. We can both shoot a bow, skin and dress our kill."

Ka-an smiled. "What are your names?"

The taller boy answered. "I'm Ard, and this is my younger brother, Arn."

Ka-an liked these boys. "Grab bows and fill a few quivers from those weapons over there. Find short swords, too." When everyone was ready, Ka-an waved to Liam and started off, the old man in the lead.

Rat didn't move after he dropped down into the hold, waiting for his eyes to adjust to the dark. Muted light came through the hatch. Rat saw the problem right away. The broken ends of the oars were stuck into the ground and jammed against the oar openings. The ship was effectively pinned. Rat grabbed one of the oar handles to see if they could be moved. He strained and twisted but couldn't move the broken oar. Maybe two or three men could pull a handle up from the earth through the oar opening? He had to try something. He backed away from the fractured shaft and tumbled backwards, head over heels, thumping his head on some kind of box. He swore like a sailor and then broke out into a loud, continuous laugh: the great Rat, chief of the Shadowmen, cracking his skull in the dark—his supposed element.

Liam heard the thud, foul language, and laughter. Confused, he climbed up the deck to the hatch, pulled himself through, and dropped to the ship wall, where Rat had rolled to after playing the fool. Consequently, Liam dropped onto Rat and that brought on another wave of laughter and shouts. The slaves outside began to worry. Were these the men they were to follow?

Liam and Rat finally got control of themselves and stood.

"What are you doing?" asked a confused Liam.

Rat was still chuckling to himself when he explained the situation with the broken oars. "Then as I was moving away and going for help, I tripped on a spar and hit my head on that box. Then, I rolled under the hatch holding my head and that's when you decided to drop in."

Both men smiled as Rat rubbed his head, but Liam's attention was on the box. It was small, easily held in one's arm. It was bound in iron and it looked very old in the gloom. The wood was ancient and gave a well-worn, brown glow even in the weak light. Liam was drawn to the box. It seemed to call to him. He began to move towards it. Rat spoke to him, but Liam wasn't listening. His full attention was on the box.

Rat grabbed him by his right arm and shook. "Li, Li, wake up—what's wrong? Li, wake up."

Liam stopped moving towards the box and slowly turned his head towards Rat. "What ?"

Rat was shaken. What had happened to his brother? "Li, you went into a trance once you saw the box. You couldn't hear me, didn't see me. Are you alright?"

Liam blinked and tried to understand what Rat was saying. Was something wrong with him? His gaze fell on the box once more, and he felt the overwhelming pull again.

Rat didn't wait this time. He pushed Liam back against the ship wall and shoved him down into a sitting position. Whatever was working on Li's mind didn't seem to be touching his. He pointed at Liam and said one word: "Stay".

Looking around the inside of the ship, he found a lump of iron, probably used as ships' ballast. He lifted it in both hands and walked over to the box. The ingot grew heavier. Rat lifted the block of iron over his head and brought it down on the center of the box.

Liam screamed as the box shattered, and he jumped to his feet. He shoved Rat out of the way and stared into the ruined box. A small bag sat at the bottom of the chest. Liam grabbed it. He thought it was leather, although he didn't want to guess what kind. The bag seemed to vibrate in his hands. He undid the leather strap that kept the bag tight and put his hand inside. Liam gasped as he drew out a simple white stone. The stone was warm, just like the one on his chest, just like the one worn by the People's king. Liam slid the rest of the bag's contents into his hand. He counted nine more white stones of various sizes, all extremely white and smooth. He knew instinctively they were identical to his. The power, he thought. The incredible mind-bending power he now held in the palm of his hand. No wonder the warriors were trying to escape: they controlled the power of empire and knew it. Liam couldn't imagine any circumstances where the King would have let these stones out of his personal control. Had Vardar collected these stones during his long lifetime? Of course, he had. Liam knew the King of the People had lived a long and extraordinary life. These daring soldiers-turned-thieves must have looted the collected stones from the castle before it had collapsed. Well, they paid the price for their crime. Would Liam and his friends pay the same price for possessing the mysterious sky stars?

Liam poured the stones back into the bag and tied the strap. "Rat, keep these safe on your person. They are more valuable than anything you will ever handle." Liam didn't want to hold the white sky stars. The one he wore scared the hell out of him and he didn't know what nine of them would do to him. Better Rat, who wasn't affected by the small rocks, carry and protect them.

Rat took the bag, weighed it in his hand, and then stuffed it down his tunic. "I'll tie them to my body as soon as I can. Right now, we have to get these pegs out of the sand. When you get out the hatch, send all of the young men down here. I need some muscle. Also, send a few swords down in case we have to hack our way through these cursed sticks."

Liam nodded and silently pulled himself up through the hatch. He did as Rat asked and sent a dozen strong backs down into the hold, four of them carrying swords. Liam moved as if in a dream. The stones had affected him deeply. All his life he had seen himself as different, unique. At times that vision of himself kept him going, the life of a slave not very conducive to a positive self-image. Then he had met the King, who had almost conquered him with power like his own, and now he found a bag of stones, as easily as if it were a bag of candy. Were these things so common across the earth? Did his stone really mean nothing after all? Would he meet others wielding the white stone power? He had no answers. Again, he could only go on.

Liam heard shouting and the hacking of swords. Rat was pushing his men hard. He had no choice. Liam followed their progress through the deck of the ship as they worked down the side. After a time, men came boiling out of the hatch, sliding down the deck to the rail. Shortly after, Rat did the same.

"The pegs are out, Li," he said. "We can try to move the ship into the river."

Liam nodded his head and turned away. He looked inland, wondering when Ka-an would return. Without realizing, he took a few steps towards his friend, worried, as usual. Would this ever end? Decision after decision had to be made with no real knowledge to base them on. He was beat up. He had no answers. Looking to the northern canyon wall, he could only see hazy rivers of red marking the lava flows that would, in time, come for them, if they remained much longer.

Liam dropped his gaze lower and thought he saw a large group of natives moving towards them. This couldn't be good. Just as he turned to ask Rat to get the ship into the water, a large piece of the canyon dome fell next to the ship, half in the river and half on the shore. Rat was thrown over the rail, crashing against the deck of the ship; Liam was knocked to the ground. The others were frozen in fear.

Liam got up and ran to Rat, who wasn't moving. Liam got down and lifted Rat's head. "Rat, Rat, please. Rat, wake up." Rat didn't move. Liam checked and found that Rat was breathing shallowly. AT least he was alive. Before Liam could do anything else, shouts broke out from the other slaves. They were all pointing to the north. Li motioned to one of the slaves to stay with Rat, got up, and joined the other slaves. He saw what they saw. There wasn't one group coming but two. Liam didn't have to see who they were to know one was led by Ka-an, while the other was a group of the People after their blood.

Liam turned to the slaves and shouted, "Everyone against the ship and push for your lives." The slaves understood what was happening; they needed no further encouragement. None would be slaves again; they would rather die first. The ship moved slowly, very slowly, across the sandy shore. Liam thought quickly. Getting the ship into the water was the first priority, but setting up some kind of defense was also necessary. Liam remembered the earlier attack on this same ship by People looking to escape. He remembered the bowmen and their deadly flights of arrows.

"I need two men who have fired a bow," he bellowed as he ran to the weapons cache. Two men left the group pushing the boat. Liam pointed to the bows on the ground. "Each of you take one and grab arrows. Follow me."

Liam grabbed a bow for himself and a quiver of shafts. He ran towards Ka-an as the rabble closed in on him.

As Ka-an drew closer, Liam realized there were only three people approaching. Ka-an and the two boys ran for their lives; the old man, their guide, was nowhere to be seen. Liam stopped behind a low ridge of stones that had been pushed up from the ground by the quakes. He and the other men nocked their arrows. "Shoot over our people's heads," Liam commanded.

They began to shoot. Whether by luck or skill, their first three shafts brought down three of the People. The pursuing horde fell over the bodies and each other. By the time they got moving again, three more shafts claimed two more bodies, and this death from above stopped their charge. The People were puzzled. They didn't know where the arrows were coming from. They couldn't see Liam and his companions behind their wall. Three more shafts whistled into the group, wounding one more.

By this time Ka-an and the two brothers, Ard and Arn, were behind the wall with Li. The brothers immediately nocked arrows and let fly. They were far better shots and two men fell dead. It wasn't by luck. Then five shafts flew, as all the men shot together, and that broke up the mob. The People began to run, but only out of bow range. Someone led them and whoever it was, wasn't finished with Ka-an or any of the hated, human slaves.

Liam grabbed Ka-an. There was no time to pick off the remaining attackers. Li dragged Ka-an toward the ship, which was upright in the water. The brothers and the others followed, Ard and Arn letting loose the occasional shaft to keep the mob at bay. Liam reached the boat and saw a rope ladder hanging down the side. Six men fore and aft on the beach controlled the ship with ropes found stored in the hull, without which the ship would have floated downriver by itself.

Liam looked for Rat and couldn't find him. He scrambled up the ladder, followed by Ka-an and the rest. Rat was lying on deck, back against the mast stump; his head was slumped onto his chest.

Liam shouted and pointed, "Ka—Rat". No more was needed. Ka-an ran to Rat, carrying a bag Li hoped was filled with medical supplies.

Liam ran to the side rail. "Release the ropes," he ordered. "Get on board." Twelve men moved as one. Ropes dangled fore and aft. Men climbed the rope ladder two at a time. Li gave another command: "Move four oars to the starboard side." No one moved. Then he understood and pointed: "This side; this side." These men didn't know starboard from larboard.

Men disappeared down the hatch to move the second-tier oars over. Liam ran to check on Ka-an and Rat. "Ka, how is he?"

Ka-an shook his head. "I can't wake him up, Liam. Something is wrong with his head. What happened to him?"

"He was thrown against the side of the ship." Liam had to make a decision. "Ka-an, leave him. I need you to go down below and work the men on the oars. They don't have any idea what to do down there."

Ka-an was torn. If he left Rat, Rat could die. If he didn't get the ship moving, they could all die.

"My decision, Ka-an," Liam said. "Not yours."

Ka-an stood up, looked Liam in eye for what seemed like an eternity, then went to the hatch and disappeared into darkness. Ka-an never saw the enemies' feathered darts as they began to fall.

Chapter 38:

Dancing Fools

Celine was actually laughing. She couldn't remember the last time she really laughed because she thought something was funny. Her four followers had been converted in roughly the same manner she had been by the Mother. Today, Celine had taken her acolytes on the road to practice their mind invasion and control techniques. Five women walking alone along the ravaged roads of Athlan was a rare sight. The effect on local thieves and brigands was about the same as dragging a fishing lure through a teeming sea: something would bite. Sure enough, after a short walk, on an isolated stretch of road, a ragged band of men approached the sauntering group of women and quickly surrounded them with obvious bad intent.

Celine was constantly amazed by the ability of men to sink to the level of rabid animals. These poor examples of masculinity were no exception. They leered and laughed, poked and prodded. Obscene remarks and questions, sexual suggestions and horrible gestures rained down upon the once-women. The sisters were grouped in a loose circle facing their tormentors. None of the Little Mothers moved. They watched Celine, waiting for her to react. Celine, meanwhile, was waiting for the leader of this rabble to reveal himself. Rabble was rabble. Once the leader was removed, groups like this quickly dispersed. She didn't have long to wait.

A very large, very fat, very greasy man with long black hair and a thick black beard flecked with grey stepped forward. He had one large eyebrow, which hung like a ledge over two black, beady eyes. His right hand rested on the pommel of a long knife, while his left held a massive quarterstaff. He was a muscular man encased in a mountain of fat. He towered over Celine and her charges.

The brigands began to chant his name: Gnash, Gnash, Gnash… over and over again. Celine knew the group was working itself up to do something and Gnash, or whatever his name really was, would act first. She waited and sent a psychic message to her people: "Wait for me." No words were spoken between the Little Mothers because none were needed.

Gnash took another step forward. He was puzzled by these women. They didn't seem afraid. They weren't cowering or screaming for mercy. Instead, they stared at his men with cool eyes and calm demeanor. He needed to make that change in a hurry.

Gnash twirled his staff over his head and around his body. The staff whistled through the air and constantly moved closer and closer to Celine. Gnash figured she was the leader, and once she went down the others would panic. Then the fun could begin. Gnash moved his weapon faster and faster and, just as he was about to crush Celine's head with a lightning strike, she struck, using her power s of control and stasis, Mother's gifts to her.

The staff froze in midair. The pressure exerted on the big man's arms snapped his wrists like twigs. He howled in pain.

His followers were utterly confused. Why wasn't Gnash crushing that small woman like a bug? What was wrong with him? Why wasn't he moving? Why was he screaming like a woman?

Then it got worse. A man named Targ, someone they had met on the road, pulled his rusted sword and began hacking away at his new gang friends. Before anyone could move, he had cut down two thugs and was working on a third.

Targ was greatly confused. Why was he killing his own mates? Why were his arms moving with such precision and speed? This was bad, but things quickly got worse. Gnash suddenly planted his staff in the ground and rammed his own throat down onto the upper end, which wasn't sharpened. The wound was massive and ugly. Blood gushed from the gaping hole in his throat, running down the staff in a heavy, red river of death.

Gnash didn't die right away; he continued to push the staff up into his brain again and again. Even when his eyes rolled up into his head, even when his stentorian breathing stopped, even when he was clearly dead, the body of the man called Gnash kept trying to push the staff up through the top of his skull. Those brigands still standing quickly lost their aggressive tendencies and began to run, but they could not run fast enough.

Six of the original twelve ran down the dusty road to nowhere. Their escape ended in mid-stride. Each man fell face first into the dust.

Celine let Gnash's mangled body fall. She knew each of her charges controlled at least one man lying in the road, and that Oak and Beech controlled two. Celine said: "Do what you will."

The Little Mothers looked at each other, smiled, and faced their captives. The ragged men popped to standing positions as one, picked a partner and began to dance. The women knew how to dance; in fact, they knew many dances. The men, despite having never danced in their ugly lives, executed the most wonderful steps together, dipping and swirling as if they were performing on stage. And they laughed as they danced, for the women believed dance to be a thing of joy. When the men began to laugh, Celine began to laugh. Her acolytes began to laugh. Then one man dropped to the road, wriggling like a worm. Then another, then another, until all the men flopped around on the ground, their feet shaking in the air, raising a cloud of dust amidst their own laughter.

Celine had seen enough. Vocally, she called, "Stop."

The men ceased moving. Some faced the sky, while others rested with their faces in the dust. The women were no longer laughing.

Celine called to the men, "Stand." Each man stood without coercion. She said, "Apologize." One man made an obscene gesture and turned to walk away. Celine stopped his heart, and he fell dead in the dust. The other men began apologizing profusely. They fell to their knees, begging for mercy and promising to never do anything like this again. Gnash made them do it. They had lost their families. They were hungry; they were starving. The excuses for their behavior rolled on and on.

Celine silently asked, "Mothers?" After a moment of silent conversation, each former Sister closed her eyes and as they did, each man felt a tremendous pressure in his head. Each man could actually feel his mind slipping away. They began to scream in panic and fear. In the end each had his mind completely erased. Six men stood in the road with no memory of who they were or where they were or of anything else. They were mindless drones. They were doomed to wander the island incapable of any coherent action. They were walking dead. A simple death would have been merciful. The Little Mothers had proven their power, and they had proven their ability to kill. More than kill, the Little Mothers showed a very pronounced mean streak. Celine was certain they would need it.

She had seen enough. Her wards were capable of killing and much more besides. That was why they volunteered and why they were ultimately chosen. Mother had told Celine that if the Little Mothers passed the test, they would go on to the Ban Castlean at once. Apparently, the battle for the planet was ready to begin. Celine and Mother had discussed this. Celine and her followers would wait in the hills just above the Ban Castlean. Most people couldn't climb that mountain face. The Castlean had never been attacked from those heights. Celine and her crew would have no difficulty moving through the ancient rock face. From that perch they could watch whatever action was about to unfold. Celine wasn't sure how they would participate in the final battle. She would wait for instructions from Mother. She looked forward to the fight. She looked forward to seeing Liam. He had no business in the middle of the coming struggle, but somehow she knew he would be there, eventually. They would meet again.

Chapter 39:

Fire and Water

Liam's back was to the shore. He watched the starboard oars ply the river. They had no rhythm, no unity. Some bit into the water and some skimmed the top. Skimmers moved back faster than biters. The result was a constant clash of oars, which resulted in a ship that went nowhere. If they didn't pull together soon, the ship would be carried back onshore by the current. Liam turned to yell down the hatch when the first arrow hit the deck.

"What the..." he said aloud. Then a thick flight of the shafts hit, and the screams began. His crew was being slaughtered. Liam's head whipped towards shore, and what he saw shocked him. There was an armed force of the People where before there'd been only a badly armed rabble. A competent commander had kept these troops together through the chaos. The ad hoc force had archers as well as foot soldiers. Liam saw that while the archers fired, the foot soldiers were hammering together rafts with whatever they could find. These troops had tools and they knew how to use them.

The dome had become an oven. Sweat ran down Liam's face and back. He screamed over the din to Ka-an. "Get them together, Ka-an. We have to get out of here."

He couldn't wait for a reply. Grabbing the two brothers and the other two archers he'd worked with before, Liam lined them up below the ship's starboard rail. He put his arms around them as they crouched. "Listen: just put shafts into the soldiers. Don't aim, don't expose yourself. Just shoot." The boys needed no further encouragement. They took turns popping up over the rail, shooting their shafts as fast as they could. The other slaves moved and fired much slower. They had plenty of heart, but it didn't take long for one of them to catch an arrow in the chest. That left three bowmen to attack over one hundred troops. The odds were not good.

Liam stayed low, his eyes just above the rail, trying to locate the commander. He didn't know the rank markings of the People, but he knew the trappings of command. He'd been living the life of a commander for months and months. He looked for someone surrounded by troops, someone giving orders. He looked for soldiers giving some type of salute. While he studied the enemy, he saw a long red glow through the mist, far in the background. He couldn't see all that clearly, but he thought the red worm of flame was crawling across the landscape—crawling towards the soldiers...and the river.

As he watched, the soldiers on shore grew excited. They began pointing behind them. They, too, had seen the red threat. Liam knew what it was: lava, flowing down from the northern wall. The soldiers all looked to what must have been their commander and that reptile-like leader first pointed toward the lava flow, then toward Liam's ship. His meaning was clear: burn in the lava or capture the ship and live. The soldiers redoubled their effort furiously and soon launched their first raft. More soldiers were on the raft than should have been. All wore haphazard, miss-matched battle armor.

Liam shouted an order: "Shift fire to the raft." Three bows twanged and three soldiers fell into the river. The raft was close. At this range it would be hard to miss. Another flight left the ship and three more monsters dropped off the raft. But at the same time another flimsy raft left shore loaded with men. Li saw he was playing a losing game. The ship was still only limping along and continuously

collided with refuse in the river. Liam worried about the oars snapping. Then where would they be?

He peeked over the rail again and once more found the commander who had now moved to the water's edge. He was directing his men onto the rafts. Liam nocked an arrow, took a deep breath, and stood. He instinctively estimated distance, wind and angle. Arrow pulled back to his cheek, he was oblivious to the shafts whistling into the ship around him. His fingers let the shaft fly. Liam immediately nocked another arrow and let that one fly, too. The first hit the commander in the back, but stuck in his armor. The commander turned toward the ship to scream his defiance and caught the second arrow in his throat. Liam watched as his counterpart sank to his knees, then pitched forward into the sand, snapping the arrow as he planted his face in the earth.

The soldiers on shore rushed to their commander. Liam checked the progress of both rafts. The first was floating downriver, covered with bodies, shafts pointing to the sky. The second was alarmingly close to the ship. Ropes still hung down fore and aft.

"Keep shooting" Liam called, as he ran to the bow, picking up a sword along the way. He dropped his bow and gave the rope a mighty two-handed slash. The rope parted. Liam dropped the sword and picked up the bow again. He fired into the raft as fast as he could. At the same time, he noticed that the ship was making better headway into the river. Ka-an finally had them rowing together.

Liam checked the raft again. Ard and Arn had wreaked havoc on the soldiers, and the raft was turning back. Li examined the shore. The troop wasn't moving. They stood around their dead commander, heads down. Liam looked beyond them. The lava flow was much closer. The soldiers would soon have to scatter.

Ard and Arn joined him in the bow. The other slave bowman was dead. Only the boys made it. Bodies littered the deck. The military monster's archery had been brutally effective.

Liam hadn't noticed how many had died. He felt a little sick. He had been so wrapped up in everything, he hadn't had time for the living or the dead. He began to walk towards the hatch to thank Ka-an, but froze. A cold sweat broke over his entire body. His blood turned to ice. He shook. There was his brother, his friend, Rat, who sat, peacefully pinned to the broken mast with three shafts through his chest. Liam's legs turned to jelly and he collapsed, senseless, to the arrow-studded deck.

Later, as the ship slowly made its way with the sluggish current, Ka-an still sat next to Liam, who now rested on a bed of blankets that had been found below. Ka-an cried quietly. Rat was no less his brother.

Through his tears Ka-an watched both shores for any type of threat. It was difficult to see much through the smoke and steam. When an opening in the curtain appeared, Ka-an saw appalling destruction.

Everything was burning. People lined the shores looking for salvation, but the river was filled with floating bodies. There was no salvation now, only death. The dome continued to crack and fall in a deadly rain. Ka-an didn't know where they were going, but he knew they had to get there fast. Once the dome really started to collapse, it would go in an instant and there would be no hope.

Liam began to mutter, then began twisting and turning, shouting in his sleep.

Ka-an grabbed his arms and put his weight on Liam's chest. "Li, Li, wake up. Wake up, Li."

Liam came to his senses, and awoke crying out, "Rat, Rat, oh no, no, Rat."

Ka-an held him until he became still. Moments passed. They held each other, the loss beyond words.

"I'm alright, brother," Liam finally said.

Ka-an pulled back and said, "He is our brother. We will not forget."

Liam nodded. "Have you...?"

"He lies at rest aft, wrapped in blankets. Anytime you wish, Liam."

"Help me up Ka."

Both men struggled to their feet, supporting each other on the slightly rolling deck.

Liam remembered his duty as commander of this ragged band. "What's happened, An-ka?"

"We left the soldiers behind. With the coming of the lava flow, they scattered, leaderless. Since then we have tried to stay center stream. Ard handles the tiller, and Arn stands watch in the bow. Things are falling apart quickly. It's only a matter of time before we get crushed from above, get burned to a crisp, or get a giant tree trunk through our hull."

Liam smiled. "Situation normal in other words."

Ka-an laughed softly, "Exactly."

Liam walked up front. He found Arn at his station, eyes riveted on the river. "Arn, my name is Liam. I watched you and your brother earlier. Both of you are fine young men. Your father should be proud."

Arn took his eyes from the water and spared a look at Liam. "Our father is dead. As is our mother, sisters, and one other brother. We have only each other. We stick together." Arn returned his attention to the river.

Liam stood still. Such strength and bitterness from one so young. He would need to talk to the older brother. If these two weren't Outcasts at heart, he didn't know who was. Athlan was being torn apart; the people of Athlan were destroying each other, yet men like Ard and Arn still came forth in times of need. Athlan was still capable of producing superior men and women. While life was crumbling, particularly here in the forgotten kingdom of the People, there was still hope, still resolve. There was real courage in the world. Liam turned away. He would say one last goodbye to his brother before Rat was given to the river.

Debris fell everywhere. As Liam approached Rat with Ka-an at his side, Arn and Ard shouted at the same time. "Forward, look, straight ahead."

All eyes turned downriver. Li and Ka-an ran forward. A cloud of smoke covered the river. Nothing could be seen. Liam shouted: "What? What did you see?"

Arn answered: "A giant wall, a mountain face. The river seems to run right into the mountain."

"How far?" asked Ka-an.

"Ten bow shots, maybe a few more."

We still have time, thought Liam, *but what to do? How do you get ready when you don't know what's coming?* "Ka-an, put more men on the oars," he ordered. "Get whatever weapons we have left here by the bow. Medicine, food, water—whatever we have that's useful, get it piled here.

If we have to abandon ship, I don't want to leave anything useful behind. Is there any rope in the hold?

"I'll check," Ka-an said, disappearing down the hatch once more.

Liam stood behind Arn, straining to catch a glimpse of what was hidden in the mist. The dome continued to collapse. He saw giant splashes ahead and to either side. On both shores snaking rivers of fire made their way down to the water. Steam hissed and obscured the land. What would they find under the mountain face? He couldn't help worrying. What would try to kill them next? Would An-ka survive, or would he? To Arn, he said, "If we get out of this, I'd like you and Ard to join Ka-an and me. We hope to meet the rest of our people on the coast."

Arn looked him in the eye again. "If we get out of this, perhaps Ard and I will let you and Ka-an join us." He smiled a wide smile that lifted Liam's heart. Yes, there was still friendship in the world. *You could do a lot with friendship*, Liam thought.

He had lost track of time staring into the wall of smoke and thinking about Rat and Ka-an and how strangers became brothers.

"There." Arn pointed and Liam looked down river. There it was. Not clear, but certainly a mountain face. Arn was right. The river seemed to pass directly under or into the mountain. They were getting close, maybe four bow shots away. Then he looked up, and his heart broke.

Ramparts. Ramparts had been carved into the mountain face, and they were manned by monsters, hundreds of them. Archers, spearmen, and even catapults, as if the Outcasts needed more stones hurled at them. This must have been the last redoubt of the monster kingdom. The most secure place in the vale. Unassailable for as long as the mountain stood. And it appeared as if the mountain was still standing.

They couldn't pull to either shore. Death waited there. They couldn't go back. They had to get into the tunnel, take their chances with the men on the wall. How many times had they faced situations where all choices were bad? How many times had they been forced to go ahead no matter what? How does that happen? Why did it always happen to them? Why did their people always pay a blood price, when all they wanted was to be left alone?

As usual, Liam had no answers, but once more he would take responsibility. And then the world changed again. The men on the battlements didn't shoot boulders down on them; they shot flaming balls of something—it didn't matter what—and their first shot hit the ship aft, wiping out the tiller, Ard, and…Rat.

They were burning. Arn screamed "No!" but it was too late. His brother was gone in the blink of an eye. No rhyme or reason—a good young man gone, and all of the wonderful things he could have done erased. Rat was also gone, along with the leather bag of stones Liam coveted so badly, but Liam didn't have time to mourn for Rat or the stones. He would cry for his brother if he survived and, as for the stones, well, maybe it was better for everyone if they vanished forever.

Liam ran to the hatch. "Ka-an get up here with your men. Bring the oars with you. Now, now" Arrows began to whiz overhead. They thudded into the deck.

Ka-an couldn't make it through the hatch because the first slave through caught a shaft in his chest and hung dead over the opening, half in and half out. Ka-an struggled to move the man.

Liam grabbed the body under the arms and tore the dead man from the hatch. Arrows fell like rain. Liam checked on Arn. He sat on the deck, protected from arrows by the prow. His head was in his hands, knees drawn up. He wept for his older brother.

Ka-an got up on deck, and the slaves below, far safer than the people on deck, passed the oars up. Liam and Ka-an grabbed them and threw them to the deck.

"What are the oars for?" Ka-an breathlessly asked.

"We can hang on to them if we have to jump—we can float. I don't know if these men can swim."

Men pushed up through the hatch. The oars were all on deck. There was no time. The rear of the ship was burning fiercely. Another fireball sailed overhead into the river. Liam felt the tremendous heat on his face as it passed. He moved to the prow and examined the gaping maw bored into the base of the mountain. The river seemed to disappear. There was no other way out. Arrows continued to fall. His men were being hit. He grabbed Arn with both hands and lifted him to his feet. "Ka-an, we must jump. Oars."

Liam and Arn ran to the oars, grabbed their own, and leapt overboard. Ka-an and another slave followed immediately. The rest of the slaves did their best to follow, but most didn't make it. The hail of arrows was even greater than it had been. Every piece of the deck was punctured with shafts; every slave left on deck was pinned by multiple missiles. Twenty, or so men still lived, but only seven made it into the water.

The ship was an inferno. Liam and Arn were turned around when they hit the water. As they flowed into the cave below the mountain face, pulled along with all of the other garbage in the river, they watched the boat burn and finally begin to sink. Both thought the same thing: a fitting funeral ship for their brother. And then they were swallowed by darkness as the current sped up. The tunnel became smaller and smaller.

Powers Revealed

In complete darkness Liam felt as if he was being carried downhill faster and faster. Arn held on and said nothing. Liam hoped that Ka-an was behind him, but he didn't really know. The roar of the water was deafening. He wasn't sure how long he could take the buffeting. They were being beaten against the tunnel walls, against tree trunks and boat parts and anything else in the river. His arms grew weak. Water filled his mouth. Liam thought this might be the end and just as that thought seemed to find a home in his brain, the bottom fell out. He plummeted, the oar, still tightly gripped by both Arn and himself, now floating above their heads.

Chapter 40:

Cost of Doubt

Croi had left the tunnels. His work there was done. A brigade of armed Ravers awaited his command to attack. The time was very near, but not all was ready. Croi still had to move his commanders and their troops to the plain of the Castlean. He had to make sure the great ships of Afrik rested off the coast of Arcasaid, just beyond the horizon. They would carry him and his surviving men away from Athlan after the battle.

He sat in one of the hidden temples of Graxas, surprisingly close to the Ban Castlean. The temple was completely underground, carved from solid bedrock, while a ramshackle dwelling, long abandoned and decayed, stood aboveground. Standing on the edge of the plain at night, swathed in darkness, Croi could see the watch lights moving along the castle rampart. During the day he watched the lost people of Athlan clamor for entrance into the castle from inside his decrepit hovel. He felt confident in his plans. Things were progressing well. Soon the Castlean would be surrounded and, while the Gardai's attention would be on an interesting demonstration he had prepared, his Ravers would strike from the sewer below the castle. Who knew—perhaps the nature of his demonstration would draw the Gardai out onto the plain. If that happened, they would be caught between hammer and anvil. There would be no escape.

But the mentors in his head whispered, "Caution, caution, Croi. We have been here before and always have they escaped. Beware the Warrior, Croi. Beware overconfidence."

He was not overconfident. His basic plan was to have the Ravers attack as he staged his diversion. His underground force would split as it entered the castle courtyard. Half would attack the living quarters to find and kill Kon-r Sighur and the others would storm for the gates to open them. His Ravers on the plain would wait for the gate to open and then they would charge as fast as they could. It may or may not be fast enough. This was the one weak spot in his plan. Once inside, though, the slaughter would be enormous. Croi's forces outnumbered the Gardai by more than five to one. On the other hand, if he could draw the Gardai out, his weak spot wouldn't matter…ah, then blood would flow for all to see. Perhaps he would modify his display somewhat. Yes, yes. He would modify part of his plan. With the Gardai outside of the impregnable walls of the Castlean, the slaughter on both sides would be magnificent, a spectacle his Master, Dorchada, would reward him for.

Bas Croi reached out to his commanders in silent communication: "Move to your final positions and stay hidden. Do not advance on the castle. Once in place, all commanders come to me." Croi placed the image of his location in their minds. Final plans had to be explained. The battleground had to be studied. He didn't doubt the resolve of his commanders, but he wanted one last chance to reinforce his orders.

The world was changing. Bas Croi knew this. Three of the Four were gone. The strength of the Council was a thing of the past. The coming death of Athlan, both physical, as the island nation erupted in fiery destruction, and militarily, as his Ravers and Captains killed the last Warrior and wiped out the famous Gardai, was his time of ascension. He was happy, but he was worried. Change was also a curse; results could go either way. His plan was good. His pieces were almost all in place. He could taste victory, and yet there were too many new developments, too many new players on the field. Powers never before encountered had appeared. The problem for Croi was lack of intelligence. Who were these new powers and who did they support? What were their agendas? Did they work for him or against? If they worked for him, he would surely know. The Master wouldn't throw them into the fray without telling him, would he? Promises had been made. He expected great reward for his efforts. Would his Master renege? Would he....

The room became ice cold. Vapor froze in midair and fell to the ground. Oddly enough, Bas Croi began to sweat. Breathing became difficult. Croi felt thousands of insects running up and down his spine. He experienced real fear for the first time in a long time and collapsed to his knees. A voice filled his head until he thought his skull would explode.

"Do you doubt me, Croi?"

The Bas Croi could not answer. He couldn't speak. His master, the Angeal Dorchada, had come to Athlan.

"Answer me, slave, do you doubt me?"

Croi tried to swallow. He couldn't. When he answered his voice came out as a dry croak. "No, Master, never."

"Never, Croi? Perhaps I misread your thoughts just now. Did I?"

Croi couldn't think. He felt like a bug pinned to a board. The red-hot light of interrogation burned in his brain. He began talking but had no control over his words. "Yes, yes. I doubted you. I'm worried. New forces have appeared on Athlan. How do I know you, even you, can help me defeat them?" Croi couldn't believe the words that came from his mouth. Dorchada was silent. Croi would not look up. The silence stretched to infinity. Croi's eyes, filled with sweat, burned. His muscles twitched; his brain screamed in agony. He was paying the price for doubting his master.

"I have sifted your mind, Croi," Dorchada said," and I have searched this cursed planet for the beings that torment you. I cannot directly interfere here. You are my prince on this cursed orb. However, I have sensed the presence of another power, one that lingers across the surface of the planet. I have sensed a new independence but cannot discern who wields this power. Neither is a threat to your mission. Are you the man to orchestrate this great event to a successful conclusion, or should I end your existence now and find a replacement? Other qualified candidates exist. There is no shortage of depraved humans who would do my bidding. Answer, Croi."

The pressure lessened in Croi's head. He breathed easier and spoke: "I have been trained for this and this alone. You know my commitment. Domination is my life and I have offered my service willingly. If you find me deficient, kill me. The answer is simple. I have planned and our forces are in position. If you tell me there are no problems, I believe you. I am ready. Give me your approval, Angeal."

The Angeal Dorchada was in the room, but incorporeal. He was a force, a dark presence, not a physical body. He could be felt, however, and the Bas Croi felt him now. Croi saw images in black and red: huge wings blasting heat unbearable; fire and Sulphur; screams of pain coming from nowhere. He felt Dorchada enter his own body. He felt tremendous power. Croi felt as if he was dissolving. He felt his body burning, turning to ash. His mind went up in flames and, for a brief moment, he ceased to exist.

The Angeal brought him back. "You are now reborn. You are now rededicated to your task. Can you feel the difference? Can you feel the strength I have given you?"

Croi stood under his own power. The Angeal Dorchada had withdrawn. Croi did feel something. He felt different, more concentrated, denser somehow, more potent.

The Angeal said, "I see your plan and I approve. I have given you power—power to kill on a vast scale. Your plan requires this power and you now possess it. Use it only when needed. It will dissipate with use. I cannot offer you more. You would not survive having such strength for long. Your body would waste away. Remember my visit, Croi. Remember the pain. You must have faith in me, Croi. Destroy the Warrior. If nothing else, destroy the Warrior. Do you understand?"

Croi had no time to answer. The Angeal Dorchada impressed these words on Croi's brain with what seemed to be a molten branding iron. It felt as though a wall of fire engulfed Croi, burning him to his very black soul. Croi collapsed, his head crashing on the flagstones. He remained there writhing in cold flame throughout the night.

Chapter 41: A Father's Despair

The western shore of Athlan was a long line of mountainous defense, except for one perfect geographical feature: the harbor at Arcasaid. The harbor was an exquisite example of man improving nature through artistry, engineering, and craftsmanship. Originally, the harbor resembled an elongated watermelon with the western end cut off. Ocean winds and waves blew directly into the harbor. This lack of protection created havoc for anchored ships. On the eastern end of the harbor the Black River ran down from the Ban Castlean. The river, running underground when it sunk beneath the walls of the Castlean, rose to the surface some distance from the walls and became wide and deep as it spilled into a tidal basin where water levels rose and fell more than the height of two tall men, one standing on the shoulders of the other.

Millennia ago, the same creatures who built the Ban Castlean decided the harbor needed drastic improvements. Giant blocks of basalt were quarried from the mountains and moved to the harbor. Some were used to construct the quays that ran the length of the harbor on both the north and south sides. The quays did not, however, solve the problem of an open harbor mouth. That task was left to an unknown genius who designed and built huge walls of the hewn black rock. One wall extended from north to south, approximately three-quarters of the way across the harbor mouth. The second wall ran from south to north. It also covered three-quarters of the harbor mouth. The key design feature was the space between the two walls, which was almost six longbow shots in width. A ship entering the harbor had to sail or row south of the North Wall, as it was called, then turn the ship north to row to the northern end of the South Wall. By the time both walls were navigated, the ship would be crawling into the main harbor and could either anchor in the harbor or tie up to one of the quays. The design also made every ship that entered the harbor a sitting duck for the Gardai who manned the walls.

In addition to protection from invaders, the design protected the harbor from western gales. The two offset walls acted as baffles, breaking the power of wind and wave. The face of each wall was adorned with carved figures of power and knowledge. Massive men in bas relief, the kings of ancient Athlan, stood tall in their young strength, wielding weapons of power or offering scrolls of knowledge and peace. The beauty and glory of this stonework struck first time viewers dumb. The scale was too vast, the accomplishment too great. The ancient message was clear: those who approached the harbor of Arcasaid had a choice: war or peace. Only fools chose the former.

From a defensive point of view, no ship could sail uncontested into Arcasaid harbor. Too many maneuvers were required to navigate between the walls. Those same ancient battle engineers placed a variety of weapons atop the wide walls when they were built, and those weapons had been continually improved as weapons of war became more deadly. Each wall towered over the tallest ship's masts. The width of the walls themselves could accommodate fifty troops walking shoulder to shoulder. Even today, the thin blade of an assassin's knife could not be inserted between any two basalt blocks of either the North or South wall. Weapons capable of launching stones, burning spheres, and giant javelins were placed on each wall in such a manner they could fire in all directions. Complementing these massive weapons were recurve bows capable of accurately firing wave after wave or normal-sized arrows. No ship could pass into the harbor if defenders on the wall decided to deny such passage.

As a further defensive move, two great chains had been forged in the early days of Athlanean strength. Once extended, they blocked the openings between the North and South walls. If an invader broke the first chain and attempted to run the gauntlet of the North and South walls, the second chain would trap them in place long enough for the Gardai on the walls to destroy the ships below. These chains, however, were now coiled at the bottom of giant towers at the end of each wall. In fact, the chains had not been used for generations. Military threats to Athlan had been nonexistent in recent history. Ships wishing to enter the harbor docked on the southern shore and were inspected by port officials before being allowed to pass. Any ship trying to skip this requirement was savagely attacked. If the ship survived, all goods were confiscated and crew members were enslaved. Most ships did not survive.

Just below the top of the North Wall a large platform had been constructed on the seaward face. A wide gate allowed soldiers to exit the wall and access the platform, which was mostly covered by a large bronze bowl. Behind the bowl was another vast bowl tilted up on its side, this one made of polished silver and inside the bronze bowl was a black mineral mined in many places outside of Athlan. Athlan traded for huge quantities of the substance every year.

Every evening the mineral was loaded into the bronze bowl and set afire. The mineral, called *kol* by native miners around the Inland Sea and in Afrik, burned brightly for a long time. From the sea the flame could be seen for miles and miles because the polished silver bowl behind the bronze receptacle gathered, magnified, and reflected the rich flame far out over the ocean, warning ship captains away from the walls. Mariners of the world talked about the Flame of Arcasaid. The number of ships and lives saved by the light was incalculable.

By this light the fighting ships of Afrik had navigated the final leg of their journey. Wasir Obenga Owonga commanded the small but powerful fleet. All three ships were in fine condition, even after they had run into the giant white ship that burned their sails. Owonga had no idea who maned that wonderful vessel, but it had sailed into the Southern Deep, while they had remained true to their course. He put the strange ship out of his mind. Owonga was sailing west and then would go north until he saw the Fire of Arcasaid. At that point Owonga's ships would raise sail and throw out sea anchors for the night. The ships would stay together. His instructions were to do this every evening until the Fire of Arcasaid did not appear. That was his signal.

Once the fire was out, the harbor was his to attack. He would overcome the Gardai defenses, he would wait for a personage called the Bas Croi and the people Croi brought with him. He was then to sail under Croi's command to wherever Croi wanted to go. *Simple enough*, he thought. He was commanded to do these things by his new god and he would obey.

Owonga's story was a strange one. For most of his life he was a farmer and a good one. His life was full. He had a wife and five young sons to follow in his footsteps. He was tougher than most, with a wide body, if somewhat short. His arms bulged with muscles, and his back was strong. His ability to think, however, was what set him apart from most of his people. So did his religion. He didn't believe in the gods others prayed to. He figured one god should be good enough for everyone. His problem was this: which one? This was a difficult question. Who was to say what was real and not real? Ever practical, he lumped all of the gods together in his mind and prayed to that one, great big jumble of a god. It seemed to work. Life was no worse than it was before, and his farm and family continued to flourish.

Then one day, his oldest boy, Jamat, was leading their prize ox in from the fields when a large snake raised its coiled body directly in front of the ox. The snake struck. The ox bellowed and shook its massive head. Jamat was pierced by a horn, lifted from the ground, and dashed to the dusty earth. Dead.

Owonga heard the bellow. He ran to the fields and saw the ox running away. He knelt by the body of his son, twisted and broken on the ground.

Powers Revealed

Owonga's world changed. He cried and screamed in anger. He put his head in the dust and pounded the ground. "Jamat, Jamat, Jamat," was all he could say, but no answer came. Jamat was gone and so, too, was a large part of Owonga.

As the days turned into months, Owonga withdrew into himself. His wife told him to pay more attention to his other children, that being with them would help him with the pain of Jamat's death. But the exact opposite was true. Being with them only reminded him more of Jamat. He found he could not enjoy his other boys because Jamat was gone. He began working harder than ever. He spent longer hours in the field. When it rained, he found other chores to keep himself busy. He all but ignored his sons and wife. They stopped talking. The once happy and prosperous family was still prosperous, more than ever, but there was no joy, no happiness. Those things had disappeared with Jamat's bright smile.

Owonga decided to go hunting. He was a good man with either bow or spear. He could set snares and make pits to trap the wiliest animal. His family already had plenty of meat, but that wasn't why he hunted. He hunted to get away, to be alone. He figured to be gone for six or seven days and packed accordingly. He said goodbye to his wife, but the boys weren't around.

Owonga knew the route well. He walked steadily, neither quickly nor slowly. He tried not to think. He concentrated on the ground in front of him. When dusk fell, Owonga found shelter beneath the root system of a fallen tree. The roots had grabbed earth as the tree tipped over. This created a perfect roof. Owonga took out his flint and straw, gathered twigs and branches, and built a fire. He was alone. He was warm. He was comfortable. He built the fire a little larger and stared into the flames. For the first time since Jamat's death, he was completely numb, which brought a certain kind of peace.

Owonga remained in this trance for some time. The night moved on, and stars wheeled across the Afrik sky, but he didn't notice. His eyes were locked on the flames. The wood burned down, creating a bed of coals that burned black, red, white and hot. He found himself reaching for them. He wanted to hold one of the scorching brands. He grabbed a large coal and let it rest in the palm of his right hand. He felt nothing.

Just then, a voice spoke to him. "Owonga, you seek an end to pain, do you not?"

Owonga didn't know who was talking, but it didn't matter. "Yes."

"Good. Do you feel the searing pain of the hot coal burning through your hand?"

Owonga looked at his hand closely. The coal had burned the flesh of his hand down to the bone, yet he remained completely detached. "No, I don't."

"You feel nothing because I control the pain. Do you believe me?"

Owonga was out of his depth. Was this a god? "I don't know what to believe." As soon as he said these words, the pain of fire wracked his body. He screamed like he never had before. He smelled the stench of his burned flesh, but he could not move his hand. He cried aloud for mercy, but none came. The blazing coal finally dropped through his savaged palm to the ground. He was released from the power that held him and he collapsed to the earth, destroyed hand held tightly to his chest.

"Owonga, listen to me. Your life is like your hand: useless and painful beyond words. You know this, do you not?"

Owonga could not speak, his jaw clenched. He had heard the words, though, and agreed with them.

"Good, you do not have to speak. I see your thoughts. Goodman Owonga, I can take the pain away and give you a useful life. You have seen my power. Are you interested?"

Owonga squeezed his eyes shut. Was he going mad? Did he burn himself?

"No. What is happening is real and it happens because I will it to happen. I have made an offer to you. I have proven my power. Accept now, or go back to your pitiful, depressed life, less one hand."

Owonga was overwhelmed. But if the pain would stop and if he could forget his son...

"Yes, you will no longer remember Jamat, your wife Mara, or your other children. You will begin again, Owonga, and we will work together."

Owonga wept. Deep down he didn't want to leave his family; he loved them and knew he was needed. But he was weak. His son's death shattered him like an old pot. He didn't want the pain, no more, never again...

"I am yours," he said, and he found himself whipped by a gale of laughter. Wasir Obenga Owonga, husband, father, and master farmer of the Ashar valley, ceased to exist.

Chapter 42:

On the Board

Cean and Kon-r had spent the night talking. Neither Warrior could sleep. The end of Athlan was very near. They could feel it. Last night they had talked about everything under a full, pale, smoke-streaked, yellow moon. Cean had asked personal questions. He wanted to know how a Warrior lived: would he ever have a woman or children? Could he have any kind of normal life at all?

Kon-r had answered. Past experience said those things were impossible. Always had been impossible. But who knew, really, what the future held. There had never been two Warriors alive before, either. Things were changing. Maybe the old rules would change, too.

The sun came up weak, covered in wispy clouds, more dirty orange than red. Smoke dulled the landscape. Kon-r and Cean skipped breakfast and walked up through the city, across the empty sand combat square, and entered the Warrior's Hallway. Both men waited for their eyes to adjust to the perfect dark. They then moved as one down the hall, their sandals slapping softly. Neither looked right or left. There was no need. The stone representations of the Warriors of the past, 12 heroes dead these many years, lined the walls of the sacred passageway. The Warriors had come alive for Cean's testing and confirmation. Would the live again? Cean felt a thrill from his toes to the top of his head. He walked a little taller, held his head a little higher. Soon, he heard footsteps in the hall other than his or Kon-r's. They were falling in behind the past Warriors of Athlan. They all marched in step towards their destiny, one unit of the best soldiers the world had ever seen.

Dark turned to grey as they approached the Hall of Heroes. Grey became soft yellow. Yellow became bright white, and the Warrior unit stood before the Cath Angeal. However, she was no longer a woman. Now the Warriors were faced by a man, as far as they could tell. He was very tall, very severe, and fully armored, which was part of the problem: neither Cean or Kon-r could clearly distinguish the Angeal as man or woman because of the brilliance of the armor. Their sight was clouded. Kon-r couldn't tell if the armor was white, silver, or something else altogether. He had the impression in his mind that the metal wasn't metal at all, but some type of molten flame which had formed a hard carapace around the Angeal's new form.

Cean looked up at the ceiling panels where he had seen such wonderful things before. The ceiling was blank. He scanned the walls of the chamber, looking for the beautiful images of his first visit. The walls were blank as well. There were no distractions in the Hall of Heroes today. The stories of glory had been told. The past was exactly that: the past. This meeting would deal with the hard realities of the present, no frills and no promises.

The Angeal spoke. "The time has come. The final battle for Athlan, for this Earth, this planet is at hand. Warriors of the past, you have been summoned from your rest one last time. Do you accept the summons?"

The once-dead Warriors answered "yes" in firm but low tones. Kon-r and Cean said nothing.

"Warriors of the past, will you follow the commands of Kon-r Sighur and Cean Mak-Scaire?" the Angeal said.

There was no hesitation. "Yes," the ancient Warriors said, in the same calm, quiet tone.

The Cath Angeal nodded. "Very well. I cannot tell you the outcome of this battle. I know not. It has ever been thus. I cannot help you fight, nor can I command your actions. The battle is yours to win or lose as you will."

The Warriors listened and waited. They hoped for more.

Indeed, the Angeal continued. "You have often wondered who your enemy is, or has been, for these millennia. This time, the enemy, my counterpart, has crossed the line. He has interfered, trying to give his followers the advantage. Rules have been broken; a door has been opened. You have the powers you need to win. Whether you do or not is up to you. Behold your adversaries." Figures materialized in the wall panels. Twelve fully armored giants with the red gleam of death in their eyes and one other, smaller, almost frail, being with a hood covering his features, wrapped in a robe that shimmered with reds, yellows, and black. The creature's eyes were burning coals in the darkness of his hooded existence.

"The small one is the Bas Croi," the Angeal said. "He is the chosen of my adversary, the Angeal Dorchada. Croi is the descendent of many like himself, all tasked with resisting the Warrior and Gardai, all pledged to the destruction of everything that we consider good. They have prepared the way for this day for as long as you have toiled in my service. The Twelve are his captains, spirits that have come down through the ages, inhabiting body after body, but never changing their evil essence. You see your foe. Now you know why you have been summoned."

The Warriors studied the images. Their resolve grew strong. There was no fear in their hearts. They knew the horrors of battle, and while they were not eager to slay, slay they would. They readied themselves for whatever was to come.

Kon-r seemed content. Cean, however, was not. Why wouldn't they win? Were the famous battles of the past for nothing? After being immersed in Gardai and Athlan history so intensely, Cean had begun to feel good about his role, the Warrior tradition, and the strength of the Gardai. Now he doubted. Had the Gardai, led by Warriors like Kon-r, like himself, been over-confident?

Cean stared directly into the Cath Angeal's eyes and found the Angeal staring right back at him.

"You doubt, Mak-Scaire." It wasn't a question. It was a statement; perhaps a condemnation.

"Yes," he answered. None of the other Warriors took part in this mental communication. They were shut out.

"Why?" asked the Angeal.

"Too much is withheld from us. We fight and die but you pull the strings. There are rules, you say, but we don't know them. Our enemy is led by someone just like you. The Bas Croi and his men are just like us. We are placed on a board not of our choosing and you say to play, fight, win, lose—it is all up to you. If it was up to us, we may decide not to play at all, as I chose not to play when tested, but we must play or die, because this is the game you have created and we cannot escape."

A Warrior with doubts had emerged; impossible, but true. The Angeal knew this conversation could only take place with the newest Warrior. Doubt did not exist for the others. Things were changing, even within the confines of the Angeal's own power. The Angeal wondered if change had come to the other side as well, though it probably had not. That side followed their own rules, and their values were different to say the least. Of course, Cean was right. What would he think if the Angeal told him she didn't really know where the rules came from either? The universe was a machine that contained wheels within wheels. The first cog never came in contact with the last. They all did their best to understand and when they couldn't understand, they found something they could believe.

He couldn't lose this one, however. If the coming battle proved inconclusive, which many of them did, he would need Mak-Scaire to continue the tradition of the Warrior and the Council, because the cycle would repeat itself again and again across this Earth until a final victor was determined.

"I will not play word games with you, Cean. Like you, I am also on the board. I, too, must play my part with little room to maneuver. Study the Bas Croi."

Cean shifted his gaze to the panel holding Croi's image.

"This is more than an image, Cean. You see Croi as he really is, as if he were standing right there for you to touch. What do you feel?"

Cean stared at the eyes. He could feel the power, the hate, the need to inflict pain. He shuddered. "Evil, Angeal. I feel evil."

"Would you walk away? Will you refuse the challenge, or, as you say, will you refuse to play?"

Cean wanted to say, "Wait—you and the others like you created the evil. You have stacked the game. I have no choice. I must fight." But he remembered the Angeal's words. If he was on the board, and the Angeal was on the board, who else was on the board and how many battle boards were there? The harder he thought, the more confused he got. Kon-r had explained this. Kon-r's mind had gone down this path and others many, many times. There always came a point where thinking failed. Cean had reached that point. He was thrown back upon himself, alone. He would fight because he had to fight. He wasn't happy, but happiness had nothing to do with it. He said nothing, did nothing. His eyes never left the Angeal's. He didn't bow in submission, nor did he apologize for his doubt. The

Angeal and Warrior became equals, something that had never happened before.

Interrupting, Kon-r asked, "What are your instructions, Angeal?"

"I have no instructions, Kon-r. I have only advice, and it is this: When they come, and they will come very soon, watch your back. The Dark operates through stealth and misdirection. They will make you look one way while they do something elsewhere. When you think you have things under control—that is the most dangerous moment. I cannot see their plans; they are hidden from me. Remember what I have said. Remember your training and remember who you are. This is your fight. This is my fight. This is our fight, a battle we must join for our own reasons." The Angeal looked at Cean as he said these last words. "More is at stake here than our lives. Yes, I, too, can cease to exist. Concentrate on doing your best, and the rest will take care of itself."

The Warriors were strangely subdued. There was no rattling of weapons or shattering war cries. An end was near and they felt the weight, wondering if they would suffice.

The Angeal saw them all as the young men he had recruited through the long years. He was neither optimistic, nor pessimistic, having been through this before. He hoped but kept his hopes to himself. Hope was a fragile flower, easily crushed on a battlefield.

"Kon-r," he said, "get your men ready to defend themselves. The storm approaches even as we speak." The Cath Angeal vanished. The men were alone.

Kon-r led them out of the Hall of Heroes, down the Warrior's Path, and out into the sunlight. The stone sentinels guarding the Hall entrance for centuries snapped to attention. Gardai and Masters practicing on the sand gaped in wonder at the magnificent cadre walking onto the sand. The Gardai and their venerated teachers dropped to their knees out of respect. The past had returned from the dead. Surely this was the end of times.

Chapter 43:

Who will live...

The Ban Castlean had been carved from the mountain in one piece. There were no seams, no joints, no weak spots. The walls, immensely high, were also tremendously thick. Within the walls were stairways and halls that connected evenly spaced watch towers. Men could travel within the walls in complete safety. Also within the walls were rooms that could be used for barracks, weapons storage, commissary, medical needs and planning.

Some time ago Kon-r had moved his personal quarters into the wall, just to the west of the main gate. In this way he would always be close to the point of attack and could always see what was happening outside the gate. The gate itself was made from an unknown metal, light but immensely strong, whose secret had been lost to time.

The sun would be up soon. Kon-r heard men moving. He had ordered the Gardai to man the walls. They would be fully prepared for battle, if today was the day.

He hoped for the return of companies sent out on their normal duties both on the island and overseas. He was concerned for the missing men but wasn't worried about the security of the Castlean. One past Warrior manned each of the twelve sections of wall. Each Warrior had commanded the armies of Athlan. They could handle a company of Gardai. Whatever move the Bas Croi made outside the walls would not threaten the people within. Perhaps Croi could fashion catapults. Perhaps he could throw stone and fire. The Ban Castlean would not crumble; it would not burn. The non-combatants—wives, children, fathers, and mothers of the Gardai—were hidden within the Castlean, safe from threatening missiles. There was plenty of food; Athlan would destroy itself before their food ran out. Weapons were abundant. While everyone worried about the fate of the island itself, no one worried about the coming battle. Kon-r knew this was good and bad. He remembered one of the Cath Angeal's warnings: "Watch your back."

He was uneasy. If the Bas Croi was as accomplished as the Angeal had said, he would know better than to make a futile frontal assault on the Castlean. It would not—could not—work. His people would be slaughtered. What was his plan? Kon-r couldn't see it and because he couldn't, he had made up his mind in the night. Cean must leave the Ban Castlean as soon as possible. Kon-r had already sent a runner to wake and bring him to Kon-r's room. There were things that needed to be said. No doubt Cean would put up a stiff argument. Kon-r knew the boy wanted to fight by his side. He felt it was his duty, felt it would be cowardly to run. Kon-r would feel the same way.

Sighur's room was simple: a cot and blanket, a wooden table and chairs, a wash basin on a stand with a towel. There was a fully stocked weapons rack within easy reach of his cot. On the table were candles and papers. One scroll contained a list of names. These were the people Cean would take with him. Kon-r had considered this list very carefully. Wherever Cean went, wherever he landed, the skills of Athlan would be needed. A military presence was a given, but he would also need doctors, farmers, craftsmen of all kinds, and men of science. Cean would need people who knew how to run a government. He would need women to make families and put down roots. Traders and judges—all were required, but which ones should Kon-r choose? Only so many could leave. Who left, lived; who stayed, died. Kon-r had to play at being god and found he didn't like the job.

Kon-r's door was open. Candles lit his windowless room. The light was soft and shadows filled the corners. Kon-r looked young again. Cean stood outside, looking in. For a moment he thought he was looking at himself. Cean remained stock still, unwilling to break the peace. Kon-r's concentration was complete. Cean finally knocked softly on the door jamb.

Kon-r looked up and smiled. "Come in. I have nothing to offer in the way of food. Have you eaten?"

Cean shook his head. "No, I was on my way to the kitchens when your messenger found me. Food can wait.?"

Kon-r waved to a seat. Cean sat on one side of the table, back to the door, and Kon-r sat on the other.

Cean studied the papers on the table. There were scrolls, but there were also maps, some beautifully colored, some with actual texture, depicting mountains and valleys, streams and major rivers. Cean raised his eyes to Kon-r's but said nothing. He waited.

Kon-r seemed to be laboring, struggling to speak. "Cean, I'll say this plainly: one of us must leave the Castle and Athlan. One of must survive the coming battle and the destruction of our home. Last night I made the decision. You will leave and you will take many of our Gardai and citizens with you."

A thousand questions raced through Cean's mind. He knew this decision was coming. He knew Kon-r would risk his life to save Cean's. He even knew it was the right thing to do. But he was a Warrior. He could not run. "But Kon-r..."

"Stop." Kon-r raised his index finger and said again, in a soft voice, "Stop."

Cean stopped. There was no compromise in Kon-r's eyes. Sadness, maybe, but no room for negotiation. Kon-r knew Cean's arguments before Cean could express them.

Mak-Scaire sat back, his fight gone. Two men faced each other, the weight of the world resting on both.

Kon-r pushed the scroll across the table. "These people will go with you. I can spare two companies of Gardai and one Warrior to lead them."

Cean thought about the journey. "Two questions, Kon-r: how do we get out and where are we going?"

Good, Kon-r thought. *He accepts his role with a level head.* "Let's discuss the last question first. You will leave from Arcasaid harbor. Ships await you there. They are provisioned for many months at sea. They are fully crewed, including Gardai captains and sailing masters. These men can take you wherever you decide to go." As he said this, he opened a map unlike any Cean had seen. It displayed the world, with Athlan at its center.

Kon-r put candles in brass holders at each corner. He leaned forward, as did Cean. "Here is Athlan. I have sailed to every land mass

Powers Revealed

that is on this map and many that aren't. I've seen much beauty, Cean, many places where you could live and prosper. None, however, are empty. People already live almost everywhere, and where they don't live, you don't want to live there, either. Wherever you go, you will find friends and enemies."

Cean listened but became impatient. "Kon-r, pick a place. I can't."

Kon-r had considered this, of course. He knew where he would go, but would it be the best place for Cean to go? His eyes moved over the surface of the world. East was Afrik—no good. To the west was a huge land, extending north and south as far as a ship could sail. The natives were full of fight, but the lands were rich. To the south there was nothing. To the north there was a chain of islands that arched across the Muirseol Sea. Each island was different in nature. Two were very close together. One, the farthest west, had a temperate climate, rich land and friendly natives that were few in number. Cean would need friends, not enemies. His power would be weak to start. It was also an easy island to sail to. Any captain worth his salt could sail this route blindfolded. So be it.

Kon-r went over everything. In the end, Cean was satisfied with the travel plan.

"The first question, Kon-r," he said. "How do we get that many people out of here? Do we leave through the front gate and wave as we go?" Normally, Cean's joke would have been funny. Kon-r didn't even smile.

"No", he said, "you will go through long forgotten castle sewers. These sewers once drained into the Black River. The Black will take you down to Arcasaid harbor. Once there, you know what to do." Kon-r opened another map. This one showed the defunct sewer system beneath the castle. Cean's route was marked in red. "Close the door."

As Cean got up to do so, Kon-r blew out the candles. The room turned pitch black. Cean looked back to where he remembered the table being. He couldn't see anything at first, but then he saw strange red lines shimmering in midair.

"Come here," Kon-r said.

Cean made his way back to the table. He stumbled into a chair leg.

"Sit down."

He did, mesmerized by the red lines. "What you see is the map of the sewers. The red lines are your escape route. The lines illuminate in the dark. You will be in the dark. Look closely, Cean. Could you follow this route in darkness?"

Cean felt confident. He would get out with his people. "When do we leave, Kon-r?"

"Get your people ready today. Tell them to keep possessions to a minimum. They will have to travel fast, and the tunnels may be narrow. I will notify the Gardai and Ro-Fannin. He will be your Warrior commander. He will follow your orders, but you would be wise to follow his suggestions. The Gardai will be ready to march in two hours, but I suspect you will not be leaving until tomorrow before dawn."

Kon-r and Cean spent many hours together that morning in private discussion. The sun was high in the sky when they opened the door of Kon-r's room and walked out into the sunny courtyard in silence. Both studied the ground, looking neither to the right or left. They stopped and spoke in soft voices. No one heard the words. Their embrace was brief. Cean turned towards his quarters and Kon-r went to take his place on the wall.

Chapter 44:

Darkness Falls

Athlan rumbled and shook. Smoke filled the air, blotting out the moon and stars. The night was black. The flame of Arcasaid burned all the brighter. The keepers of the flame were devoted to their duty, but they were not what they once were. In days long past a special Gardai detail was in charge of the flame while companies of Gardai rank and file guarded both the North and South walls. To advance in the Gardai, service on the walls was mandatory. Weapons were maintained. Guards changed on time, every time. There was no chance, absolutely none, of the walls falling to an aggressor; there was no chance of spies moving secretly between the walls. The harbor was secure. A safe Arcasaid was a matter of Gardai faith.

On this night the people guarding the flame were retired Gardai and young men and woman who volunteered to feed the fire because it was fun. The walls were patrolled by Gardai invalided out of the service due to injury, loss of limb, or disease—all acquired serving their country. Working on the wall, for the most part, was a now low intensity reward for service rendered. There had been no attacks on the harbor in generations, and so, the mission to protect the harbor and the great walls lost importance. And, while both walls were once defended by multiple companies of hardened warriors, on this night no more than a handful of seasoned fighters were dispersed among fifty or so of the old, young, and infirm. All was quiet. Most guards slept, dreaming of past campaigns.

The harbor itself was a mess. Lanterns lit the quays. Shadows distorted reality. Real Gardai, although not as many as should have been on duty, kept Athlaneans away from ships tied to piers. The people of Athlan wanted to escape the dying Island. The ships were Gardai ships, provisioned and manned by Gardai officers and sailors. Kon-r Sighur himself had ordered them to be protected at all costs.

The citizens raved and screamed for salvation. The ships must save them. There was nowhere else to go. More than one Athlanean had felt the sharp point of a Gardai spear that night.

The Gardai commander, Captain Dan Bo, had his hands full. Standing on the deck of the warship *Angeal*, he knew he couldn't hold the line. He needed more men. Motioning to his aide, he said, "Take two men from the ship's crew. Take off your uniforms. Dress as civilians. Get up to the Ban Castlean. Tell Kon-r I need at least one more company to defend the ships and I need them fast."

The young aide saluted and vanished. Bo then turned to the captain of the ship and said, "Captain, I need half your men on the dock, right now. Arm them with pikes and form a second line of defense behind my men. Put archers into your rigging, too. We may have to shoot our own citizens this damned night."

As the Gardai were busy with crowd control, a band of men dressed in black swam through the dark waters of Arcasaid harbor. They carried their weapons on their backs. Only their heads, wrapped in black cloth, were above the waterline. Spread out, they were invisible. Led by a young man, once a talented worker in leather, these men had lived beneath the Ban Castlean for months. They had been specially picked by the Bas Croi for their skill, strength, and intelligence. He had worked with and on them. Once normal people, they were now fanatics, dedicated to the destruction of the Gardai. The leader, called Matai, saw the proof of his Master's words: the Gardai did have ships ready to save other Gardai. The Gardai would leave the rest of the people to die as Athlan perished. The Gardai had to be destroyed.

Matai had lost his entire family in a fire. He wandered aimlessly, finally joining a ragged group of homeless men and women, just like him.

They had met a larger group and on it went, until one day a giant of a man stood in the middle of their road, blocking their path. He spoke to them of great things, of food and warmth and shelter. He asked them to follow him, and they did. Eventually, Matai found himself armed, sitting in tunnels and caves that were dark, wet, cold, and smelled of things Matai didn't want to think about. He learned to fight and survive.

One day a hooded figure called his name and beckoned him to follow. The old man—at least that's what Matai thought he was—took him deeper into the tunnels and caves. There was no light. No warmth. But there was life. Matai began screaming and didn't stop for a very long time. The boy who had entered the tunnels with the old man did not leave the tunnels. Something else did. A creature named Matai, but very different, very much a demented killer completely subservient to the bloody will of the Bas Croi.

The black-clad men moved silently through the water. They had one mission: to destroy the Light of Arcasaid. The flame had to be quenched. The Northern Wall would be plunged into darkness for the first time in its history. There would be death this night. Matai had been trained well. He wasn't sure why the flame had to be extinguished, but the Bas Croi had ordered it done, and so it would be done.

Matai could see the South Wall. He motioned to the others. The small group closed up and swam to the South quay in a tight group. Reaching the ancient stone, Matai eased his way up the slick stairs, constantly looking for Gardai sentries. None were on duty.

The group moved out onto the docks, following Matai's lead. His primary job on the South Wall was to kill anyone he found. He could leave no one alive to warn the North Wall guards. Blending into the shadows, the group crept silently over the old stone, extinguishing each lantern they came to, skillfully killing each person they found. The bodies were slid, unnoticed, into the harbor.

Matai and his men climbed the stairs within the walls. Knives flashed in the dark; garrotes noiselessly crushed throats; short, exquisitely sharp swords were used expertly. One real Gardai put up a brief struggle, stabbing one of Matai's men through the heart, but the Gardai paid for his valor. In a surprisingly short time only the men in black remained alive on the South Wall. Kneeling in the shadows, they peered across to the North Wall. Guards walked along the parapet; no one over there was alarmed.

Matai and his team reentered the water and swam to the North Wall. The water was rougher here, colder, and the swim took a long time. They were tired when they dragged themselves up another set of stone stairs. Again, no one was on guard. Eleven black forms hugged the wall as they began the second phase of their task. Lanterns were extinguished and Matai led his assassins up into the wall.

Alert Gardai attacked from a side storage room. Lanterns were smashed. Men fought and died in the dark. When it was over, Matai and a few of his men had survived. None of the Gardai did. But the battle, short and brutal as it was, also alerted those above.

There was no time now. Matai ran up the steps, knife in one hand and short sword in the other. The real Gardai were dead, but the rest of the watch charged towards the small group of killers.

Matai found the door to the beacon. He ran out onto the platform while the remainder of his men blocked the door and fought a holding action. The guards on the platform, young boys and girls, didn't know what to do. The platform was small; there was nowhere to go once the door was blocked. Matai killed them all. The bowl that held the fire was red hot. The mirror behind the bowl reflected heat and light out to sea. Matt felt like he was in a furnace. How was he to put out the fire? He never knew how large the bronze bowl actually was. He looked for water, but there was none.

He could hear his men fighting and knew they would be dead soon. He was running out of time. In frustration he howled into the night. Something heard his anguished cry. Matai felt strength flow into his body as he became possessed. Disregarding his own pain, he placed his palms against the giant, molten bowl and pushed. His flesh sizzled and burned. He screamed in pain and joy. The bowl began to shift, spilling liquefied kol onto the stone. He shoved harder and screamed louder. He walked through the fire, pushing until the giant bowl slid off its foundations and slowly toppled into the sea. The Light of Arcasaid was extinguished. Matai, the once talented leather worker, was also no more, another mindless sacrifice to the Dark, having been scorched to ash by the fire he had destroyed. His men died in the doorway. Mission complete. And out to sea an ex-farmer gave orders to a murderous crew.

Chapter 45:

The Servant

The day and night went swiftly for Kon-r and Cean. Kon-r held council after council with the Warriors, as well as his officers. Weapons were distributed, food was brought to the wall, duty rosters were prepared and reviewed. The trappings of war were fully wrought.

Cean spent his time gathering the people on Kon-r's list. In many cases they didn't want to leave the Castlean and needed to be convinced. Once persuaded, however, they needed to select and pack their goods into small, portable bundles. This proved to be a real problem. No one wanted to leave anything behind. Asking them to leave was one thing; asking them to leave behind their possessions was quite another. Cean, literally, had to go through each person's packs, eliminating useless articles. Packs had to weigh less than thirty pounds and could be no wider than the back of the person carrying it. Cean spent all day on this task, and still the stubborn Athlaneans tried to hide precious gems and other valuables on their persons. Cean couldn't blame them. They were going to an unknown land to face an uncertain future. All they had known was being destroyed, all they had believed was proving false. Their possessions offered a certain amount of security.

Each person carried a small amount of food and water. Neither Cean nor Kon-r thought their escape to the harbor would take much more than half a day, but it was good to be prepared for surprises. There were children in his group as well. Cean didn't like it, but it would be too cruel to separate parents from their children. Some civilian men asked for weapons and were provided with them.

Cean figured he would have almost three hundred armed men when he left. The Gardai he could count on. Ro-Fannin he could count on. The rest, who knew? Cean told his people they would leave before dawn. They had to be in the courtyard by the western wall before sunrise. Cean told them he would not wait. If they wanted to live, they would be there.

The night was quiet. No threat presented itself. Kon-r and Cean walked the walls together, offering a word of praise here, encouragement there. The Gardai were in good spirits.

Kon-r said, "They are amazing men. The best troops the world has ever seen. They willingly serve on this wall, knowing they will not survive the destruction of Athlan."

"Much like you, Kon-r," Cean answered.

"Aye, lad, we were all trained the same way, I guess. We all shared the same beliefs, fought for the same cause, lived together and died together."

Kon-r said, "Cean, maybe you know this, but perhaps not. You cannot make people follow you. They must want to follow you. They want to follow when they see three things: competency, hard work, and trust. Your people need to know they can trust you to work for their good and that you will do that well. They will know how good you are at your job by how well their lives go. It is a simple equation, but extremely demanding. Never set yourself above them. There are very few leaders, but many men who desire power. Your people will follow if you lead well. The paradox of command is this: they follow, but you are the servant. You must be dedicated to their welfare, not your own. Your superior abilities must be used to attain their security and prosperity. The Gardai have followed me and every other Warrior for exactly those reasons."

Cean didn't answer. None was required. Maybe this was the final lesson, the greatest of all.

They found themselves standing over the main gate. Leaning on the parapet, each man was silent, wrapped in his own thoughts as they looked out over the inky black plain below. Cean reviewed his escape plan again and again. He had planned for every contingency he could think of, but what had he missed?

Kon-r knew he was well prepared. Experience had taught him his trade. He worried about the Bas Croi. How would he trick Kon-r? Where would the surprise come from, for come it would as sure as the dawn.

"I must leave, Kon-r," Cean said. "The time draws near. The sun comes."

Kon-r nodded in the dark. "Yes, I know. I wish it were not so, Cean. Go. Do your duty. You have been prepared. You are sufficient to your task."

They did not embrace. Everything had been said. Cean turned to walk away. Just before he descended to the courtyard, he heard Kon-r say, "Never forget us, Mak-Scaire. Never forget."

Cean continued down the hard stairs, unable to speak. Tears rolled down his face. He couldn't decide whether Kon-r was father, brother, or friend. In the end it didn't matter. He was losing family. Walking away from Kon-r Sighur felt like another of the Cath Angeal's tests, but this was real and it was tearing him apart. He reached the bottom and walked towards the courtyard. Earlier, he had put his own pack and weapons in a nearby doorway. He opened the pack one more time to make sure the maps were still there. He buckled on his sword and slipped his long knife into his sash.

Slinging his pack over his shoulder, Cean turned to see the Gardai drawn up in formation with Ro-Fannin at their head. He stood at attention, as did the troops behind him.

Cean wasn't ready for this but said, "At ease, men." Feet shifted and they relaxed slightly.

"All present, sir," said Ro.

Cean walked to Ro and quietly said, "Thank you Ro. I have no experience. I will depend upon you and your men to get us through whatever lies ahead."

Ro carried a short throwing spear as well as long and short swords. He met Cean's gaze. "You are in command. I do not understand, but I trust Kon-r and the Cath Angeal. You have my life and the lives of these men in the palm of your hand. Use us well, young Warrior." Ro smiled and that smile meant everything to Cean.

The travelers congregated in the courtyard. They were tired and worried. Cean could see many were weighted down by packs that were obviously larger than directed. He shook his head. Either they could carry the weight or they couldn't. Hopefully, their packs wouldn't get them killed.

Cean drew a map from his tunic. It was a copy of the tunnel map. He handed it to Ro. "This is our route. Will you take point for us?"

Ro studied the map. "What is your plan?"

Cean realized he had not discussed his plan with Ro. Would his inexperience get them all killed? "I would like you to take point with a third of your men. We will space Gardai at the head with you, in the middle with an officer, and at the end of the column with me. Our people will travel between Gardai elements. We can protect them and they won't get lost. Does this make sense to you, Ro?"

Ro waited a heartbeat and said, "Yes, it does, but I have a question: How are we to see in the dark? How are we to find our way? Your map may glow, but the tunnels don't."

Cean was stunned. He had made a serious mistake already. Was he just stupid? He stood there with his mouth open. First Ro began to laugh, then the Gardai officers joined in, and then the rank and file laughed at him as well. He was a failure already.

Ro slapped him on the back. "They aren't laughing at you, young Warrior. They are laughing with me. There is a difference." Ro commanded them. "Attention all." Each man stood ramrod straight. "About face." Officers, as well as troopers, faced the other way.

Cean didn't know what was happening. Were they leaving? He looked at Ro, who pointed to the nearest officer. Cean didn't know what he was pointing at, couldn't...and then he saw them. The officer was carrying three short torches tied to his pack. Cean saw that every Gardai had three torches attached to their pack.

"You will learn, Cean," Ro said. "Let's hope most of us are still alive when you do." Ro smiled again, commanded, "About face," and the Gardai were ready to go. "Your orders, sir?" he asked.

Cean, now a very humble Warrior, said, "Get them into the sewers, Ro. Let's get out of here."

Kon-r watched it all from the wall. Ro-Fannin, Cean Mak-Scaire, Kon-r Sighur: three Warriors, with eleven more on these walls: *The end of times, surely*, he thought. He wished he had had more time with Cean. The boy needed to learn so much so quickly—maybe too quickly.

He watched them descend into darkness. Kon-r never liked fighting in the dark. There was too much chance for confusion. Men slaughtered their own. Every Warrior had been taught the stories, except Cean. No time. They never got there. Ro was Cean's best chance of survival.

He watched until they were gone. Cean was the last to enter. He hesitated before dropping down, turned and raised his hand in a final farewell. Then he was gone.

Kon-r felt his heart jump in his chest. This was hard. He turned from the courtyard, walked stepped up onto the firing step, and concentrated on the plain below. Cean had beaten the sun. The Ban Castlean faced east by southeast. The sky lightened. Soon the plain would be bright. The mountains behind the Castlean would be red with reflected sunlight. Kon-r could see rivers of fire far to the south. He smelled Sulphur in the air. The earth trembled. He closed his eyes, admitting to himself how tired he was. His mind drifted to past battles, past friendships, victories and loses. He remembered the feel of the ocean wind on his face. He was young and the world had been open.

"Kon-r, Kon-r, wake up, sir, wake up!"

Kon-r's eyes snapped open. He had drifted away. The sun was up and the plain was lit. He saw the strangest sight. Eleven large men, giants, stood in a line, equally spaced across the plain, just out of bow shot. They wore red armor. Each wore a large sword and carried a tall spear. The spear tips glittered in the sunlight. The enemy was here, but what a strange way to present themselves. And what were they going to do with only eleven men, no matter how large they were? He checked the wall left and right. All was in order. The red giants below did not move; in fact, the sun moved across the sky and they remained perfectly still. Kon-r didn't move, either. The Angeal's words kept repeating in his head: "Watch your back, Kon-r." His back was protected by a mountain range. Where was the danger going to come from?

Then hundreds of people surged forward from the tangled edges of the plain. They were all armed, but they were ragged. By some unseen and unheard command, the entire group stopped, forming a line between the giants. All stood still, as if waiting. The plain was eerily quiet. No sound escaped the enemy formation.

All Gardai were now on the wall. No words passed between them. The sight below was strange beyond belief. Kon-r could sense the worry among his men. He needed to do something.

"Commander Yost," Kon-r said.

"Sir," answered the Gardai officer.

"Load a javelin and take your best shot."

"Yes sir." Yost moved to a mechanical javelin launcher. He shouted "Load," and two crew members loaded a long, thick projectile with a hardened metal point. They cranked back on the bow line and the shaft followed. The crew locked the bow line and shaft in place. "Aim," Yost ordered, and the crew aimed their weapon at the red giant that stood almost directly in front of them. Yost screamed, "Fire!" and the crew knocked the locking mechanism away. The shaft sped from the track in a high, beautiful arc.

The crew was certain of a hit, but the thermals outside of the wall shifted the shaft slightly to the left of target. Nonetheless, the deadly quarrel pierced the body of a normal-sized soldier and pinned the unfortunate man to the ground. Gardai cheered along the wall.

Kon-r called out, "Silence."

The wall fell silent. The Red Giants and the soldiers between them made no sound. Not one man moved to check on their dead comrade.

Kon-r could only think of one thing: "Watch your back, Kon-r." Something bad was happening, but he couldn't figure out what it was. Just as he was about to leave the wall to check on Cean's progress, a figure in black slowly made its way out onto the plain. Kon-r assumed it was a man, although the head was completely covered by a loose hood. The man walked deliberately to the center of the line. He stood slightly in front of the central giant. The man carried a large black walking staff. He stood still and silent for a few moments, as if thinking, then flipped his hood back.

Kon-r saw a thin face under a bald head. The eyes looked red, but that must have been a trick of the light. The man seemed to look directly into Kon-r's eyes. *The Bas Croi*, he thought.

Kon-r could feel the Bas Croi trying to search his mind. Then a voice filled the plain. "Sighur, come down. Sighur, come down. Sighur come down." The giants began to chant the same words, then the soldiers began to do the same.

The chant grew louder and louder. The men on the wall could think of nothing else. The chant filled their heads, reverberating off the mountain face. The Warriors looked to Kon-r for direction. He shook his head. He would ignore Croi's challenge. They would wait; theirs was the position of strength. The chant went on and on. Gardai nerves were frayed. After what seemed to be forever, it stopped. The plain went deathly still.

Chapter 46:

Dark Fire

B as Croi stood before the massive gate, out of harm's way. He was unsure of what to do next. He had positioned his captains on the plain simply to draw attention to them. Croi wanted Gardai eyes on the plain, not focused within the Castlean itself. Croi expected his fifth column to have already attacked, but clearly, that had not happened. He waited for the gates to swing open, but that didn't happen, either. He began the chant because that was all he could think of to keep their attention on him. He wanted to give as much time as he could to his force below the castle, but nothing was happening. Something was wrong. Perhaps the attack had failed. Such thorough planning and training all for naught. He had sent one of his captains, Sith Ast, to lead the underground force. What power could stand against him and his tunnel-trained army?

He couldn't worry about that now. He was on the brink of failure, and failure was unacceptable. Croi shivered with a strange mix of fear and pleasure. He did not want another visit from the Angeal Dorchada, and yet he was drawn to that power like a moth to flame. Croi stood perfectly still, hood covering his head and face. He had to come up with another plan fast. The gates must be opened. The key was Kon-r Sighur. What would make him leave the safety of the Ban Castlean and expose himself and his men? What would force his hand? Croi remembered the Angeal's last words: "You will need it." Yes, the force, the strength Croi received from the Angeal. How to use it? How to manipulate Sighur?

What was the primary duty of the Warrior? The answer was easy: to protect the people of Athlan. Croi considered possibilities. And then he had it.

He sent a message to his captains. "Bring up our people. Do it now." The captains moved for the first time since taking their positions at dawn. A whistle passed over the plain. Thousands and thousands of Ravers ran to the front. The captains formed them into successive lines. Croi's force covered the width of the plain and was at least fifty ranks deep.

Standing on the wall, Kon-r was shocked by the number of armed people waiting in perfect, military order. His Gardai could do no better. Kon-r studied Croi's troops. They were old and young, men and women. Ordinary people, the forgotten, abandoned citizens of Athlan. Croi had crafted an imposing force of the dispossessed. They were desperate and dangerous. They were the aggrieved. Kon-r lowered his head and closed his eyes. These were the people he was supposed to protect, but he had failed. The collapse of Athlan weighed on his soul.

Croi ordered his captains back into position. Croi held his staff over his head with both hands, parallel to the ground. His captains did the same with their spears. The Bas Croi began to hum a soundless tune. He concentrated, gathering the power recently given to him. The air around Croi began to throb. The ground reverberated with hot power.

Kon-r felt the vibration in the stone walls of the Castlean. Every Gardai could feel the same. Croi became a red blur. Heat emanated from his body. Kon-r shielded his eyes, but he was mesmerized. A small red sun burned on the plain below.

Croi's captains began resemble Croi. They became red, pulsing clouds of hate. Streaks of power shot from Croi's staff. The power lines connected with the spears of his captains. Soon, there was a solid, thick line of pulsing, red and black flame that crackled and smoked, connecting Croi to his captains.

Kon-r was horrified. This was beyond his experience. The rank and file of Croi's army stood taller, as if they were drawn to the fiery cable. They dropped their weapons. Croi lowered his staff to waist level and the captains did the same. The power still crackled and sizzled, a fiery chain from one end of the plain to the other.

Croi uttered a loud cry and the first rank of his army walked directly into the fire line. Kon-r couldn't believe his eyes. Every one of Croi's troops literally cut themselves in half on the bar of power. Severed bodies collapsed to the ground. There was very little blood. The massive wounds were cauterized immediately by the sunlike power bar.

Croi uttered another startling cry and the power line disappeared. His men lowered their spears. Croi set the end of his staff on the ground. The dead were left where they fell. Kon-r's Gardai stood in shocked silence; each man wondering what it would feel like to be killed that way.

Croi pulled his hood over his head again and kept his army in stasis. *Let them ponder that for a while*, he thought with a crooked smile. Then he issued the next silent command, "Move up the next rank."

Chapter 47:

Heated Thoughts

Celine rested in magma. She didn't burn or suffer. She was the fire and the fire was her. Upon waking she searched for Mother, as a child seeks their precious blanket or favorite doll. Finding her on the other side of the planet, she extended her earth sense to Athlan, her reason for existence. Her wards, the four converted Sisters, were in the mountain above the Ban Castlean. They watched the proceedings but could not be seen, being part of the rock face itself.

The battle had begun. Players moved across the vast board of earth. People were dying. Their deaths didn't bother Celine. People died all the time and, as Mother had told her, humans were not part of her plan. They were "other" than Mother.

Celine was fully aware of the Bas Croi and his minions. Those sneaking through the sewer tunnels were not hidden from her.

Liam, the slave leader, had had a rough time and she wasn't sure if it was over for him. Celine was sad to see the Valley of the People destroyed. The valley had been a uniquely beautiful part of her earth. Their valiant king and his race went back to the beginning of life on the planet and they had never injured the earth. But their time had come, and life would go on without them. Sad but normal. The Gardai were safe behind their walls, but that might change quickly for many reasons. She saw the new Warrior entering the tunnels below the castle. There would be a bloody battle there. And one small ship braved her northern seas, following a dream. She wondered who they were and if they would find what they sought?

Mother had been right: time blocked her from seeing the results of these human efforts. And because they were human efforts, she had no control over them. Celine now fully understood Mother's frustration. Events were happening without her, as if she didn't exist. People were determining their own fate and, for those who understood, the fate of her planet and, therefore, herself.

The real problem was that these humans were being driven by the Paladins of the Travelers, the Angeals Cath and Dorchada, both far beyond her power. She hoped Mother could handle that part of the challenge. If humans had gone to war by themselves, neither she nor Mother could have cared less. Humans always went to war. They couldn't help it. They were deeply flawed, but that was alright. The pattern had repeated itself over and over and would again. However, the interference of "gods" and "beliefs" made this conflict "unworldly," as in, not of this world. This was anathema to Mother.

Celine knew her time was approaching. Who would she side with, if anyone? All choices were dangerous. Would her acolytes be ready to act? Would she? As Mother said, there were no guarantees. Celine would wait and watch, hoping that her best course of action would reveal itself as events unfolded. What else could she do? Closing her incorporeal eyes and becoming one with the earth's fiery core, her last thought was of a slave boy's warm kiss.

epilogue

Now, the machinery of war cannot be stopped. The die has been cast and who lives or perishes is largely a matter of circumstance. The Celestial Powers look forward to another contest in their endless battle for dominance, while their human pawns must, ultimately, pay the blood-price for the overreaching ambition of the eternal Travelers. Caught between these implacable foes are those of earth simply trying to live with dignity and freedom. Not all is foretold, however, and there is considerable room for independent action unlooked for. As everyone knows, dealing with humans can be extremely frustrating.

C. T. Fitzgerald

About the Author

C.T. Fitzgerald was born in South Buffalo, New York. While attending Canisius High School, Canisius College (B.A.), and Canisius Graduate School (M.A.), he also worked as a union card-carrying longshoreman (Local 1286) in the grain elevators of Buffalo, in the blast furnaces of Bethlehem Steel, as a bartender where his father and grandfather tended bar before him, and as a licensed teacher for the City of Buffalo. He attended Kent State for his Ph.D. in Literature (2004), and he has been married to Kathleen for 45 years. They are the parents of Ryan, Craig, and Tim and the happy grandparents ("Pops" and "Nana") of Lachlyn, Shea, and Emelia.

Dr. Fitzgerald is weak in religious faith, but strong in the hope that we go to a far better place when the ballgame is over. Being a philosophical Cretan, Dr. Fitz's religious beliefs have been simply stated in the past: "Do unto others as you would have them do unto you." If humanity actually followed this easily understood rule, the world would be a much better place.